Ruins Terra

Ruins

TERRA

Edited by Eric T. Reynolds

Hadley Rille Books
PO Box 25466
Overland Park, KS 66225
USA
http://www.hadleyrillebooks.com
info@hadleyrillebooks.com

The stories contained within this book are works of fiction. Any resemblance, unless noted by the author, to actual persons, living or dead, is purely coincidental.

RUINS TERRA
Copyright © 2007 by Eric T. Reynolds

ISBN 0-9785148-5-8
ISBN-13 978-0-9785148-5-3

To Katsuyoshi Sanematsu

Acknowledgments

"The Ruin" copyright © 2007 by Skadi meic Beorh.

"Python" copyright © 2007 by Jenny Blackford.

"The Outdiggers" copyright © 2007 by Jean-Michel Calvez.

"The Chamber of Azahn" copyright © 2007 by Thomas Canfield.

"The Moment of Glory" copyright © 2007 by Brendan Connell.

"Seagull Inn" copyright © 2007 Adele Cosgrove-Bray.

"The Tomb" copyright © 2007 by Leila Eadie.

"Rock Visions" copyright © 2007 by Floyd V. Edwards.

"Amazon Library" copyright © 2007 by Lisa Fortuner.

"Rising Tide" copyright © 2007 by Sharon Hurlbut.

"Icebound" copyright © 2007 by Kate Kelly.

"Moss Memoirs" copyright © 2007 Lancer Kind.

"Maximum Entropy" copyright © 2007 by Kfir Luzzatto.

"Rats in the Walls" copyright © 2007 by Lyn McConchie.

"A Glint Through Smoke and Flame" copyright © 2007
        by Michael Merriam.

"In Every Place that I Am" copyright © 2007 by Adrienne J. Odasso.

"It's a Temple" copyright © 2007 by Gareth Owens.

"Airholes" copyright © 2007 by George Page.

"The Last King of Rona" copyright © 2007 by Stefan Pearson.

"Introduction" copyright © 2007 by Eric T. Reynolds.

"The Boy Who Found Atlantis" copyright © 2007
        by Jacqueline Seewald.

"The Guardians of Llarazan" copyright © 2007 by Stoney M. Setzer.

"Pilgrims" copyright © 2007 by Ted Stetson.

"After the Stonehenge Bombing" copyright © 2007 by Ivan Sun.

"Clonehenge" copyright © 2007 by Douglas A. Van Belle.

"Burrow" by Joel Arnold, first appeared in the magazine *Burning Sky*,
        copyright © 2002, reprinted by permission of the author.

"The Tour Guide" appeared in the April 2003 issue of the on-line
        magazine, *Denovozine*, copyright © 2003 by Angeline Hawkes,
        reprinted by permission of the author.

Front cover art copyright © by Bob Eggleton.

Back cover and interior photographs copyright © Hadley Rille Books.

Editorial assistance by Rose Reynolds and Laura Reynolds is appreciated.

Contents

Introduction by Eric T. Reynolds   13

Rising Tide by Ann Walters   15

Icebound by Kate Kelly   19

The Moment of Glory by Brendan Connell   33

A Glint Through Smoke and Flame by Michael Merriam   39

Pilgrims by Ted Stetson   41

The Outdiggers by Jean-Michel Calvez   43

The Last King of Rona by Stefan Pearson   49

The Ruin by Skadi meic Beorh   85

Rock Visions by F.V. "Ed" Edwards   87

The Chamber of Azahn by Thomas Canfield   113

Maximum Entropy by Kfir Luzzatto   121

After the Stonehenge Bombing by Ivan Sun   135

Burrow by Joel Arnold   147

Python by Jenny Blackford   155

Seagull Inn by Adele Cosgrove-Bray   161

Clonehenge by Douglas A. Van Belle   171

It's a Temple by Gareth Owens   175

The Guardians of Llarazan by Stoney M. Setzer   183

The Tour Guide by Angeline Hawkes   195

The Tomb by Leila Eadie   201

The Boy Who Found Atlantis by Jacqueline Seewald   207

In Every Place that I Am by Adrienne J. Odasso   211

Amazon Library by Lisa Fortuner   213

Moss Memoirs by Lancer Kind   215

Airholes by George Page   219

Rats in the Walls by Lyn McConchie   227

Introduction

You turned off the highway a few minutes ago and are now bouncing along a remote dirt road across a barren desert region of New Mexico. The sun will set in a couple of hours and the slanting light is already causing smaller hills to cast long shadows that drape across the rolling land of scrub brush and outcrops. The distant mesas bask in the late afternoon sun while puffy clouds float high above.

You endure the washboarding effect of the road while your seatbelt keeps you from bouncing around, for you will soon reach your destination: the dwellings of the Ancient Ones.

The road crests a hill then descends into an ever-expanding valley that opens into the heart of Chaco Canyon, a now-desolate place that was once inhabited by thousands. The sheer walls of the canyon bound the wide valley, and there along the base of the bluffs you see a brown structure—a "great house" several stories tall, still standing after nearly a thousand years. Dozens like it are scattered across the valley.

You leave the car and hike toward the silent edifice. You enter a different world, stopping a few meters short to gaze at the building that may have once housed hundreds of men, women and children. The clatter of daily work echoes through its windows and around the courtyards. You hear the songs of their lives, the laughter of children, the voices of commerce, the building of shelter. This and the other buildings were the center of the world for a vast network of peoples, an advanced society that prospered despite harsh conditions, a people who could brave much of what the natural world would send their way for hundreds of years. Until at last they had to abandon the valley.

Ruins have fascinated us for centuries. They provide a connection with the past, telling us about a culture no longer there, or of one that has moved on to new places.

In this book we present twenty-five stories and a poem about many kinds of human ruins from all over the world. You will find several genres represented including science fiction, fantasy, horror, gothic and mainstream. Each deals with how humans make sense of the ruins around them, whether natural or artificial.

Enjoy your travels into these fascinating realms of humanity.

Eric T. Reynolds
Chaco Canyon, New Mexico, USA
May 2007

Ann Walters has a Ph.D. in physical anthropology and has worked on numerous archaeological excavations in the American Southwest. She is keenly interested in the connections between the past, present and future. Her fiction has appeared or is forthcoming in Kalliope, Quarter After Eight, SmokeLong Quarterly, flashquake, THEMA *and others.*

Modern human activity has a knack for destroying the artifacts of ancient cultures. But sometimes it inadvertently protects them, for a time . . .

Rising Tide
by Ann Walters

A grey ceramic pot leans against a masonry wall under blue sky and red stone. Unlike the rare cylindrical jars—tall straight-sided vessels reserved for ceremonies—found at Pueblo Bonito in the heart of Chaco Canyon, this one is not unique. It isn't special in shape or function like a pitcher or ladle. It's not even a decorative bowl, superbly adorned with dizzying black-on-white geometric patterns. It is a simple corrugated cooking jar in pristine condition, sitting where it has rested for almost a thousand years.

The pot isn't made in this narrow side canyon. It is brought here after being created by an old woman in a prosperous town. A pueblo of five hundred rooms on the west bank of a large arroyo, the town is a massive four-story structure towering above farm plots and trash mounds. The woman digs the clay herself from damp ground where a seasonal stream trickles into the main tributary, using a paddle fashioned from the branch of a piñon pine. She sits kneading it in the shade of the tall sandstone walls.

She's been making pots a long time. She is skilled, but her arthritic fingers have lost the dexterity to produce fine lines and intricate patterns. Painted wares are no longer possible. The glory days of youth behind her, she no longer creates for beauty. Her focus now is function, durability, the production of cooking pots for everyday use. With concentration she can still work the kaolin into thin ropes and coil them on top of one another to form jugs, jars and bowls. Her fingertip presses uniform corrugations into the exterior of the coils, giving the vessels a texture that is both easy to hold and pleasant to the eye.

This particular jar is a gift. The pueblo's heyday is waning. A third of the rooms stand empty already and more families will leave in the spring. Strangers are rumored to be encroaching on the borderlands, although no one can say if they come from north or south. Some speculate they are angry gods, coming to survey the results of the punishing drought they have wrought for the past dozen years. Others think the gods are forgiving, withholding the rains only to remind people that life and livelihood are gifts easily taken away. Most people simply understand that crops can't grow without water and that the appearance of *others* usually means trouble.

The potter is too old to leave but she doesn't mind. Generations have lived and died here. Why should she be different? Her grown son and daughters will go, joining their families with a handful of others heading northwest toward the mesas. She gives them what gifts she can: a pair of fine twined sandals woven from spun yucca fiber for her son, the inlaid turquoise pendant that belonged to her own mother for her eldest daughter, and a necklace of beautifully shaped bone beads for her younger daughter. The three older grandsons each receive a bundle of wooden arrow shafts and a notched arrow point of red chert, the newborn a blanket lined with turkey feathers. To her only granddaughter, a girl of seven years and endless smiles, she gives the corrugated pot.

With a blessing on her lips and a rift in her heart the old woman watches them go. The girl walks last, the jar swaddled in a layer of corn husks within a yucca bag over her shoulder. She clings to her grandmother, resisting the rent in her world, until her mother pulls her away. Dust follows their footsteps, and the old woman stands alone in pink morning light, hand held high in farewell, long after the air has cleared.

On the trek they meet many others. Some have come far and are moving farther still from their ancestral homelands, places no longer safe nor sacred. They tell of marauders who kill and take what they want, and of struggling farmers forced from their lands. Even without such tales it is clear that people are scattering like corn pollen blown from an open palm. The group lengthens their journey, searching for a spot secluded enough to be safe and fertile enough to sustain them.

It takes months to build their new home high above the creek in the shelter of an overhanging cliff. Strenuous labor is required to break up the sandstone and shape it into uniform blocks. Although the masonry is rough by the standards of their old home, the pueblo of forty-three rooms and two kivas fits snugly into the alcove. It is soon filled with the hum of conversation and the scrape of mano on metate. The smells of wood smoke and roasting cornmeal hang beneath the stone ceiling. Feet shake the dirt floor in ceremonial dance. They are thankful to have escaped the violence, famine, and disease, though life is harder here and bereft of the loved ones left behind.

They live here for less than three decades, a single grain of time. The girl so cherishes the corrugated pot that she uses it seldom. She can't bear the thought that it might break or wear out. She likes to hold it, looking closely to see fingerprints preserved where the old woman indented the clay over and over. She remembers the laugh that always started down in grandmother's belly, fighting its way up and out in a burst of merriment, and how the old woman brushed her long hair with a bundle of ponderosa pine needles, jet ear ornaments shimmering against the grey of her tresses.

Even the day they leave in haste, before dawn, before the raiders come, the girl—now a grown woman—picks up the jar and places her finger in her grandmother's print. Her husband calls and the baby shifts in the cradleboard on her back. It is time to leave. She sets the pot down. To move quickly, their loads must be light. The pot will stay behind.

*   *   *

The plain grey corrugated jar remains in the cliff-dwelling, set close against the wall inside the doorway, waiting for a family that never returns. Decades stretch into centuries. Protected by walls and roof, overhanging cliff, and arid environment, the pot remains unaltered by time.

A party of soldiers, fortune-seekers in gleaming breastplates and helms, follows a brown-robed friar through the main canyon. They don't notice the narrow rincon, never see the already ancient Anasazi dwelling. Their eyes look only ahead to a dream of seven golden cities, fables of glory and wealth spurring them ever forward. What do they care for crumbling pueblos and old pots?

By the time cowboys follow grazing herds of cattle along the river, most of the pueblo roof has collapsed. Rooms are exposed like lidless containers, their contents laid bare. Stones fall in piles before the dwelling, creating miniature scree slopes made up of building debris and the detritus of ancient lives. They are unheeded tumuli, marking lives no one remembers. Strays need to be rounded up and steers gathered for market, and the horsemen ride on, following their own bottom line of survival. Still the pot sits, unmoved, unbroken, unseen.

People work far down the main canyon. The sounds of engines and explosions batter the stone landscape like the vengeance of indignant gods. Juniper and scrub brush grow in ancient trash piles, and behind them the red walls of the ruin are indistinguishable from the sandstone cliffs. The doorway has long since disintegrated, exposing the grey corrugated jar to the view of anyone who climbs above the canyon floor. No one does.

When the machines finish, only the gentle burble of liquid echoes from one steep wall of rock to the other. The reservoir fills inch by inch, consuming the canyon until the perfectly preserved pot is covered by waves and water achieves what time has not, swallowing the fingerprints of the past.

Kate Kelly's fiction has been published in Hub Magazine, The Willows *and* Murky Depths. *She lives by the sea in Southwest England and when she is not writing she masquerades as a Marine Scientist. As the researchers in this story discover, there will be consequences of global warming, both expected . . . and very unexpected.*

Icebound
by Kate Kelly

Dr. Tom Johansson stumbled onto the bridge, rubbing the sleep from his eyes and blinking at the sunlight streaming in through the salt-caked windows. The ship rolled and he reached out a hand to steady himself. He could hear the captain barking orders through the ship's intercom as the ship rolled again, beam on to the driving Atlantic swell.

"What the hell is going on?" he shouted, but nobody seemed to hear.

The captain was studying the radar screen, hands placed on either side of the console to steady himself as the ship continued its turn and started to pitch into the waves, salt spray smacking against the bridge windows.

"Full speed ahead," he said, his jaw set firmly beneath his grizzled beard.

Tom glanced out at the scene ahead. The crew had set the wipers going on the windows and he could see in the distance, falling and rising amidst the swell, the dark shape of another ship, a black shadow against the blue and white of a wind kissed sea, spume streaming from the tops of the whitecaps. She vanished between the rolling hummocks of steel blue water, to rise again, nearer.

He marched up to join the captain, the pursued ship an orange blob on the radar screen before him.

"What's going on?" he demanded once more.

The captain turned towards him and Tom could see the fury in his eyes.

"Bastard cut our tackle," he snarled, gesturing with a work-hardened hand towards the fleeing ship. "Thinks she can get away with it."

Tom felt a cold shudder pass up his spine.

"Were there fish?" he asked in a low voice.

The captain shrugged and turned back towards the radar and the retreating ship.

"No, of course not."

"Then what's your problem?"

"What's my problem!" exclaimed the captain, his face flushing red beneath the grey of his beard and his blue eyes narrow. "My problem is people like that who think they can just cruise in here and take our fish, and employ dirty tactics to stop us taking the fish that are rightfully ours! They think they can just help themselves! These are Danish waters you know, and that . . . " he jabbed a stubby finger towards the bridge window, "that's a Spanish ship!"

"There are no fish!" Tom shouted slamming his fist down hard beside the radar screen. The captain blinked but didn't flinch.

"I am the captain of this ship," he said slowly.

"Captain of a trawler with nothing to trawl for. This ship has been chartered by the Norwegian Government and while we are at sea, I am the Norwegian Government!"

The captain glared back at him. "I've fished these waters my whole life," he muttered.

"As did your father and his father. I've heard it all before," said Tom. Then he took a deep breath. He felt sorry for these fishermen. A deep-sea trawler in a sterile ocean that once had teemed with life. But now their nets were empty, their livelihood gone, and many of them, like this man, were still struggling to come to terms with what had happened.

"So we've lost our nets. We weren't going to catch anything anyway. But we've still got a lot of research we can do, measurements we can make. We're trying to help you know."

The captain didn't answer but gave a swift nod to his mate and Tom felt the throb of the engines ease as the ship slowed. He stared out at the sea and sky. The sun was low on the horizon, as low as it ever reached at this time of year in these latitudes, meaning it was around midnight. He scanned the horizon but the Spanish ship was lost from sight, although he could just make out a dark shadow where the sea met the sky. He scowled.

"Is that land?"

The captain nodded and prodded the chart laid out on the table beside the radar. "Yes. We're just here and that'll be that promontory there."

Tom frowned at the chart.

"But we're miles from the survey area! How long have you been chasing that ship?"

The captain shrugged in response.

"Do you know these waters?" Tom asked.

The captain gave a half grunt. "If you could call them waters. They used to be ice. You never used to be able to get this close to land. It was fast ice all the way, and the land was white. They call it Greenland and it really is green now."

Tom ignored his tirade. "Can you take us in closer?"

"I guess so."

"Good." Tom nodded and stifled a yawn, running his fingers over the coarse stubble on his chin. He felt tired, but there was no point in going back to his bunk. "Then we'll deploy the plankton nets and make some measurements here before we return to where we're supposed to be." He directed a pointed stare at the captain who paid him no heed. He sighed. "Let's see what's going on at the bottom of the food chain," he added and turned to leave the bridge.

Tom stood up and stretched, feeling his joints unlocking and his sinews clicking back into place. Gelda, one of his research students, a young woman with flame red hair and face a mass of freckles, was peering through a microscope on the lab bench beside him, and a tall lanky student was preparing the next plankton net for deployment. Tom felt the decks shifting beneath his feet, but the ship was moving a lot less now that they were in the lee of the headland. He turned towards the girl.

"Anything?" he asked.

She didn't pull her face away from the eyepieces but the gentle shake of her head told him: "No."

He frowned. Surely the oceans couldn't be that dead? After all, the problems with the fisheries were caused in the main by human activity; over-fishing depleting the stocks below a critical threshold for recovery when the fish populations were already under stress, trying to adapt to keep pace with the changing ocean circulation. But the plankton? There had to be plankton!

He turned towards Daniel, the male student, thinking that maybe he ought to take a closer look at those nets. Maybe they had the wrong mesh size, maybe they were torn, but a flurry of footsteps signaled the arrival of Freyja, the third of Tom's students, who had yellow hair like buttered straw. Her face was flushed and her eyes dancing.

"Tom, you'd better come up to the bridge and take a look!" she said. Gelda pulled her face away from the microscope and looked up at him and Daniel paused, net in hand. Tom grinned.

"Come on then," he said.

Freyja led the way up to the bridge, her boots clattering on the metal stairs and Tom could hear the other two research students close behind him. The coast was nearer now, high cliffs of black basalt. The captain was scanning the coastline through a pair of binoculars, which he lowered and offered to Tom as he joined him.

"What do you make of that?" he said.

Tom studied the cliffs, at first seeing nothing but barren rock, but then, where the cliffs dropped down to sea level and the water was marked by the muddy stain of a river outfall, he noticed the huts.

"A settlement?" he said, and the captain nodded.

"Looks like it. Nothing on the chart though. This was once a glacier."

Tom could see the telltale ridges of moraine, piles of debris left by the retreating ice. The huts were huddled against the hillside above, but he guessed there may have been more, on lower ground in the path of the glacier, swept away by the scouring of the ice.

"Can you take us in closer?" he asked.

"Don't see why not," said the captain. "You going ashore?"

"Yes."

"Then I'm coming with you."

"But I thought the captain was supposed to stay with his . . . " the blonde girl started to say but Tom silenced her with a glance. He looked at the huts again. They had to be very old. They had to pre-date the glacier—a glacier that had come and gone. And he wondered what people could have lived here.

They drove the RIB onto the steeply shelving beach of black volcanic shingle and pulled her clear of the lapping waves, the captain making her fast. Tom stared around at the landscape before him. It was hard to imagine that only a decade ago this whole area had been icebound. But the ice was retreating at an unprecedented rate, the ice sheets that had once covered the great landmasses of Greenland and Antarctica now almost gone, their last remnants being discharged into the oceans in a muddy torrent, like the turbulent orange tinged waters of the river that now flowed where this glacier had once crept.

He stared up at the huts and frowned. From the beach they looked familiar in shape. Freyja had brought the video camera and she panned around the landscape slowly as they climbed the slope to walk among the ruins. Tom could see how little actually remained of them, just the walls, a jumble of piled stones. In some he could see where a hearth must have once been, and in others he could clearly see the entrance, an outer wall curving around to provide extra protection against the wind.

The captain scowled and scratched his beard.

"Nobody's lived here for a long time," he grunted. Tom smiled, inhaling the unfamiliar smell of a foreign land.

"A very long time," he said. "If I'm not mistaken this is an early Viking settlement.

The captain stopped scratching and scowled at him from beneath heavy brows.

"Vikings?"

"Definitely Vikings," said Gelda, brushing a strand of red hair away from her face, grinning at them and pointing to a large slab of rock jutting out from the ground beside her. "Look what I've found."

Tom joined her and ran his hand over the rough surface of the stone. It was heavily eroded but the pattern of lines and symbols was still discernable.

"Runes," he said. "I wonder what they say."

"I can read them I think," said Gelda, looping the rebellious strand of hair back behind her ear. Tom glanced swiftly up at her.

"You can?" he said, and Gelda grinned.

"But what are Vikings doing here?" said the captain.

Tom smiled. "The first Vikings came here with Erik the Red," he said. "It was during the last warm period, around 900 AD, when Greenland really was green. It was good fertile land and they farmed it for hundreds of years. Then the climate changed and the ice encroached. They perished. It's a classic example of what happens when people fail to adapt to their changing environment."

The captain ignored Tom's dig.

"Doesn't look very fertile to me," he grunted, looking around at the barren landscape.

"Give it time," said Tom. "This part of Greenland will soon be green as well."

"And this is one of those settlements?" said the captain.

Tom nodded and Gelda squatted down on her heels, running her fingers over the ancient writings. "Interesting," she muttered, half to herself.

Daniel scrabbled over the loose stones to stand behind her, sweeping his thick hair back into place with his hand.

"What does it say?" he asked, but Tom could tell that he wasn't really interested in the runes, his eyes fixed on Gelda.

"I'm not sure," she said. "It says something about suffering the same fate as those that came before. It talks about the ones who lived on the red hill."

"An earlier Viking settlement?" Daniel suggested.

"Perhaps," said Gelda scrutinizing the next set of runes. "I don't know these symbols," she muttered.

Tom stared around at the barren landscape. There was nothing growing here as yet, for the soil was poor and the centuries of ice and snow cover had left it all but sterile. He looked around for the plant life that should have been beginning to encroach, patches of small, tough green plants, moss and lichen covering the exposed rock, but as yet there was nothing. He assumed there hadn't been enough time yet since the ice here had melted and he found himself wondering just how quickly the ice sheets were now retreating, how long before they would be gone.

And there was something else that bothered him. Something missing but he couldn't tell what. He frowned and scuffed the toe of his boot in the barren earth. This land had once been fertile, and it should have been again. But for now he could see the bare, exposed rock, and all its folds and structures, and his heart gave a faint lurch as he noticed that the hill behind the settlement was made of red igneous rock.

"The red hill," he said, pointing.

Daniel grinned. "Well let's see if I'm right," he said. "Care for a wager?"

"No thanks," said Tom, "But we'll take a look anyway."

It was clear from some distance as they approached, that the hill was the site of another settlement. Gelda had lingered by the runes and had had to run to catch up with them, and Tom could hear her breathing heavily after the uphill jog. He scowled at the ruins up ahead. There wasn't much left.

"It's a walled city," said Daniel giving voice to the thoughts that were tumbling round in Tom's head. "I doesn't look Viking to me."

25

"I don't think it is," said Gelda.

"No," said Tom. "It's something else. This could be really significant."

He paused before the city walls. Up close like this he could only guess how high they must have been, now crumbling into dust, shattered by the action of the frost and snow. Yet from what was left he could see they had been magnificent, the masonry finished to a high standard, as good as anything he had seen in the ancient world.

And to their left was a gateway, guarded by two mighty statues.

"Wouldn't fancy meeting them on a dark night," said Freyja zooming in on them with her camera, and Tom had to agree with her. The statues were of reptilian figures, badly weathered but in places he could still see the pattern of their scales carved into the rock. Their eyes had once been set with stone but were now just hollows and the stubs of white limestone were all that remained of their teeth. But even without fangs they were monsters to chill the heart. He felt an involuntary shudder crawl up his spine as he passed between them and entered the city.

Inside, the city had not survived so well. There was little to see of what must once have been houses and temples but mounds of rubble, in places almost indistinguishable from the heaps of moraine that the glacier had left as it retreated and over which they had clambered to get here.

"Definitely not Viking," said Daniel, glancing across at Tom with a grin. "Guess it's lucky for me you're not a betting man."

Tom didn't answer him. He stared around at the remains of the city, wondering who had built it, trying to imagine what it must once have looked like. But there was little enough left to give him any clues and all he could do was guess and imagine.

"There's not much to see here," said Gelda, stopping beside him. "It's not Viking but that's all I can say."

"And it's not Inuit," said Freyja. "They don't build cities."

"Maybe it's the ancestors of the Inuit. Maybe they once built cities, back when they first arrived here," suggested Daniel.

Gelda shrugged. "Interesting idea. But there would be other cities."

"Unless they were all buried under ice." Freyja said.

Tom kicked a stone and watched it skitter across the bare earth and rebound off one of the rubble walls. He laughed.

"We'll take some pictures and head back to the ship," he said. "Log this find and report back. They can send out a proper team of archaeologists to take a look. Our job is to study the oceans."

"Good," said the captain, his voice gruff, as he wiped the sweat from his forehead with a grimy handkerchief and started back down the hillside towards the black beach where their boat was waiting. "Seen one ruined city you've seen them all."

Tom saw Daniel look at Gelda and shrug. But for some reason she didn't laugh. She looked quite serious as she turned to follow.

A shout of alarm made Tom shiver; he could hear rocks falling somewhere up ahead. The cries grew fainter as if coming from below ground. And he realized that something had happened to the captain. He couldn't see him anymore; just hear his muffled cries. He started to run.

The students arrived at the scene before him and he pushed his way between them, peering down, trying to see what had happened. He breathed in a sigh of relief when he saw the man below him, scrambling to his feet, rubbing the back of his head and cursing loudly, his voice echoing amongst the rocks. He had lost his footing on the surface of the glacial moraine and had slipped down its flank as if it was scree, leaving a scar of freshly slipped stone and earth behind him like the track of a grey dusty avalanche.

But then Tom noticed something else, and Gelda must have noticed it at about the same time.

"More ruins," she muttered beside him.

"But better preserved," said Daniel.

The captain had stopped swearing and was staring up at them.

"You going to stand there gawping all day?" he growled.

"No," said Tom. "We're coming down."

He set off down the uneven slope, feeling the loose rock sliding beneath his feet. He could hear the others following behind him and occasional stones rolled down past him, gathering speed and bouncing off others, causing them to start sliding as well.

The captain was looking around at the ruins when they joined him. Tom followed his gaze. The scree they had scrambled down was part of one of the larger moraine deposits left behind by the retreating glacier, but the area they were standing in had escaped the scouring of the ice. He studied the morphology of the landscape. It would need a more detailed survey to confirm for sure, but his initial assessment was that the ice had been steered away from this location by a sill of hard igneous rock. And it was into this rock that an entrance had been carved, guarded by the same two reptilian monsters that guarded the city walls on the hill above.

Gelda was kneeling down, looking at the masonry that marked the remains of the foundations of ancient buildings that had once stood in this place, then she glanced up at Tom.

"Some sort of temple, I think," she said. "These dragon things are incredible."

Tom nodded. Unlike the carvings on the city gate, these were well-preserved, white limestone teeth and eyes inlaid with black obsidian. Their scales almost glistened. Beyond the entrance he could see nothing but darkness, a stream of murky orange melt water flowing out from between the statues.

"Are you getting all this, Freyja?" Tom asked, and Freyja nodded as she panned around the scene with the camera, pausing to zoom in on the carvings, a strand of blonde hair drifting from under hood across her eyes.

"Let's take a look inside," he said, pulling a torch from his pocket and leading the way to the temple entrance. The stream of melt water backed up against his boots leaving behind an orange residue when he lifted his feet. The cave was damp and stank of decay.

Tom paused, looking around the cavern. The others dispersed, Freyja panning with her camera, Gelda studying the carvings and writings on the walls, which were like no script that Tom had ever seen.

He caught her eye and she shrugged her shoulders in response.

"There are some more of your runes here, Gelda," said Daniel. Tom glanced across. He was squatting down in the muddy orange water running his fingers over the base of a broken stone pedestal. Gelda hurried over to join him, splashing through the water, for the floor of the cave was flooded, a giant puddle flowing out through the cave entrance.

Tom joined them and Gelda looked up at him, her eyes wide, her fingers tracing the patters of the runes.

"'Death came from the skies,'" she said.

"It's some sort of altar I think," said Daniel straightening up. "Only it's been damaged." Gelda continued studying the runes.

"The ravages of time?" Freyja suggested. The cameras whirred as she zoomed in.

"No," said Daniel. "This has been broken on purpose. Desecrated. Look."

The top part of the pedestal had fallen backwards, and Tom could see the scars of the tools that had been used to fracture the rock. And something else: attached to the top of the pedestal but now half submerged in the swirling opaque waters was a lump of rock, its surface glinting metallically in the light of his torch. He moved around to take a closer look. The water was deeper here and he stumbled slightly as he felt it start to trickle in over the top of his boots. It was bitterly cold and numbed his toes. He stooped down and touched the rock, gazing with wonder at the intricate patterns the metal made on its surface. His fingers tingled at the contact.

"It's a meteorite," he said.

"Death came from the skies," said Daniel. "Do you think it wiped out this civilization?"

"I doubt it." Tom straightened up, feeling suddenly light-headed. The enormity of what they had found was overwhelming. The excitement was making him shake. "They built this temple to it though. I guess it probably killed a lot of people, but it didn't wipe them out."

"It must have left a massive crater," said Daniel. "They'll probably be able to find it now that the ice has retreated."

"Yes," said Tom reaching out with a hand to steady himself, his head spinning.

"Are you all right?" asked Daniel.

"I just need some air."

He felt Daniel take his arm. The melt water splashed his legs and the cold was biting. Then he was out in the brilliant sunlight once more and he could feel its warmth. He blinked to clear his vision. The captain was sitting on a rock looking at him.

"You don't look too good," he said.

Tom shook his head. He could sense the students hovering around him and feel their concern. This was silly. He struggled to pull himself together, but when he tried to stand he nearly fell. He leaned back against a slab of rock.

"We'd better get you back to the ship," said the captain.

He felt Daniel take his arm and pull him to his feet. Gelda was walking beside him. He pulled in drunken lungfuls of air and his head started to clear.

"What did the other runes say?" he asked.

"Don't worry about it," she said, glancing at him, her eyes dark.

"No, tell me. It'll make me feel better."

"They said 'Death came from the skies.' I guess that was your meteorite. The Vikings clearly thought it was responsible for what happened to them and assumed it was the same thing that had happened to the people who built the city. That's why they defaced the altar. Of course, it didn't save them. Nothing could stop the ice."

Tom grinned.

"Fascinating," he said.

"But there's one thing bothering me." Tom glanced around at her, the movement making him dizzy.

"What?"

"It's just that this settlement is very old. One of the first, yet it was abandoned early on. Other settlements in Greenland persisted for hundreds of years. This one was abandoned before the ice came."

They had reached the RIB and Daniel lowered him onto the

shingle. He looked around. The captain and Gelda were preparing to launch and Freyja was still filming. Daniel sat down heavily beside him, and Tom suddenly noticed beads of sweat breaking out on his forehead, his dark hair damp. He was shaking.

An icy chill shivered up Tom's spine. He looked out towards the others. Freyja was filming the river, its outfall of swirling orange melt water dissipating into the ocean. And he realized what it was that was missing, what had been bothering him ever since the set foot on shore. There were no seabirds, yet the skies and the cliffs should have been full of them. He looked back out at the ocean.

"It's water borne!" he gasped.

"What is?" said Daniel, looking at him, a deep intensity in his eyes. "What are you saying?"

Tom felt his vision starting to blur, and then the black shingle of the beach was rushing up to meet him. He clasped with his fingers against the grit and sand. It all made sense now, the barren landscape, the sterile ocean, two ancient races, their buildings crumbling to dust, the desecrated temple, and now this. It had been sealed in a temple, trapped beneath the ice, but now the ice had melted and water would carry it, whatever it was, to wherever the ocean currents took it.

"Death came from the skies," he gasped.

Brendan Connell was born in Santa Fe, New Mexico, in 1970, and currently lives in Ticino, Switzerland, where he teaches English and writes. He has had fiction published in numerous magazines, literary journals and anthologies, including McSweeney's, Adbusters, Nemonymous, Leviathan 3 *(The Ministry of Whimsy 2002),* Album Zutique *(The Ministry of Whimsy 2003) and* Strange Tales *(Tartarus Press 2003). His first novel,* The Translation of Father Torturo, *was published by Prime Books in 2005; his novella "Dr. Black and the Guerrillia" was published by Grafitisk Press the same year. In this story he tells us about victories, apparent as well as not-so-apparent. (Caution: some of the scenes may be too intense for some, particularly younger, readers.)*

The Moment of Glory
by Brendan Connell

Twelve of them dropped at the volley of musket fire, but it was ineffectual. Others, to take their places, emerged from the rich, green line of jungle which bordered the field, surrounding the fort. The Aztecs were no longer afraid of the smoking sticks or those who carried them, who they now knew were men who could die, and not the gods they had imagined them to be.

They were clad for war, many with rich headdresses of feathers, and elaborate, brightly colored costumes. Some held javelins and bucklers, while others carried slings for throwing stones. They advanced on the fort in waves, uttering chilling cries of death, strange and ferocious. In those grave hours there was not a man among the Spanish who would not have given up all the gold they had won to be out of Mexico, at home, in safety.

The eastern side of the fort had been set fire to the previous day and was now charred and half broken through. Six of the thirteen arquebusques were being used to defend it, as well as a number of muskets and around forty archers. The western side was under the command of Pedro de Alvarado, with three arquebusques and over sixty men.

The sun had not yet risen over the line of jungle. The light was the somber, almost mystical light of early morning. Birds and monkeys cried out from the trees. The Aztec warriors were heedless of the dead which littered the field and advanced, many running, spurred on by the desire for vengeance.

"Fire!" de Alvarado screamed to the arquebusques.

The fuses were lit simultaneously and, a moment later, the cannons fired, two at the same instant, a third slightly after. The balls leaped into the oncoming crowd. One ball fell short, landing in a puff of dust at the feet of the advancing enemy. Another took off a man's head. The third knocked over several men, leaving them bloodied, dead or senseless.

The Aztecs cheered and surged forth. They seemed to take delight in the battle and the knowledge that they had many men to spare, while the Spanish were relatively few.

De Alvarado's whiskers bristled with well mastered fear. Strands of long black hair came out from beneath his helmet and clung to his brow and cheeks, which were clammy with sweat.

He could clearly make out the features of many of the Aztecs. One, obviously a lord of some sort, waved a scepter in the air and rallied his men forward with angry cries. His white teeth formed a slash on his face and the sinewy muscles of his forearms could be seen.

De Alvarado ordered the archers to shoot. A flock of arrows sprung in the air, whistling as they left the bows. Over half the arrows found themselves embedded in human flesh. About fifteen men had either been killed, or fallen with serious wounds, but the Aztec's number did not seem in the least diminished. Those in the forefront, seemingly the most savage, neared the fort and began slinging stones which fell like hail within, some crashing against the armor of the Spanish, one or two even knocking hard against exposed flesh.

The muskets were reloaded. With a strange, metallic taste in his mouth, which he knew to be the taste of war, Pedro de Alvarado ordered them to fire at will. The men kneeled, took aim and fired through the ramparts. The lord, with his white teeth still showing in a vicious grimace, was hit by a ball in the throat. He reeled back and fell, blood trailing across his breast and marking his chin.

"Bravo!"

De Alvarado turned. It was Cortes.

"Yes," he replied. "But for every one we kill there are a thousand more waiting. They don't believe Montezuma is alive."

"I do not believe he will be for much longer."

"Then we must fly."

The Aztecs were already scaling the walls of the fort, constructed of mud and timber. Soldiers with pikes cautiously leaned over and speared them as they neared the top, aiming for their heads, necks and bellies.

What Cortes said about Montezuma was true. He lay prostrate in a dug out room surrounded by four guards. Shivers coursed his spine. His skull was cracked and his hair stiff with dried blood. The rock that hit him had come, unwittingly, from one of his own men, three days earlier, as they pelted the fort.

His mind drifted back to the early days. In order for him to assume the position of emperor, Montezuma had had two thousand eight hundred neighboring lords murdered, including his own brother. For his coronation war he took five thousand one hundred prisoners for sacrifice. When he returned to his palace, he had the entire staff killed, even those he had smiled and laughed with, because they had seen him in the role of a human.

That first sacrifice was a blood bath. He was adorned with a bright, down cape, his legs and arms decorated with dyed turkey feathers. He stood at the top of the sacred pyramid and watched as his minions dragged the victims up the steep steps. Some howled in terror, begging for mercy. Others, those who were not cowards, came forward without argument, ready to meet an honorable death.

One by one they were tied to the sacrificial table. With a knife made from the sharpened snout of a swordfish Montezuma performed the rights. He plunged the blade into their chests and plucked out their still beating hearts, then held them up to the sun, dripping with blood, as an offering. Placing them on tortillas of corn he consumed them, the warm essence of his enemies sinking into his belly.

The people down below danced and sang, waving their arms in the air. The young men, aroused by the blood, chased the laughing females and pleasure girls off into the jungle. Montezuma had the flesh of his enemies divided amongst his people. The women cooked the meat in large clay vessels and served it, decorated with golden squash blossoms.

Montezuma, drunk with death, continued, hour after hour to participate in the sacrifice. Some, frightened out of their wits, tried to crawl away on all fours, like animals. With these he was particularly cruel, flaying them alive and draping their skins over his back while they looked on, eyes crimson with terror. When he cut open their breasts the blood would sometimes gush forth, spurting high in the air, and then reside into a slow gurgle, like a brook running out of the wound. He rejoiced in this and plucked and consumed the hearts until, exhausted, he could no longer stand, and his stomach protruded, gorged with the fruit of his cruelty.

Montezuma grinned as he remembered this, and his last breath parted through those twisted red lips.

"We have no choice but to retreat," Cortes told de Alvarado, when it had been ascertained that Montezuma was dead.

The other did not disagree. Over half of his men were wounded and a great many were dead. They were better armed, certainly, but they lacked the necessary forces. The Spanish were terrified and weary beyond words and every man wanted nothing more than to carry away with him his own life.

Together, in a band, they retreated through the eastern side of the fort. There were not enough horses to go around. A number of soldiers, as well as the single Haitian slave who was the property of Cortes, were compelled to go on foot. At first the retreat was orderly, de Alvarado staying somewhat to the rear, with a band of mounted musketeers in order to defend the retreating flank.

"Kill as many as you can!" he shouted to his men. "Put fear into them!"

But it was not the Aztecs who were afraid. Many dropped dead, but others ran forward, with bucklers and waving javelins, aching to see every Spaniard drowning in blood. And more came. They surged out from the jungle. The most virile formed aggressive cliques which ran on ahead, leaping through the undergrowth and over streams in order to cut off the retreat of the conquistadors.

"It's no use," de Alvarado cried to his men. "Move— Move as fast as you can!"

And, lashed with terror, the Spanish galloped away, leaving those without horses to fend for themselves, to avoid the stones and javelins of the Aztecs as best they could. The army, decimated, tore away, propelled not only by the fear of death, but by the fear that, if they were captured, they would most likely be sacrificed, their hearts ripped from their heaving breasts.

Those who were left behind were simply killed however, and none taken captive. Their blood mingled on the field of battle with that of the Aztecs, of whom thousands had been sent from this earth with musket balls cracking their skulls and arrows piercing their necks.

The Aztecs did not pursue the handful of horsemen who rode hell for leather through the dense jungle. Instead they gathered around the dead, to tend to that sea of flesh and glory in their victory. It is true that some women and children wept, but for the most part there was much joy.

The body of Montezuma was tossed into a ditch in disdain. He was dead, so it was now obvious to his people that he was no deity. Later they drew his bloated corpse out of the water and revenged themselves on it, tearing it to bits, burning it and sending the dust to the wind.

From the field, beyond the fort, came shouts of glee. Word passed from mouth to mouth that a strange discovery had been made and the

Aztecs (warriors, priests, lords and peons) all ran to see what it was.

A group of young men stood, smiles stretching their faces, a frail body poised between them, which they passed back and forth. All the people examined it and chuckled to themselves. They were amazed at the texture of the hair and the blackness of the skin, which was blistered and flaked off at the touch. They had never seen a being like this before.

The children hooted and danced around. The women wiped the tears from their eyes and could not help but grin in turn. The young men stuck out their chests and bragged to each other about their feats in the battle and debated as to the origin of this strange prize they had acquired.

It was the Haitian slave, whose spine had been broken by a hurled stone. Little did the Aztecs realize that this, their moment of glory, was the beginning of their final defeat.

Before long, the majority of these people would be dead and, a generation later, their cities would lie either abandoned or all but abandoned, the jungle swallowing up their roads, their dwellings collapsing and falling to ruin, the only visitors of their temples monkeys and lizards.

For this prize, this man they jeered and laughed at, carried with him the small pox, which would kill off in striking numbers both man, woman and child, and thus trumpet the end of their civilization.

Michael Merriam has sold science fiction, fantasy and horror short fiction to a variety of magazines, including Andromeda Spaceways Inflight Magazine, Fictitious Force, From the Asylum *and* The Harrow. *He was nominated for the James B. Baker Award in 2007, and a Preditors and Editors Reader's Choice Award in 2006. Michael is a member of the Science Fiction Poetry Association and the Twin Cities Speculative Fiction Writers Network. He lives in Hopkins, Minnesota, with his wife and an ordained cat. Visit his homepage at www.michaelmerriam.net. Sometimes, as he illustrates for us, unintentionally leading by example can produce undesired (but not necessarily unexpected) results.*

A Glint Through Smoke and Flame
by Michael Merriam

Tomorrow, I will walk into the flames. They will caress me, consume me, and I will rejoice in their embrace.

Though we do not understand, we keep the revered rituals of our creators alive. We play their parts, standing in for them until the day they return from the dust to which they fell. Now we, their beloved creations, their favored children, tend the crystallized soil, the murky waters, the cities left shattered by the power of their ascension.

It is an honor to be chosen for this holy task. Tonight, I sit alone, as those who burned before me sat, bathing in smoke and oil. In the morning I will hang the appropriate beads and shells, items I scavenged from the ruins of the once mighty cities, about my neck. Crisp, brown grass, tended specifically for this great event and woven into a skirt, shall encircle my waist.

We reenact the ritual as shown in a recording of the makers, a recording that survived to guide us. I will walk to the lip of the crater, a silent procession of my batch mates behind me. The one chosen to wear the feathered headdress will speak the ancient words, then the four closest to me in serial number will symbolically heave me over the edge.

I will descend toward the glowing, fiery pools. As my frame melts, as my capacitors, coils, and receptors turn to slag, as my processor and circuit boards dissolve, I will pray that my memory reaches the enlightened state of my makers, and that I may, if judged worthy, leave behind my physical anchor and become one with Those-Who-Designed-Us.

Tomorrow, I will join my builders. My receptors detect their ghostly forms even now, dancing in the smoke that purifies my metal shell, preparing it for rebirth into their mighty presence.

Tomorrow, I will walk into the flames.

Ted Stetson's fiction has appeared in Future Orbits, State Street Review, *and the anthologies* One Evening a Year *and* Mota: Truth. *His published books include:* The Computer Songbook *and* Night Beasts. *He has given workshops at Florida First Coast Writer's Festivals and been honored with several writing awards, including first place from the Florida Literary Arts Council and the Lucy B. MacIntire award from the Poetry Society of Georgia. In this short he shows how people can abandon a once important symbol.*

Pilgrims
by Ted Stetson

Twice a year we come to the old place. To the ruins. Some travel from far away. For most it is not an easy journey. We come when the stars shine and build a fire in the hope that they will see. If it is cold and the frozen white flakes are falling we burn the red man.

The fire shines on the tall jagged ruins and the Silent Lady does not answer. At times people have heard something, but when we listen it is only the wind crawling through the past.

After *The People* left, the world came here to loot their cities, to find their treasure. I think there was no treasure. The treasure was in *The People's* hearts and they took that with them.

Old songs tell of the streets paved with gold. The treasure seekers found no gold, only hard work. And harder work to survive.

Many that came after *The People* did not work as hard. Some did, but they didn't have their vision, didn't have their dreams, weren't able to work together. Many were loud voiced conquerors with hollow words and little else.

The People changed the world, changed history, for the better. At least that's what the ancient stories say.

For years afterward the world was torn apart by fools, by dictators, by religious wars and madmen. When the madness was over there was only starvation, disease and smaller wars.

The world forgot *The People* fed the world and cured the plagues and sacrificed their children to make the world a better place. The world in its greed and jealousy, forgot all the good *The People* did and nearly destroyed itself.

Rumors say *The People* got tired of being blamed for everything and one day they packed their civilization in their new ships and sailed to the stars. It is said they found a large uninhabited world where there was still room for them to work their magic.

I don't know. I don't know if anyone really knows. Maybe no one knows. Maybe it is only a bedtime story told to children.

But twice a year we gather by the Silent Lady with the spiked head and light a signal fire in the hope *The People* will see it and come back and take us with them.

Jean-Michel Calvez is a French writer living near Versailles. He has had four novels published as well as shorter works in numerous anthologies and magazines including an English language story in Bewildering Stories. *As an engineer in naval shipbuilding and R&D he was impressed very early by Theodore Sturgeon, Arthur C. Clarke and Dan Simmons. He has delved into other genres, as well, such as gothic, horror and mainstream.*

His second English language story appears here—a poetic tale where he shows that humankind's intrusions into the natural world can result in strange influences from above.

The Outdiggers
by Jean-Michel Calvez

All that happened, you know, is the result of a stupid event, quite ridiculously, almost nothing. Midnight. A noise outside, repeated, then disturbing: a wooden shutter that you left half-opened, by thoughtlessness or laziness. And full moon beams have taken advantage of it, flooding down, bleaching the white field of your sheets, crawling in every corner of your bedroom, diluting any shade on the walls, penetrating your dilated pupils as deeply as a sword in a chest. Your fingers are wrinkled on the woollen blanket, you can't sleep in such an intense light; you blink, you hate her.

A sleepless night, for sure. You already know you will not sleep. So you sit up at first trying to shift the target of this damned ghostly light that disturbs and fascinates you. Then you stand up because she—the moon—eats away your night because she disturbs you, tickles you.

But it is too late for the beating shutter, no way to fix it. The evil is there now. You cannot bear it anymore so you flee.

In vain, for outside the effect is even worse and you can't escape. Even with eyes shut you soak from head to foot in this flowing *sea of untranquillity*. So you walk, thinking over what happens to you tonight, searching for a way out, to get rid of this fate. But if you do move, it's you, only you; this damned moon doesn't leave—she is still there—over you, striking you, mocking you. Everywhere her pale intrusive light is flooding, dissolving everything up to the night itself. Stars are almost darkened, turned to silence and forgiveness. This night trees have rapacious shadows like an old woman's clutched fingers, they are claws on your road. So, you walk again, seeking after some harbor of peace, a still place you would know by daylight that would remain familiar to you in these dark times. Well, maybe the fountain square would fit? Here you are now this night, its quiet and discreet waterfall sounds strange and odd like the sound of blood flooding from a wound of lively stone. So where else can you hide now? Which silent place around would fit you? At night everything is noisy and disturbing up to the slightest defect in surrounding silence.

Right now a moving shadow spreads over the square's paved stones, like a cloud blown over you by a bewitched wind. You don't breathe anymore and you jump and hide behind the fountain's vertical totem, your nose stuck against the rough, unfriendly grain of the slippery stone, concealing that intimate shadow that is yours, that is you.

Then begins a painful wait, frozen with unformulated dismays.

Suddenly he, not just a shadow, appears. His arm is lengthened, deformed, stretched over the ground by a huge black suitcase that bends his silhouette like a bow, or a forgery. His shadow tightens, stretches, still extending as it covers the fountain where you hide.

You hold your breath and wait.

Till you see what happens, and who this is. You can breathe, now. For it is . . . Jim, this guy! Nothing stranger than Jim! All that trouble, all that fear for nothing! At once, you emerge from your wet hiding place, yours arms raised in order to welcome your old acquaintance, a large smile drawn on your lips as if a joke: "Hey, Jim! Here I am, too! You shook me, you know!"

But it is too early or not quite as clear as you thought! This idiot does not recognize you tonight; he ignores you, as if he wished he has never known you, or never seen you. Strangely, meeting you seems to get him into trouble: no smile, no gesture to reassure you, no word (one single word would be nice, a password that could be your name, nothing more, would erase at once any misunderstanding). But Jim appears to feel quite uneasy, terrified, frozen, as stiff as a ramrod, his eyes empty, his face pursued, his shoulders tilted by this tense arm pulling him towards the paved stone.

Finally he speaks, but in a rough breath, nothing in common with the usual voice you knew: "Hey, it is only you?" You can see a vague and clumsy smile on his face, he looks moony, awkward as if he was trying to roll his first cigarette in one hand.

That is not a question but a matter of fact, maybe a disturbing one for him. Anyway, you will answer, you have got to break this wall of silence between you, first of all—

"Oh yes," you tell him, laughing louder than you should. "Insomnia, tonight. The moon, I think. Well, don't really know. What the hell? Couldn't sleep, that's all I know."

He puts down his suitcase too fast and almost lets it fall. But the weakened lock fails (because the suitcase is overweight?) and the suitcase opens, just like that. A flood of fresh, black humus spreads silently onto the pavement, with smells of autumn leaves and mushrooms. The soil spreads over your shoes. Raising your nose, you fix onto him. He still looks bizarre and stiff, paralysed by surprise, or embarrassment, or shame or, maybe, by horror? His eyes look crazy under the pale moon. His other hand opens and releases a tool you have not seen yet, as you were enticed by the dark mass of the swollen suitcase. His garden hoe rings on the paved stone like the first knock of midnight.

Like a gong, this signal takes him out of his awaken dreams. No smile, he just bends, picks up his fallen tool and then, strangely, brandishes it high over his head like a pickaxe. You speak to him to break the silence—

"Hey, Jim, could I help you? Where are you going? Can't sleep, just

45

like me?"

No answer, he just groans, a strange kind of prayer, somewhat imperative, his voice embraced by a terrifying urgency: "Get away, man!"

Is he sick, hallucinating, mad, or even worse? You can't admit that you don't understand, you have got to dissipate this misunderstanding between him and you. You try an ultimate riposte.

"Hey, old chap, it is me! Hey, Jim, don't you see it's me?"

His hand quivers, then falls. He brushes his forehead with his dusty jacket sleeve, raises a glance towards the moon illuminating—or observing?—this surrealistic scene, shakes his head, then speaks at last, but with a sigh, and in a hollow tone that you've never heard from him—

"It is too late, too late, now . . . "

"Of course, it is late!" you answer at once. "It is exactly why I wonder what the hell you . . . "

And you shut up, disappointed or lost. For it seems you are not on the same wavelength. You dealt with time, but he is speaking of . . . you. So, too late then? But too late for whom, and for what? You feel despair while the shadows close like a net or a black glove on a pale hand around you. Nothing left then, apart from his well of moonlight, this round cold eye above you, flowing immaterial but in almost tactile streams, as a polar draft that penetrates and freezes your bones and moulds your mind in a maleficent and odd will.

Now my sheets remain cold and flat each night of a full Moon. Of course, I can see Jim, I often see him, he is a good friend; let's say he was. During the day, he is cool and kind, a little bit moony just as I am, but his eyes—and mine, too—are somewhat encircled, crazy or too distant, flooded by a suspicious pale light at some very specific periods of the month, excessively regular and cyclic.

What about me? you will wonder. Since our strange encounter in the square, I am still soaked to the inmost depths of my soul by these Moonbeams. So, I bought a small garden tool, too. The handle of which was much too long for proper use in narrow spaces, so I sawed it to the length of my arm. I bought a large suitcase, as well, a rough and strong one.

And, naturally, I found my own subterranean work as if it just waited for me. It is located under the northern wall of the church, a place that was still available for work, clean and still intact. The same way, Jim has been working hard for several moons on his own digging place, under the southern hillside. I never visit him, but am sure he is there; sometimes I can hear him from my own gallery, hitting hard and digging out as if he were deaf or addicted—or moonstruck. He works relentlessly since the very first night, that night of his meeting with the full Moon and, at the same time, with another *outdigger*, after a night of insomnia, drawn by some greenish beams fallen from the night sky.

We all suffer, we all have broken backs and members, muscles and bones, worn out by this gigantic, never ending task. Nevertheless, as moonlighters, we never complain or tell anything to each other or to anybody else, we, the *outdiggers*. Evoking such a penalty in the daytime would be inconceivable, heretical, suicidal.

On full Moon nights, when Moon beams are streaming and goading and bathing us, urging us to move, we go to our secret and silent digging places, as if we were a kind of spectral travellers. There, like underground miners, we sweat blood and water in the heart of dark, narrow and dirty galleries, and we carry away full suitcases of black earth extracted from deep foundations, under ancient moist walls.

There, underneath, hidden from daylight and human eyes, are the ruins of my life.

That's because the Moon loathes these sacrilegious buildings that rise anywhere, assaulting her sky. She needs and wants ruins, where her pale beams will have free access to caress the tepid ground, and will delight in the flavor of earth's nourishing humus.

Some night will be in ruins, too, this church we undermine on its base in a rhythm of ants, digging out full suitcases, throwing dirt in the river in order to dilute it and keep the secret. One day it will collapse and fall into ruins—as will all these black buildings that make no sense and make insult to the serenity of the Moon, those buildings forcing their jagged shadows into its pale round light, boldly assaulting its face of ancient silver, far older than they are. Because—have no doubt about it—*outdiggers* are legions, they work hard and, without being aware themselves, they are waiting for you, too, to enlist you one night when your turn comes.

Distrust them if that bothers you, if on a night of insomnia, you meet one of these slow, bent and old-looking silhouettes, heavily loaded, walking towards the banks of the river close to your house. Distrust them, or be called by Moonbeams, too.

Flee him, flee them, if you still have time.

Otherwise, join them. You will when you have no more choice.

And your life, too, shall fall into ruins.

Stefan Pearson's publishing credits include stories in Nova Scotia: An anthology of Scottish Speculative Fiction *(alongside Ron Butlin, Charlie Stross and Ken Macleod), and the horror anthology* Read by Dawn. *He lives in Scotland where he sets this suspenseful tale rooted in history and legend. (Caution: some of the horror scenes may be too intense for some, particularly younger, readers.)*

The Last King of Rona
by Stefan Pearson

Seven herrings
Feast for a salmon;
Seven Salmon
Feast for a seal;
Seven seals
Feast for a small whale;
Seven small whales
Feast for a great whale;
Seven great whales
Feast for a cionarain-crò;
Seven cionarain-crò
Feast for the great beast of the ocean.

—Translation of traditional Gaelic rhyme

How I came to be reunited with this benighted isle is no small mystery, and one I'm forced to mull upon impotently while the tempest flails against the *taigh geall*. Would I have chosen to holiday at Dornoch with the good Doctors Rutherford and Seward had I known duty would call me back to Lewis? I doubt it. St. Andrew's or the new course at Musselburgh would have sufficed just as well, and my clubs would be less inclined to rust. I can only hope that buffoon Merchiston keeps them well oiled in my absence.

I'm broken from my reverie by an unholy groan that issues from the flue, as if Boreas himself has the croft under siege. Leaden panes rattle in their frames like cheap dentures, and a thin pall of smoke drifts upward around the mantle. I stoop to cast another slab of peat onto the fire.

"Would you like more tea, Doctor MacCulloch?"

My host, Mrs. MacCagie, seems wholly unperturbed by the storm, and I'm gratified that she addresses me in English—though remnants of the old tongue lurk like rude cousins in the backwaters of my mind, I have no desire to make their reacquaintance.

"Thank you kindly, Mrs. MacCagie."

She refills my cup before taking a seat opposite on the other side of the fire. "A grim business," she says, swilling her own.

"A grim business indeed. Did you know either man?" I ask, shuffling my feet closer to the flames.

"No, not personally, although Murdo was my sister-in-law's nephew."

"Murdo MacKay? Which of the two was he? The one found bound in his plaid?"

She frowns, staring into the depths of her cup for a moment. "That's right, Doctor. From the accounts I've heard, Murdo was already sewn into his plaid, as if for burial. It seems poor Malcolm hadn't the strength to drag him to the graveyard."

I nod, hands drawn into a peak—an affectation I picked up at Surgeon's Hall and seem unable to shake off. "Yes, he must have expired before he could finish what he'd started. Of course, we'll find out for certain soon enough." I pull aside my woolen blanket and step up to the tiny window. "If this damnable squall ever lets up."

There is an uneasy silence.

"Are you learned gentlemen sure that it's necessary to disinter the men? I mean, it seems wrong to me. 'Let the dead lie,' the people are saying."

"Really? The other Ness folk? I'm sure Donald would like to bring his father's remains back to Lewis and give them a proper Christian burial." I find the Gaels pagan superstitions irksome. But what can one expect at the extremities of empire?

"Oh, no doubt, Doctor, no doubt . . . But that's not the whole of your business, though, is it sir? If you'll excuse my meaning."

"Indeed it isn't, my good woman. No, a post mortem will be carried out on both unfortunates before they are re-interred."

Mrs. MacCagie shudders visibly. "You know, an old woman from Barvas had a premonition that something was amiss on Rona before the *Lilly* set sail."

"Really?"

"Aye. Granted she makes no claims to the sight, though by her account, some verses of scripture upon which she'd prevailed had given her a deep sense of unease, and she feared for the men's lives."

"Is that so?"

"Apparently, after the *Lilly* returned and she heard the tragic news, she claims she dreamed that very night that Murdo Mackay had stood before the foot of her bed, dripping with blood, and recited the first two verses of the 73rd psalm."

"As any good apparition worth his salt no doubt would." My attempt at humor fails to lift her saturnine mood. I clear my throat and retake my seat. We sit for a while in silence, each lost in our own thoughts.

"If it's all the same to your good self, I think I'll retire," Mrs. MacCagie says after a time, putting her empty cup aside and rising from her chair. "No doubt the storm will lift through the night. I noticed John McBain's cattle were facing away from the *Clach Stein* this afternoon, so no doubt the wind's on the turn."

"I'm sure it is, Madam," I nod. "I shall retire myself shortly."

"Good night then, Dr. MacCulloch."

"Good night, Mrs. MacCagie."

The single-masted cutter *Vigilant* awaits our party at the pier. As the goodwife Mrs. MacCagie predicted, the storm abated in the early hours and the day has dawned as fairly as can be expected; that is to say there is a light south-westerly bearing spatterings of a thin, melancholy rain, and slate grey clouds grind across the sky. Fine weather for passage to Rona, no doubt.

"Good morning to you, Doctor MacCulloch." A bedraggled MacKenzie making his way towards me. He swats vigorously at his ruddy face—he is no doubt as plagued by the detestable midge as I am.

"A good morning to you, Doctor MacKenzie. Did you sleep well?" MacKenzie was late arriving in Ness and spent the last two nights in one of the sodden, dung-infested *taigh dubh*.

"Not a bit, sir! When the rain wasn't penetrating the roof, the wind piercing the walls like a hail of icy arrows, and the beasts lowing like Grendel with indigestion, the stench was enough to banish any hope of oblivion."

"The weather bodes well?" I opine, ignoring his outburst.

"I'm assured it does, sir." He dabs black dots from his face.

"Then I shall rest easy, though I fear I may be prone to the sea sickness. It's been a long while since last I took to water. Not discounting some pleasure boating on Duddingston loch summer past." I smile good-humoredly.

"Well I assure you that makes you an infinitely better qualified jack-tar than myself. Care for a wee dram to steel the spirits?" says that good doctor, offering a neat silver flask.

"Thank you, but I'd rather not. I suspect I'll need my senses raw to our peril if I'm to stay on my feet."

"As you will," he says, shrugging and taking a healthy swig.

The *Vigilant*'s crew are already aboard, about their business, some of the men helping our party load equipment and provisions. A small crowd has gathered at the harbor mouth, a handful of sullen villagers from Ness, Habost, Eoropie and the likes. I have not made the acquaintance of some members of our party yet—Dr. MacKenzie I have met once before, and though I feel he may be a little too fond of his drink, I believe him to be a competent doctor and of good character. The law is represented by Mr. Ross, deputy procurator fiscal; a dour and Presbyterian Caliban, and by Superintendent Gordon Morrison, a local bobby of good standing with whom I have passed no more than inconsequential pleasantries. The final three are local men, none of whom I have yet met. The first two are both young fellows, one by the name of John Weir, and one named Angus MacKay. Both were members of the party that came across the dead shepherds and interred their remains a month past. The final of our number is none other than Donald MacDonald, Malcolm MacDonald's surviving son. A more dour and ill-favored looking fellow I have never set eyes upon.

As I watch from the quayside, checking one final time that my Gladstone is packed and contains all the necessary implements of my trade, two bright pine coffins are struggled unceremoniously aboard.

The passage to Rona takes the *Vigilant* the bulk of the day, and it is early evening by the time we sight a leaden wedge of grey looming slowly from the mist. Before long, the island emerges from behind its watery veil, its flanks flushing coyly with verdant green at our approach. Rugged black rocks fringe the shoreline and the agitated specks of wheeling white gulls dot the cliffs beneath *Leac an Taulure* like bone chips in a snow globe. Rona is a welcome sight after lengthy hours at sea. My stomach has been turning cartwheels, and as I predicted, I spent a fair part of the journey with my hatless head lolling over the side. Dr. MacKenzie, on the other hand, seemed in fine fettle, and even found time to engage in a game of cards with one of the *Vigilant*'s crewmen. I managed to take some thin broth at midday, but dared not eat any more for fear of losing it. I am now ravenous.

At length we take sail, drop anchor off *Geodha a Stoth*, and make ready the skiff. Once we are ashore, the *Vigilant* will leave us and make around the cape and on to Loch Erribol about its fisheries duties. The cutter will return for us in three days time. Our official labors shouldn't entail more than a day's work, and I confess that I welcome the opportunity to indulge in a little amateur ornithology; a keen hobby of mine, and one I rarely get to indulge at the taxpayer's expense.

A deceptively large swell hinders our attempts to load the skiff and it is with some irritation that we lose one of our only two spades over the side. After four trips to and from the shore, the skiff is rowed back to the *Vigilant* one last time to load aboard the coffins, a task it is soon apparent it is ill-suited to. It is difficult enough to lower a coffin aboard, but once stowed we find it nigh impossible to reach the oars. Some debate ensues, before the skipper, a dour Grimsby man, suggests that we tow them one at a time behind the skiff. "It is only a short journey to the shore, and they are unlikely to be swamped." Just to be sure, we tack the lids down with a couple of short nails and diligently row them to the rocks. Superintendent Morrison and Donald remain ashore and maneuver them out of the water and to safety. A dozen black heads bob nearby in the swell, watching our ungainly endeavors with what must be some amusement.

Our provisions and supplies finally ashore, we begin the long trudge up the gentle green slope of *Leathad Fhianuis* and on to the ruined village. The drizzle turns slowly to a more resolute downpour and one would be hard pressed to witness more wretched specimens than we. It is our intention to take advantage of the depressions and deep-set walls of the settlement to make camp. Donald, John and Angus are adamant that we should not stay in the "house" until Murdo and Malcolm's remains are properly laid to rest.

"Would you rather we joined them?" blurts MacKenzie on hearing this. "Damn you foolish boys, it was no doubt exposure that sent the shepherds to their graves anyway! It's madness not to hole up in the only building on Rona with a roof!"

At that Donald casts aside the rope with which he is pulling one of the coffins and makes as if to strike the tactless doctor.

"Now, now, Donald!" Thankfully, Superintendent Morrison steps forward. "We'll have none of that. Remember, this may not be Lewis, but from this day forward and until the moment I step back into the boat, I am the law on Rona and you'd do well not to forget that."

Donald spits some Gaelic curse that I do not catch and retrieves the rope. No one speaks again until we make it to the skeletal remnants of the village.

On first impressions, one would be forgiven for wondering where the village is! So feeble and sorry are the scattered walls, trenches and turfed-over ridges, that to the casual observer it looks like little more than some elaborate sheep fank. Only St. Ronan's teampull stands out above the ground in any significant way. Next to the reconstituted black house, it is the only building in the village even partially roofed. The rest of the ruins consist of some rude trenches, low walls and a thick carpeting of sheep sharn. On the outskirts of the village proper, the grass-crested lazybeds jut from the ground like the ribs of some long-buried giant.

"This seems as good a place as any to make camp," says Mr. Ross—the first words he's spoken since we arrived. The procurator's voice has an authoritative air belying his ogre-like features, and it is with little debate that we set-to pitching tarpaulins above the exposed houses and laying out groundsheets beneath.

The work is strenuous and only made worse by the virulent wind and relentless downpour. Little is said, but it is apparent that hunger and fatigue are worrying our tempers. It is nearing seven in the evening by the time we have put the camp in some semblance of order. I am to lodge with Dr. MacKenzie and Superintendent Morrison in our make-shift tent, and Mr. Ross is billeted with the three local boys in a ruin opposite ours. Little can be heard or said over the rattle of agitated canvas but we manage to light a sorry fire from the kindling and small peats we brought with us from Lewis. We have enough kindling to light another two fires, but we will have to scavenge what timber we can from the shore tomorrow and the day after. This shouldn't present us with any real problem—not a single tree grows on Rona, but according to the Ness folk the ancient inhabitants survived for years burning the flotsam cast upon their shores.

I am utterly ravenous and it is with great relish that we finally throw sausages, eggs and victuals into a large pan that in no time is playing havoc with my senses. I feel like I haven't eaten in a week and launch myself upon my food with gusto. Our sullen moods seem to evaporate almost as quickly as our supper. Once we are fed and rested, we are soon joined beneath our canvas by the others, and a bottle of whisky is produced from within MacKenzie's voluminous coat. Angus, Donald, and Weir strike up a soulful rendition of *Failt' ort, Aran Naoimh bho neamh,* a hymn I have not heard since my childhood, and I'm much cheered by it. The whisky comes my way but I choose not to partake, even though I'm sure a wee nip would chase some of the chill from my marrow. I have an aversion to strong liquor that began in my student days, and have always found drunkards disquieting and somewhat menacing.

It is still light, and even on a sodden May evening such as this, the meager daylight will not fade for a couple of hours at least. Ample time for a perfunctory exploration of the village and its immediate environs. I may even take a walk up to *Toa Rona,* from whence, light permitting, I will no doubt be able to see the whole island laid out below me.

"In the mood for a wee exploration, Doctor MacKenzie?" I ask, making good my Mackintosh and water-proofed boots. A frown passes across the good doctor's face that negates need of answer. I am about to step back out into the squall when young Donald asks if he can join me.

Conspicuously avoiding the deceased shepherds' *taigh dubh,* our first port of call is St. Ronan's chapel. The teampull is by far the tallest building on the island. That is to say, it rises no more than a few feet above the ground, and I am forced to stoop to squeeze beneath the lintel and into the stygian cell. No sooner is my head thrust through the doorway, than an unholy noise erupts from within and I am suddenly deluged in a thick spray of foul smelling ichor. I backtrack as quickly as I can, flailing my hands before my face and scrabbling for my handkerchief.

"I forgot to mention the pious fulmars," says Donald, evidently much amused by my predicament. One cannot begin to describe quite how foul the squirted regurgitate of an angered fulmar is. It burns like acid and smells worse than the pierced colon of a three-week old corpse—a smell I have had the misfortune to encounter in my professional duties. I retch uncontrollably for a few minutes until I have managed to wipe the worse of it away. Apparently one should only enter the teampull when one is certain its avian sentinels are out, or with a bag to hold in front of your face. And even then you are not entirely safe as one of the foul creatures occupies each corner of the cell.

Were the sun visible, it would be beginning to set by the time we crest *Toa Rona*. From the highest point on the island, Rona is laid bare below us. The little island is much like a glass decanter in shape (an analogy that would no doubt appeal to Dr. MacKenzie). The thin peninsula of *Fiannuis* thrusts north for perhaps a mile, lower in elevation than the land to the south where we stand, where the bulk of the island, including the village and it environs, thrusts high from the ocean culminating in the spectacular cliffs of *Leac an Taulure*.

"Those great gouges?" I ask Donald, pointing out strange, equidistant rends cloven into the cliff face not far from the village.

"That's *Leac na sgròb*. Those claw marks were made by the feral, unholy beasts that St. Ronan encountered on the island when he was put ashore by the *cionarain-crò*. He drove them back into the sea and thon marks are all that remains of their passing."

"The *cionarain-crò*?" The name is familiar and I seem to recall hearing it in nursery rhymes when I was a small boy. "Is that not some kind of sea monster?"

"So they say. Sure and it swam to the island bearing the holy man on its back, but I remember my Grandpa Mungo telling me the *cionarain-crò* could assume any shape it liked."

"Indeed?" I smile. Donald's melancholy seems to lift a little when he talks about Rona, and his family.

"So what of the sheep? I haven't seen any." I ask as we wind our way back towards the village.

"No. We lifted them off last month. Macleod, their owner, hasn't decided whether to put his beasts back on the island."

"You don't fancy a tenure here yourself if you get the chance?"

"No. One death in the family is enough. I think if I were to spend any time here I'd be driven mad before the ship returned for me. I'll be across to the mainland next year. See a bit of the world."

"An excellent idea, young man. Besides, the isles will always be here should home beckon you back."

"Aye, the isles are always here."

Digging up the remains is a slow and strenuous process, especially as we have only one shovel. Angus and John, however, have assured us that the bodies are no more than a few feet below the surface, which is some consolation. We rose as early as we could, light permitting, but the day dawns a sepulchral grey that casts all about in a perpetual and somber gloom. Yesterday's rain persisted through the night and we passed the hours of darkness in considerable discomfort. I for one was particularly glad when what meager light there was crept beneath the corners of our canvas and roused those of us fortunate enough to be asleep. Not least because of the frightful scene that had played across the stage of my dreams. I am loathe to speak of it, but feel I ought to recall what I can, if only to put my mind at rest and banish any remnants before daylight and reason. It wouldn't do to give free reign to phantoms every time I wish to sleep.

It had been late, the wee small hours, when I'd imagined that I'd heard a whispering close by my face. A hi-pitched whispering. A sibilant chattering, the words almost beyond human hearing. Were the imparted truths spoken in some ancient and alien Gaelic? Perhaps—my comprehension seemed more complete the less I tried to understand. I can recall words . . . snippets. Tales of horror. Of bloodshed, pain and misery. Of betrayal. Of a desperate hunger. I shudder at the memory. When I opened my eyes and cast about me in the gloom, all asweat, I caught a scurry close by—a small dark shape that had sped to the edge of the canvas. I leapt to my feet in a panic, but the creature was unperturbed by my sudden movement and had simply turned and looked back at me nonchalantly, if a rat could ever be accused of being so bold. And I swear on the Almighty, in the half-light, the thing had smiled, its razor sharp fangs and eyes glistening red in the embers from our fire. Then it had scurried off. Of course, this is folly. A rat can no more smile than a seagull can tell jokes, but the experience unnerved me and sleep was a long time in returning. I did not wake the others: a rogue rat was certainly no reason to disturb my fellows. Looking back on the event, I am not so sure now whether the whole episode wasn't just some convoluted nightmare.

We take turns at the digging, but by and large, Superintendent Morrison and Angus MacKay bear the brunt of the labor. MacKenzie is next to hopeless and I fear my own efforts are far from Herculean. It is early afternoon before Morrison's shovel bites through a ragged stained blanket. The sound is wholly unpleasant, but pales compared to the stomach-wrenching smell. I'm thankful that the procurator, young John Weir, and Donald especially, are away collecting firewood.

Morrison wraps his scarf tight around his face and probes the blade more carefully until the second canvas bundle is uncovered. As the boys had predicted, the two bodies were interred beneath no more than a few feet of soil.

"Come on then, let's get these cadavers back to the village before the blasted rain starts again," I declare—in part to dispel the silence, and in part to speed this wretched affair along. MacKenzie produces his silver hip flask and takes a swig, crossing himself quickly. With that I hop down into the small hollow and begin to excavate the remaining soil with my hands. Superintendent Morrison follows my lead, although from his occasional retching, it is apparent that he is less familiar with the stench of purification than am I. Within a few minutes the bodies are uncovered sufficiently for them to be lifted carefully from their rude graves. We brought two lengths of oiled canvas in which to wrap the dead shepherds and ease their removal to the village. MacKenzie and I have no desire to attempt a post mortem in the open air unless we must. The sweating doctor and young MacKay take one set of remains, and Superintendent Morrison and I the other.

Our trudge back to the village is a solemn affair. As we step down into the lee of a low wall, carefully lowering the bodies after us, we see Donald, John Weir and Deputy Procurator Fiscal Ross winding their way across the hillside clutching bundles of flotsam. A welcome sight, especially as a thin drizzle had begun again. With some difficulty, we maneuver the bodies into position on the upturned bases of the two pine coffins we'd prepared for the occasion.

When all is made ready, MacKenzie unpacks our Gladstones and methodically lays out our tools and equipment on one of the lids. The blades and implements, macabre as they seem to some, glisten and sparkle alluringly beneath the stuttering lamp suspended above us and I feel a sense of professionalism and confirmation that has eluded me since this business begun. In truth it is a blessed relief to be working at last.

MacKenzie stokes up a small fire and sets a large pot of water to boil, then takes out his notebook and pencil ready to begin. Deputy Procurator Fiscal Ross does likewise.

"Gentlemen," for all are now assembled beneath the canvas, "Doctor Mackenzie and I have no professional qualms should you wish to spectate, but if you do choose to remain and bear witness, know that you may find what you see unpleasant, and that as a witness, your presence will be recorded by the deputy procurator fiscal and you could be called to give testimony in the unlikely event that circumstance necessitate it. I would also urge that you utter not a word and give what help you can if and when we require it. If you are at all unhappy with this arrangement, then please be so good as to leave us to our labors." I stare pointedly for a few moments at Donald, who merely lowers his eyes. All are ominously silent, but make no move to leave.

With a curt nod, I take my largest serrated knife and rip open the crude stitches holding the first canvas together. As I tug the twine free, there is a sharp intake of breath from behind me, a sudden retching, and a scramble of feet. Donald has evidently seen enough already! Weir makes quickly after him, the young lad's waxen expression denoting that his motives may not be entirely altruistic. MacKenzie chuckles.

"I did try to warn you, gentlemen!" I shout after them.

"That's Malcolm MacDonald," says Angus with levity, "I recognize the jacket."

On pulling aside the remnants of the said garment, the cadaver is better revealed. I do not bother with the usual rigmarole of taking weight and height etc., there can be no doubt the body is that of MacDonald, and his identity is not in question.

"What's that soapy stuff all over his face?"

"Please! Mr. MacKay. Another interruption and I'll have to ask you to leave. Understood?"

"Yes, I apologize, Doctor MacCulloch."

I nod. "Heavy build up of adipocere around the cheeks, the lower abdomen, and no doubt the buttocks."

MacKenzie steps closer and begins to scribble. I tug open the filthy shirt to reveal a blackened and distended abdomen, its lower portions thick with grave wax. The smell is already powerful and I do not look forward to rooting out the innards. Insects have begun their ghoulish work and the body is alive with them, which is hardly surprising considering the depth of the graves. I flick some off with a cloth. "No significant trauma to the body . . . some bruising and lividity, but these are likely post mortem." I pause to tear open the shirt on both arms. "Evidence of a previous fracture to right ulna . . . some scarring, but otherwise nothing out of the ordinary."

I quickly inhale from my lavender-soaked handkerchief.

Cutting away the grime-encrusted under garments, again, all is as expected. The cadaver has evidently been venting for some time and the distended anus makes removing the remaining material difficult.

MacKenzie passes me the scalpel as a sudden squall of wind whips at the side of the canvas, rain rattling hard all about. Superintendent Morrison steadies the swinging lantern for me as I make the first cut. I pierce the cadaver at the right shoulder and draw the blade diagonally to the sternum. Then repeat the cut on the left until both incisions meet, before drawing the blade slowly in a deep gouge all the way down the abdomen to the pubic bone to form a large Y. An unearthly exhalation issues from the abdomen, which visibly deflates as it releases its noxious fumes. I fear I may have pressed a little too hard and didn't intend to pierce the stomach at this point. For a moment I step aside, scented handkerchief pressed firmly over my nose.

It seems that Mr. Ross has seen (or smelled) enough, and quickly makes his exit with as much dignity as he can muster. Now there is only myself, Dr. MacKenzie, Young Angus MacKay, and Superintendent Morrison in attendance. On the way out, the deputy procurator fiscal passes his notebook wordlessly to the policeman.

With little struggle (the flesh has already begun to slough in some areas) I peel back the flap of skin covering the chest and drape it over the cadaver's face. MacKenzie passes me the bone cutters and I begin the difficult task of cutting through the body's ribcage. By the time I have finished and sliced away any fleshy remnants, I am sweating profusely. MacKenzie puts aside his notebook and helps me to lift the rib cage free and place it aside. One would prefer stronger lighting for a post mortem, and it is hard to tell if the flesh and musculature beneath is unusually traumatized or not—all seems to be blackened and suffused with a wan yellow light.

"Let's see if it wasn't thromboembolus that did for poor Malcolm," I say, slitting away the pericardial sac and severing the pulmonary artery. A poke around the heart's chambers with my finger is enough to determine there has been no fatal blockage.

"The heart of an ox!" I declare, wiping my finger on a nearby cloth. With a few rudimentary strokes I remove the abdominal muscle to reveal the organs beneath. I then dislodge the chest organs using the Rokitansky method, again finding nothing out of the ordinary. There is evidence of some scarring to the larynx and lungs, but that is hardly surprising for a man who spent most of his time around smoldering fires. There is, however, a light build up of fluid in the bottom of the right lung and some inflammation, which would be consummate with death by exposure. I reserve judgment but it seems likely it was simply cold and exhaustion that killed the man. I detach the internal organs in one block by severing the trachea and esophagus, then slicing away the diaphragm until only the rectum, bladder and pelvic ligaments remain. With a few more deft strokes those too are disconnected.

It is bloody work, even for a corpse as old as this, and the smells are utterly vile. For the first time since I left the shores of Lewis I'm actually glad of the squall. It carries away the worst of the stench.

"Mr. MacKenzie? Would you be so good as to help me remove the organs?"

"Of course," says he, putting aside his notebook and rolling up his sleeves.

It's no easy task to remove all the internal organs in one single block, but it is infinitely quicker and less messy than trying to remove each in turn, especially under the circumstances.

While I work on the organs on the lid of the other coffin, Dr. MacKenzie prepares to open the skull and examine the cadaver's brain. Customarily, we would extract the organ and suspend it in formaldehyde for a couple of weeks before giving it a thorough examination (brains are extremely delicate and easy to damage when uncured), but that is neither practical nor necessary at this juncture. Dr. MacKenzie and I both agreed that we would not remove the brains, but simply observe them *in situ* for any obvious abnormalities or evidence of trauma. We really don't expect to find anything of that sort, and the procedure is a formality more than anything else. I imagine I'll learn all I need from the man's organs.

The grind of MacKenzie's saw is a grim accompaniment to my investigations. At first glance, it does not seem that Malcolm was a particularly sick man, and for lack of obvious signs of disease or fatal injury, my initial supposition that the man simply died of exposure is steadily becoming conviction.

I am about to conclude my investigation and declare my verdict— MacKenzie has prized off the top of the cadaver's skull and found nothing of note therein—when, whilst checking the contents of the stomach, I see something that causes me to hesitate. In truth I'd expected to find very little in the corpse's belly. Eating heartily when you are suffering from exposure is hardly the norm. I anticipated MacKay's last meal would have been meager at best—perhaps some oats, a little thin porridge. But what I see in the man's stomach is raw meat. Raw red meat. At least a pound of rotting flesh. The stench is formidable.

"Something the matter, Doctor MacCulloch?" asks Superintendent Morrison.

"Ehm, no, I don't think so," I manage, a horrid sinking dread griping my soul. Of course, this may not be what it looks like, and perhaps, in their desperation, the two men had slaughtered one of the island's sheep or seals for sustenance? But in the boy's dispositions, no mention was made of a sheep or seal carcass being found with the two men. Besides, wouldn't they have at least tried to cook the meat? And if they were too weak to cook, then they were certainly too weak to capture and devour a sheep and eat it raw.

It is only when we move on to the initial external examination of the corpse of Murdo MacKay that my horrible suspicions are confirmed.

"And what do you suppose caused all this flesh to have been stripped from Murdo's calf?" I ask young MacKay. MacKenzie is conspicuously silent, and when he catches my eye his pallor speaks volumes. I surreptitiously motion for him to remain silent.

"I don't know, sir," Angus says, seemingly genuinely perplexed. "Some beast, or bird?"

"Are there any large predators on Rona?" I counter. "Say foxes, or badgers?"

"Not that I know of, Doctor. Least ways, no one has ever mentioned seeing such a thing."

"Maybe an otter?"

"Maybe." He seems less than convinced.

"Then rats perhaps?"

"Rats?"

"Yes, there are rats on the island after all."

"Begging your pardon, Doctor MacCulloch, but there haven't been rats on Rona in over two hundred years."

The autopsies concluded, the bodies are sealed into their coffins and placed temporarily in St. Ronan's chapel until the *Vigilant* returns. The resident fulmar's are less than happy about sharing their demesne and fly off in a fit of squawking pique. No doubt they will return when we depart the day after tomorrow.

My exertions today have left me quite exhausted and it is with some relish that I finally sit down to eat. All are present, and Young Weir and Donald have cooked us a sumptuous feast of mutton, neeps and boiled tatties. Again, MacKenzie produces his whisky, and, as the light begins to fade, the young men regal us with songs, tales and legends from Ness, Rona and Sula Sgeir.

"Do you know how the ancient Ness folk claimed lordship over the isle?" There is a shaking of heads. Weir leans forward, plucks a burning ember from the fire and lights his clay pipe.

"The previous owner of the island had died and left no heir, so it was agreed that a race would be held, from Ness to Rona, and that the first man to touch the island could claim it as their own. Of course, when news of the race got around, young men from the whole of Lewis flocked to Ness to participate." Weir reaches for a piece of wood and tosses it into the fire. It crackles and sputters. "When the day of the race finally came and all the contenders were ready, a whistle was blown and the men set off in a great flotilla.

"Of course, it's a long way here, and after a few hours the competitors drifted further and further apart. Finally, there were only two boats out in front with any real hope of being the first to reach the island."

I'm passed the whisky and this time partake of a small draught. I feel it burning in my belly, and the sensation is not wholly unpleasant.

"Anyway, both boats were neck and neck, and both men were determined to be the victor. One of them, a shepherd from Barvas, was a particularly strong rower, and had been saving the last of his strength for a final headlong push to reach the shore. When the other man saw his adversary suddenly strike for the rocks with renewed vigor, he knew all was lost. He'd spent every last ounce of his strength and couldn't hope to match the Barvas man's pace. Of course, after a time, the Barvas man looked back and saw that he had outdistanced his only real rival. The two judges that had been set down on the island previously walked down to the shore to witness the race's conclusion."

"Which was?" asks MacKenzie, polishing off the last potato.

"The Barvas man had slackened his pace a few yards from the shore and began to taunt the other man, reveling in his imminent success. On seeing this, the man—he was a Ness man himself—had been utterly enraged. He couldn't believe that he'd traveled so far and struggled so heartily, to be ridiculed by the man denying him his prize. It was too much to bear."

"So what did he do?" asks Superintendent Morrison.

"Seeing there was no hope of touching Rona before his rival, the Ness man drew his dirk and promptly severed his own hand with it."

"What the devil for?" I ask. "Did he mean to die rather than see this Barvas shepherd inherit the island?"

"On the contrary, he had every intention of winning. Taking his severed hand in the other, he hurled the bloody appendage over the Barvas man's boat and onto the island . . . As he was the first to touch it, Rona was his."

A sudden flurry of wind rips at the edge of the canvas, tearing it loose at the corner. Weir and Donald get up to secure it. The weather has been souring throughout the evening and the wind grows fierce.

MacKenzie scurries over and sits beside me, consternation writ upon his brow.

"Have you told any of the others?" he asks.

"Told them what?" For some reason I find his proximity and clandestine manner irritating.

"About what you found in MacDonald's stomach."

"No I have not. And have no intention of doing so either."

"But it was *human flesh* that you found in his guts, McCulloch!"

"Precisely," I snap, a little more vehemently than I had intended. "Do you want to be the one to tell Donald that his late father was a cannibal?" MacKenzie visibly shudders at the word. "I'm sure that I don't! Besides, what good would it do?"

"But we were sent here to see if there was any evidence of foul play, man!"

"I am aware of why we're here, Doctor MacKenzie, I don't think you need remind me of my professional duties."

"And you don't think eating the flesh of another man constitutes foul play?"

"I'm afraid that, under the circumstances, I do not."

"What do you mean! It's against God. Against nature!"

"Be that as it may, from the wound upon Murdo's body it was apparent that MacDonald ate his friend's flesh *after* Murdo had died. It was an act of desperation, not infamy. Remember, MacDonald was found in the doorway, dead from exposure. Likely the only edible thing within reach in those final days was the flesh of his comrade. I'm sure in similar circumstances we would all do the same."

"Not I," says Dr. MacKenzie, crossing himself. "I'd rather die than eat the flesh of another man."

"Physically at least," I quip.

"What do you mean?"

"Don't you Papists eat the flesh of Christ every Sunday?"

MacKenzie scowls and returns to his seat at the other side of the fire.

That noise. A faint, almost imperceptible whispering, like the stutter of a dying gaslight. Again, the words, but when I try and concentrate, they elude me. Yet even when I can't quite grasp the ancient truths being imparted, a cold dread grips me, chilling me to the marrow.

My eyes flicker open. The fire is almost dead, its embers caressed by the occasional gust of wind that finds its way beneath the canvas awning. Sparks scurry for freedom and die. All around are sleeping, except for me . . . and the rat creature squatting nearby, appraising me with its infernal red eyes. I watch as it rounds the fire and stops a few feet in front of me. The thing makes a chittering noise, and somewhere, deep in the labyrinth of my brain, I sense words forming. It wants me to follow. I attempt to will myself awake—this can only be a particularly vivid nightmare—but find myself unable to, no matter how hard I try.

"*Trobhad!*" the creature implores. I find myself wobbling uncertainly to my feet.

The rat-thing leads the way, weaving sinuously through the darkness.

After what seems like an age of groping and stumbling—the trench is impossibly long—a weak orange glow appears ahead, like that of sickly firelight playing on the wall further around the bend. Have I come full circle? The gnawing fear tells me I have not, and I begin to shake uncontrollably. I am sweating profusely despite the cold.

Inching closer to the flickering light, I notice that my verminous companion has disappeared—its work evidently done. There are noises ahead. A low murmuring. Voices! Human voices! I creep to the edge of the roughly-hewn wall where it bends at a sharp right angle, and prostrate myself in the mud before edging slowly forwards on my belly. With tears beginning to form unbidden in my eyes, I steal a glance.

It's all I can do not to cry out in horror. I stifle a guttural sob behind my hand.

One of the creatures—for human beings these wretched things couldn't possibly be—hears me and drops the severed human arm on which it had been dining, and fixes me with its feral, animal glare. I scream in terror, launching myself to my feet and running headlong back the way I have come, crashing through the darkness like a man possessed, striking against stones, stumbling in the rocks and mud, screaming into the night.

"How are you feeling, Doctor?"

"Better, thank you, MacKenzie. Please, there's no need to fuss."

"On the contrary, man! Superintendent Morrison wakes this morning to find you lying face down in the mud, battered and bruised from some nocturnal altercation!"

"Hardly a 'nocturnal altercation,'" I say, smiling weakly. "Just a bad dream. Some sleepwalking. I must have fallen."

"Sleepwalking?" MacKenzie passes me a cup of steaming tea heavily laced with whisky, which I gratefully accept. "Sleep wrestling more like!" He dabs at a bloody scrape on my right elbow with an alcohol swab. I grimace. "What amazes me most, though, is that none of us heard you about your somnambulist sortie!"

"We were all very tired," I say, shrugging. "And besides, the wind last night was ferocious."

MacKenzie looks up. "Aye, that's true. And it doesn't seem to be letting up either. I hope the *Vigilant* doesn't have any bother reaching us tomorrow."

A new fear suddenly grips me. Knowing that I have to spend one more night on this cursed island is bad enough, but I had not even considered the possibility that we may end up having to stay any longer.

"Angus, Donald and Weir are away to gather more boulders to load down the edge of the canvas," MacKenzie continues. "We don't want the blasted thing being ripped away while we sleep. Otherwise we'll be sleeping with Murdo and Donald in the teampull."

"Or in the shepherds' *taigh dubh*."

Mackenzie scowls and shakes his head. "I'd be sleeping in there tonight if it wasn't for those fool boys!"

"Don't be too hard on them, Doctor. It can't be easy for them. Donald in particular."

"That's true. I imagine seeing his father's rotten corpse hasn't done him much good. Still, he did insist on watching."

"Curiosity can be a dangerous thing," I smile.

"True," he says, straightening, appraising his handiwork. "But we would never have taken the oath with out it, eh?"

It is early afternoon, and despite the ferocious wind, MacKenzie, Weir and I are doing a little exploring.

"So tell me," I ask Weir, as we walk along the cliff tops above *Leac an Taulure*. I am making quick, crude sketches as we walk. "Does the guga nest on Rona anymore?"

"Not these days," he says, slipping a little on the wet grass. "At least, not in any numbers. There've no been gannets on Rona for as long as anyone can remember."

"But they did nest here for a time?"

"I believe so. I've heard as much. These days the Ness folk sail to Sula Sgeir for the guga."

"Guga?" enquires MacKenzie, shouting to be heard over the tempest. The good doctor is sweating prodigiously from the climb, and has lost his footing twice, even with the aid of a stout stick he'd found.

"Yes. The guga . . . it's Gaelic, for goose?" Weir nods in confirmation. "The Ness folk take the fledglings for food. They're very tasty by all accounts. Like oily, fishy chicken, so I've been told."

"Aye, that's a fair description of it," agrees Weir. We're near the edge of the cliff now watching the avian ballet below and out to sea. The wind tugs something fierce and we squat down to watch for a while.

"Aye, the Ness folk would make slippers from the birds' necks," Weir elaborates. "If you take off the creature's head and body, you can turn the neck inside out so the soft downy feathers are against your skin and the leathery neck to the ground. I've worn them myself on occasion. They're very comfortable, but they soon wear through."

We're walking back from the cliff edge when MacKenzie suddenly flies backwards into the air with a terrific yelp, his feet whipped abruptly from beneath him. He slams into the ground with a terrible thud, the wind bellowing from him like a stuck pig. Neither of us saw him lose his footing, but we scurry over to the prostrated doctor in time to see the thick welling of crimson blood ebbing into the grass beneath his head. The doctor's unseeing eyes stare straight up into the heavens.

"Doctor MacKenzie!" Weir yells. "Is he dead?" He falls upon the man, trying to roll him upright.

A sickness washes over me and for a second I can do nothing but stare, stare as a slow tide of thick blood ebbs across the ground, steaming gently as it quests for earth.

"Is he dead, Doctor?" Weir screams at me.

Recovering my wits I fumble for a pulse in the thick folds of MacKenzie's neck. I pray he is only concussed, but it is plain he is not.

Nothing.

I meet Weir's imploring gaze as I lower the good doctor's head back down onto the ground.

"I'm afraid he's dead," I hear myself say, a phrase that has tripped syrupy from my tongue a thousand times, but never before left such a bitter taste. It is only when we roll the body aside that we see the ragged black stone that penetrated his skull.

*   *   *

MacKenzie's body has been wrapped in canvas and placed with those of Murdo MacKay and Malcolm MacDonald in St. Ronan's teampull.

There is a solemnity to supper and little is said, each of us lost in his own thoughts. As the one who knew Dr. MacKenzie best, it falls to me to say a few words. Knowing little Catholic funerary, I content myself with reciting a psalm, making the sign of the cross, and leading the group in the Lord's Prayer. The Ness men sing a somber Gaelic hymn and we toast MacKenzie with the last of his whisky.

Donald is unusually attentive to the fire, yet each of us occupy ourselves with whatever minutiae we can find comfort in.

"Do you know what became of the ancient Ronan's?" Donald suddenly announces.

There are murmurs and some shaking of heads. The spluttering oil lamp hanging above our heads casts the young man in a sickly, pallid light. It is apparent from the frown bisecting Deputy Procurator Fiscal Ross's face that he deems Donald's outburst in poor taste.

Oblivious, the young man continues. "Back in the late seventeenth century there was a thriving community on Rona, and some thirty families called it home." He stops for a moment to light his pipe. "One winter's day, around 1680 by some accounts, a plague of rats suddenly descended upon the Ronans." Did Donald's eyes flick in my direction? A creeping fear begins to worm its way through my bowels. "These rats— no one knows where they came from, or how they came to be on the island—devoured every last kernel of grain, every last morsel that the islanders had to their name. They ate everything."

An eerie silence envelops us, and it seems almost as if the baleful wind that has harassed us relentlessly day and night, suddenly dies away, as if the better to hear what Donald has to say.

"So what became of the islanders?" asks Superintendent Morrison, scowling.

"What do you think?" Donald shrugs, breaking the spell. "They starved to death."

*   *   *

Superintendent Morrison is finally asleep, though judging by his occasional groans and nocturnal contortions, it is hard won. I gaze across at MacKenzie's empty bedroll and shudder. I dare not sleep, although my exhaustion is utter and nothing would be more welcome than sweet oblivion. Just one night. All I have to manage is to stay awake for one more night, and tomorrow the *Vigilant* will return and I can turn my back on this hellish rock forever. But I know that the moment I close my eyes that infernal rodent thing will be waiting for me, eager to reveal new horrors. I must not let it. I fumble for my pocket watch and squint to read the time in the last of the fire. It is a quarter past one, the night all about an amorphous black, the wind a hideous, cacophonous wailing.

This time the hissing, twitching voice claws me abruptly from sleep and my eyes fly open, my heart firing like a stoked piston. Immediately I see it, the rat thing, sitting a few feet away from me, watching, smiling . . . waiting.

"*Trobhad fèisd,*" it commands, turning its back, waiting for me to follow.

I have no sovereignty over my limbs, and inevitably, lurch to my feet and into the night. I am losing my mind. I am powerless to fight it. There is some greater will at work here, one I am incapable of resisting.

This time the rat-thing scurries out of the trench and across the open grass, a sleek blasphemous shadow slipping across the ground ahead of me. It is leading me to St. Ronan's teampull. The creature stops short at the tiny doorway, waiting for me to step back down into the trench. As I do so, it disappears inside and a faint, jaundiced light leaks from within the chapel.

I follow inside, crawling through the mud on my hands and knees. I would brave a whole army of vomiting fulmars rather than witness this inescapable nightmare. Three people—if these pathetic specimens could ever have been part of our glorious species—stand hunched over something, groping, tearing . . . chewing. Their stench is overpowering and I feel a rotten, acid sickness welling in my throat. Please Lord! Release me from this horror! I would repent all mankind's sins if only

72

you would show mercy. The disgusting creatures are impossibly thin, covered in filthy rags, the hair and faces so dirt-encrusted as to defy their race or gender. They are feasting on MacKenzie's corpse.

"*Ith. Deagh!*" one of the things says, turning to me, a lump of bloody meat in its outstretched hand. As if from afar, I see myself reach out, unable to intervene, unable to act to the contrary, and take the creature's proffering, biting down into the doctor's dead flesh. Am I really here? Is this just some new dimension to my dementia? I care not. MacKenzie's flesh tastes divine . . . a succulent, mouth-watering nirvana. It makes the blood roar in my veins like a hellish choir! I lose all sense of self, tearing into the bloody meat, pushing aside the feeble ragged things and ripping out fresh chunks with my bare hands, gorging myself, my appetite infernal and insatiable.

After what seems like an age, I stagger back to the camp in a daze as the new day struggles to breach the horizon. Cresting the edge of the trench I spy a movement from the corner of my eye that sends a sudden spike of fear and terrified lucidity through me, bludgeoning me back into the moment. Had there been someone there, at the edge of other tent, watching?

I awake with a start, gripped with a sudden panic, before coming to my senses and sinking back into my bedroll with unparalleled relief. It had been just another nightmare, and even though those horrific scenes are still lucid, branded indelibly into my memory, they were nothing more than chimeras and phantoms. I dreamt it all! I offer up a silent prayer.

Superintendent Morrison is already awake and out of the tent. I feel my spirits lift as I begin to dress. There is no water left, so I pick up the empty pail to refill it in the small stream close by. Today the *Vigilant* will be returning for us. And not a moment too soon. The weather has been worsening by the day and the wind positively rages across the island. One more night on Rona would be more than my fragile sanity could take and I fear I would pitch myself over the cliffs before facing my nocturnal tormentors again.

I climb out of the tent to see Superintendent Morrison and Donald engaged in heated debate. Nether see me and the policeman abandons the discourse and makes away before I approach.

Donald nods when he sees me, but his open expression darkens as I get closer and turns from one of welcome to one of fear and revulsion. I slacken my pace. He looks like he's seen a ghost and begins to back slowly away. It is only then that I notice the rust-colored stains marring the backs of my hands. I quickly touch my face and feel a dried iron-tinged crust across my cheeks and mouth. Blood! My hands and face a thick with the stuff. I abandon the bucket and dash towards the small stream scouring myself furiously until I'm sure that not a speck remains. My black, lumpy vomit mixes with the offending blood in the water.

"I cannot apologize enough for this ridiculous interview, Doctor," Morrison says, shrugging. He and I are sat by the outskirts of the village returning one of the canvas tents to its sack. The others are by the shore looking out for the *Vigilant*.

"Don't be foolish, Superintendent. I'm sure Donald believes he saw what he did. Besides, he's not immune to the caprices of Rona. I myself have been prey to them. We are all very tired after all."

Morrison nods.

"He says you had blood on your hands and face when he saw you this morning?"

"Blood?" I laugh whilst rolling up one of the bedrolls.

"If only it were blood!" At this Morrison's eyebrows arch. "It would be less embarrassing." I rise and take some pans and cooking utensils, stuffing them into another bag. "I'm afraid that during the night I had a very bad case of diarrhea. I awoke in the morning to find my bedroll filled with the stuff. I've had to toss my clothes and bedding away. The stench was unbearable. I must have got the stuff on my face as I slept. As I said, a most embarrassing event and one I'd be grateful you wouldn't mention to anyone. Save Donald, of course. Must put his mind at rest. Don't want him thinking us men of medicine are ravening beasts, do we?"

The lie has the desired affect, and Morrison's face visibly reddens.

"Of course not," he blurts. "I must confess I had a bit of an upset stomach myself last night. Consider the matter closed, sir."

"I appreciate your discretion, Superintendent."

Once all the provisions are packed away and our last repast on Rona eaten, we retire to the shore of *Geodha a Stoth* to await the arrival of the *Vigilant.*

As the sky begins to bruise with evening, we light a small fire on the shoreline, for warmth and to aid the cutter's progress.

It should have arrived by now.

"It's not coming," yells MacKay, after some hours, having to shout over the wind and crashing surf to be heard.

He merely voices what we are all beginning to suspect.

"We can't spend another night here!" exhorts Weir. "We've no more food and the tents and gear are already packed away! It's getting dark, too. How are we supposed to put the tents back up?"

"Calm yourself, man," booms Deputy Procurator Fiscal Ross. "We can shelter a night in the shepherd's *taigh dubh* if we must."

Donald visibly bristles at this, and is about to protest when Morrison interrupts him.

"The procurator's right, gentleman. We have no other choice. Besides, I'm sure Murdo and Malcolm wouldn't have wished us to meet the same fate that they did. It's time to put superstition aside and look to ourselves."

"It'll be a tight squeeze in there," complains Angus.

"Then at least we'll keep each other warm," Morrison snaps.

We wait until the sky is almost black and the fire reduced to embers before beginning the melancholy trudge back up to the village.

I wish it were that my heart was filled only with trepidation and disappointment, like the others. There is no room for such sentiments in my breast. Not when it is filled with this ungodly terror. I dare not even think about what infamy tonight will bring. Every lengthening shadow makes me start, and I imagine I catch glimpses of hellish scurrying things on the edge of my vision. My purchase on reality loosens by the hour.

The black house is a sad affair and contains only two cots. Donald claims his father's former bunk and Deputy Procurator Fiscal Ross, being the eldest member of our party, the other. I make a conspicuous show of taking MacKenzie's bedroll for my own (I had disposed of my own the previous day down a large blowhole to better sustain my deception).

All are sullen and say little as they make what unoccupied corner of the dwelling they can, their own. Our oil lamp is set on the mantle and the very last of our supplies boiled up into a thin broth. There are no songs tonight, save the wind keening through the walls, and exhaustion takes us one by one.

Have I slept? I think not. I am sure my eyes haven't closed since darkness enveloped us and the lamp was put out. Now there is but the feeble glow from the waning fire for comfort. I shuffle a little closer to the hearth but there is little heat to be had.

Where is my nemesis? Perhaps, as I have not slept yet, it will not come? Perhaps, last night's hellish business concluded, it is finally done with me? I wish I could believe that, but I fear it is not so. No matter how hard I grope for a rational explanation, where else could the blood have come from but from MacKenzie's cadaver?

I make my move when I am certain all are asleep. I have been dreading making this charnel pilgrimage all day, but know that I must take it.

Outside, the wind is still fierce, St. Ronan's teampull a lump of dark swelling from the ground about it. Down in the trench and before the chapel's low door, I take out a small candle and strike a match. The first goes out immediately but with the second I manage to coax a tiny flame from my candle, shielding it the best I can with my hand.

As soon as I enter, the smell is overpowering. The teampull has a congregation of no less than three decomposing corpses. Thankfully the doctor's body will not have begun to rot yet, especially given the cold, but it doesn't stop the vapors emanating from Murdo and Malcolm catching in the back of the throat making tears blur my eyes.

I steal up to MacKenzie's corpse and lift my candle. And almost swoon in horror at what its sickly light reveals. It as I feared, and worse. Great hunks of flesh have been ripped from MacKenzie's body. There are bite marks in profusion, tears and rends peppering his blooded flesh. I cry out, unable to stop myself, dropping my candle and bolting headlong for the door when I see a stooping figure entering the teampull.

"Leave me be, Satan spawn!" I roar, launching myself at the figure in abject rage. Will these beasts ever leave me in peace? I have my fingers around its throat in an instant, throttling the life out of the wretched thing. "I will not dine with you tonight, demon," I snarl, pushing my thumbs into its throat with all the might I can muster. The creature struggles, gurgling, thrashing this way and that, but a titan would be hard pressed to loosen the vice-like grip in which I hold my tormentor.

Eventually its struggles weaken, and I relent, but find unlocking my bloodless fingers from its neck extremely painful. I would not have known it was humanly possible to feel such hatred, such anger. I only wish its rat-thing compatriot were here also so I could grind its filthy hide into the dirt.

Spent, I collapse against the wall and rest for some time, my mind teetering on the edge of oblivion. Eventually I feel strength returning to my limbs and spend some time groping about on the floor for my dropped candle. I strike another match to it and hold the flame out to my assailant.

Donald MacDonald's lifeless eyes stare back at me, the blackened tongue protruding from him mouth, impaled bloodily on his teeth.

It is apparent that I am becoming some instrument of evil, my purpose beyond mortal ken. There can be no more doubt. If only my rat-thing mentor would come to me again, and tell me what must be done. Where are its sibilant whisperings now, when I need them most? I am abandoned by God, by reason and my hellish patron.

But how to explain this horror to the others? I could simply dispose of Donald's corpse. Drag it to the cliff edge and pitch it into the sea. But

I run the risk of it washing back up upon the rocks and being undone. Perhaps I could claim he was suffering from an acute melancholy, had confided in me as much, and must have gone out into the night to end his life? Plausible, but I would still have to drag his body to the cliffs, and again, there is the risk of discovery. No . . . there is a better way.

When all is ready and I have mentally rehearsed my story a dozen times, I crash headlong into the *taigh dubh,* waking all within, making a show of collapsing to the ground, groaning mightily. My eye and burst lip are already beginning to swell and the pain is acute. It was no easy feat to strike myself thus, but necessary if they are to believe my story.

There is much commotion and Superintendent Morrison levers me into a chair and splashes water onto my face. I wait until I am certain all are gathered and I cannot resist their urgings any longer. There is frantic shouting and already Weir has dashed out into the night, bellowing Donald's name into the gale.

"Donald," I gasp. "Donald . . . we fought." I begin to weep. Morrison shakes me vigorously until I pretend to regain my senses.

"What happened, man!" he demands. "Where is Donald?"

"The chapel . . . I followed him. He went to the chapel. Oh my God . . . "

"Get a hold of yourself, Doctor! What was he doing in the chapel? Why did you fight?"

"He was defiling the bodies . . . He attacked me."

There is a stunned silence. Angus turns and follows Weir into the darkness.

"What do you mean, 'defiling the bodies?'" Morrison presses. Deputy Procurator Fiscal Ross passes me a cup of water.

"He was eating them . . . oh my God." I hang my head in my hands, weeping uncontrollably. "He was eating the bodies."

It is our seventh day on the island. Donald's corpse has been placed with the others in St. Ronan's chapel. Before I'd left the teampull and returned to the black house, I'd made sure and bloodied Donald's mouth and hands, scraped his knuckles and wedged bits of skin between his teeth and under his nails. None suspect the truth and my version of events remains inviolate. I have since implied that Donald had an obsession with the plight of Rona's former inhabitants, and had confided in me that he was plagued by evil dreams. All now are thoroughly convinced that the boy had lost his mind.

For the next two days I am confined to the *taigh dubhu* "until my strength returns." This suits me fine, as whilst the others forage for fuel and food, and keep watch for the return of the *Vigilant*, I take the opportunity to steal to the teampull and gorge myself. I have never felt stronger, though I must confess, I begin to hunger for fresher fare.

Yesterday, Weir died. Apparently he had been foraging on the cliff face beneath *Toa Rona*, attempting to reach some fledglings, when he lost his footing and fell. There was nothing anyone could do. He was dashed on the rocks below and swept out to sea. Now only four of us remain: Deputy Procurator Fiscal Ross, Superintendent Morrison, Young Angus MacKay and myself.

"We must find a way to best divide our labor," Superintendent Morrison says. It is difficult to read the man's expression through the prodigious beard that covers his face. How long have we been here? I must confess I am losing count.

"What do you suggest?" asks Angus.

"There are four of us left. Perhaps Mr. Ross, being the eldest, and, if you would beg my pardon, sir, the weakest of us, would be best suited to keeping an eye out for a passing ship? I'm sure it is clear to us all that the *Vigilant* will not be returning for us."

The procurator simply nods.

"Doctor MacCulloch. Would you like to accompany Angus foraging for fuel? I fear we will soon run out again at this rate and the two of you can carry more." We both agree.

"I will try hunting again. After the past few day's disastrous attempts at killing a seal, I'll go back to trying to snatch birds, unless anyone has any better ideas?"

We shake our heads.

* * *

It seems like the storm has raged for weeks. I can no longer remember a time when the wind didn't scour the island like a knife, as if attempting to scrape the taint of evil from its shores.

Two days ago a ship was sighted in the distance but we failed to signal it. We could not light our sodden beacon fire in time—having run out of lamp oil weeks ago—and the tinder would not take.

Deputy Procurator Fiscal Ross grows weaker. He scratched his shin six days ago and septicemia has set in and threatens to take his whole leg. He refuses to let me amputate it. Last night he dictated his last will and testament and entrusted it to Superintendent Morrison's safe keeping. All are increasingly despondent and lost in melancholy.

Food is becoming very scarce. We have captured only two sea birds in the last two weeks and all but I are suffering greatly from fatigue and hunger.

Donald's corpse is almost eaten. Today it is my turn to forage for fuel. Before leaving the black house, I take the longest of my serrated knifes from my Gladstone and secrete it in my boot. Morrison is hunting again and Angus is to tend the beacon.

I fish a coin from my pocket and step from the *taigh dubhu* and into the wind. "Heads Angus, and tails Superintendent Morrison," I say to myself, smiling.

"Doctor MacCulloch?" Angus is surprised to see me. He would have been even more surprised to know I have been standing behind him for the last ten minutes, my blade poised behind his neck.

On a whim, I'd sheathed the knife and stepped round the boy.

"Angus. How goes the vigil?"

"How do you think? Not a thing. I'm beginning to wonder if we'll ever leave Rona. I should never have come back to this awful place."

"Now, now, Angus. Where there is life, there is always hope," I say, trying to set the boy at ease.

"Do you think so? What hope have we? We haven't seen a sail or plume of steam for weeks. I am skin and bone. I don't know how much longer I can stand it, Doctor."

I look the boy over. He is very thin. Much more so than when we first arrived. He'll be meager pickings.

"Nonsense boy, there's still plenty of meat on those bones," I reply.

"I wish that were true."

"So do I," I sigh, sliding the blade from my boot, "so do I." A brief moment of fleeting incomprehension is followed by a soft gurgling as the serrated, nine-inch blade glides quietly into his throat. I watch serenely as his life blood drains out onto the grass.

I hid Angus' body in an alcove on the shore near *Cladach Cro Eoin Dearg*. At night I return there to feast. As if complicit in my crimes, the rain scoured away all traces of blood from the ground around the pyre. We searched high and low for Angus that first day when he didn't return from his vigil, but we can only assume he met the same fate as Weir. It has been three days since he disappeared and no one suggested we search for him this morning.

Yesterday, I thought I saw a ship on the horizon. I had been tending the beacon. At first I leapt to my feet, reaching for my tinder and remaining matches, but as I was about to strike, I hesitated. I'd never really considered what I would do if I saw a ship, if there were any real chance of rescue. But when I'd strained my eyes to better make out the distant object, it had turned abruptly towards me and approached the island at great haste, faster than any ocean-going vessel possibly could. As it closed the distance with Rona, I began to discern its shape better. This was no ship, but some sort of sea creature . . . a whale or huge basking shark perhaps? Suddenly, and without warning the thing had submerged as quickly as it had come, leaving no trace of its passage except a quickly dispersing eddy. I waited for an hour after, scanning the murky grey waters and distant horizon, but it never came again.

Deputy Procurator Fiscal Ross's fever is all-consuming. You can smell the rot off him. He'll be lucky if he lasts another night.

I have lit a small fire and am boiling water, tending to Ross's wounds, when Superintendent Morrison returns from another fruitless hunting trip.

"McCulloch," says he, nodding and slumping exhaustedly into a chair.

"Superintendent." It is obvious he has caught nothing. He emanates an air of barely suppressed menace.

"What have we left that we can eat tonight?" he asks after a time.

"Nothing, I'm afraid."

"Are you sure," he says, unable to suppress an undercurrent of suspicion. Hostility even.

"Of course I'm sure," I reply. "What are you suggesting, man? That there's some secret stash of food secreted somewhere on the island that we've been unfortunate not to have stumbled upon?"

"Of course, not," he snaps.

"Well what then? Do you think I am hiding something from you? Is that it?" I withdraw the pan from the fire and rest it on the hearth.

"No, of course not. I'm not suggesting that at all." He shifts uneasily in his chair. It is perfectly plain that that is exactly what he means.

"We are all hungry, Superintendent. We are all tired. No one is blaming you that you didn't catch a bird today."

"It isn't easy, you know!" he blurts, barely able to suppress his anger.

"No one said it is," I say, in a tone that I hope is placatory.

He is silent for a while, all the time watching from beneath heavily lidded eyes. I can feel his gaze boring through me, laying bare my infamies and crimes.

"You do look a lot healthier than either Ross or myself," he suddenly says.

"I beg your pardon, Superintendent, but there are cadavers in the teampull that look as well as the procurator," I retort in hushed tones.

"You know what I mean," he growls. "You certainly look a lot better than I do. I've lost stones, where you . . . you've barely had to notch your belt."

While he talks I turn the handle on the pan towards myself. I hadn't expected this moment to come so soon, but I always knew that it would one day. In some ways I'm relieved. At least there will be no more cloak and dagger chicanery. There is a metal poker by the fire. I wedge it into the flames, the handle within easy reach.

"Would you like to know why I have not lost as much weight as you, Superintendent?" I say calmly.

He scowls. "Why?"

"Because ever since the food ran out, I have been feasting every day."

"What!?"

I turn to face him, the pan of boiling water in my hand. "I've been feasting every day, on the flesh of our fallen comrades." At first it's as if he hasn't heard what I said, like the words, being so unbelievable, have entered his skull only to be reconfigured in as many ways as possible, in any way that did not implicate the horrors his mind must only now be forming.

He is about to launch himself from the chair when I hurl the boiling water at him. He falls back screaming, clawing at his scalded face, upending his chair, and I am upon him in an instant, battering the poker into his hands and face with all the hellish strength I can muster. His screams of pain turn to slaughter-house howling as I drive the poker repeatedly into his head. I strike time and again as his screams give way to hideous gurgles, bones cracking and splintering. Eventually his struggles ceases, blood bubbling from his ruined face. I collapse back onto the floor and watch as the red pool spreads slowly across the ground. Taking a moment to catch my breath, I wipe beads of perspiration from my brow. After some minutes Morrison's chest stops rising and the Superintendent lies still.

It is only then that I notice Deputy Procurator Fiscal Ross, sat up in bed, cowering against the wall, his eyes wide with terror. Urine seeps from the edge of his bedclothes and mixes with the blood on the floor.

Ross and I live together for another three days. I talk to him as I dismember and cook the unfortunate Superintendent. He listens. On the first day he refuses to eat the dead man's flesh, but it is plain the smell of roasting meat is driving the poor man insane. On the second day he simply weeps, only ceasing for a time when I threaten him.

On the third day he crumbles. He manages to hold the meat down for a time, but eventually vomits it all back up, spending the rest of the day whimpering like scalded dog. He tries again. Later that night I press a pillow over his face and extinguish him. He barely kicks.

Ross has almost cooled when I hear a low scritching. I put on my coat and open the door. The rat-thing is waiting, a glint of satiated malice in its glowing red eyes.

"*Trobhad,*" it commands.

I follow. Strange, I hadn't noticed inside, but the ubiquitous gale has completely receded. The night is beautifully still, with an almost surreal quality, a fat gibbous moon picking out the crest of *Toa Rona* and the grassy expanse of *Leathad Fhianuis*. The sea laps like quicksilver against the shore of *Geodha a Stoth*.

Something waits for me by the rocks. A sea creature. An enormous black shape at rest in the water. I can only guess at its bulk, but the strange swell and eddies around about it suggest its visible mass is but a tiny part of it. A huge oval eye tilts towards me from beneath the water. A string of sinuous tentacles undulate around its toothy maw, padding and probing amongst the kelp and rocks.

"Streap air bòrd," the rat creature implores.

The great beast of the ocean. I wade into the surf and mount the *cionarain-crò.*

The Ruin
by Skadi meic Beorh

I came to a ruin where indecent air
revealed Ireland's sense of Ascendancy care.
Dead smiles unflinching for power and vice
exposed sudden shadows bought for good price
far less than that carried at Easter for purse;
three pieces of silver were paid, and a curse
upon the dull peasants collecting wild thyme
and other strange simples to pastoral rhyme.
Has anyone seen now the way that they go?
Which way have they gone, have they gone?

I scanned this grey house found in crumbles and thorn;
studied its garden; felt gloomy, forlorn.
I stumbled over a cross . . . Celtic shrine
destroyed by mad Vikings amused with their wine.
Has anyone seen now the way that they go?
Which way have they gone, have they gone?

A great sense of loss filled the place, beat the ground
with unseen frustration, inaudible sound.
I knew the queer feeling of roaming a land
roiling with hatred beneath frigid hand
so ready to furnish the murderous blow
empowered by avarice only Men know.
Has anyone seen now the way that they go?
Which way have they gone, have they gone?

No rain on the morrow, cobalt had turned red;
a prayer had been answered, all shepherds to bed.
Moon-scythe had arisen; a rain-holding cup.
I smiled softly then as my gaze wandered up . . .
    children at the casements, all there beckoning.
I fell to my knees as they began to sing
Has anyone seen now the way that they go?
Which way have they gone, have they gone?

Skadi meic Beorh, a speculative writer of Celto-Teutonisch descent, has authored the story collections Always After Thieves Watch *(Brilliant Book Press) and* Scary Stories For Girls *(Backroom Publishing), and has co-edited the dictionary* Pirate Lingo *(Brilliant Book Press). His first novel,* The Obscure, *will be published by Wildside Press. He has also been honored to have a tale about his literary hero Nathaniel Hawthorne appear in the anthology* Bound For Evil. *His work has most recently appeared in* Black Petals, Twisted Tongue, Ballista, Lachryma, Brilliant!, *and* The Willows *(where he serves as Contributing Editor). He may be reached at dreamer.stalker@yahoo.com.*

F.V. "Ed" Edwards is internationally known in Medical Product development as an engineer/inventor (19 patents since 1976), a speaker and author of numerous articles in the field. He served as a Tribal Health Director for three years and did considerable research on their cultural history to support needed improvements in the health services. This story is rooted in some of that expanded knowledge and also in their legends. He expresses gratitude to James Gunn for the on-line Science Fiction workshop and the critique group formed from those classes. They were a great help in his transition from a technical writer.

Rock Visions
by F.V. "Ed" Edwards

Agonizing screams from the communal birthing hut echoed loudly off the nearby hills. They brought tension to the village. Several adult women were gathered around the hut chanting an ancient prayer while exchanging expressions of sorrow and sympathy. Sweet-Girl had grown extremely huge before the delivery pains started. Men around the central campfire with the older children were uneasy.

Her mate of nine months sat alone inside the large rock and log structure where many generations had lived. Four of those generations squatted outside as insisted upon by Swift-Feet's father, a kind and gentle man known as Wise-Bear.

The family elder sensed his third son needed to avoid anyone seeing the unmanly cringes certain to follow the periodic outbursts of his mate. There was no reason to expose the man of seventeen summers to possible questions of his mental and physical fortitude. He was sure the sensitive young brave had never dreamed the coupling with Sweet-Girl would lead to such agony. He remembered the fear that clutched at his heart over the mournful cries when his mate first gave birth. The fear diminished with each of the next nine, but, so had the intensity and duration of Night-Bird's misery lessened.

After a softer screech, new born cries were heard. Swift-Feet stopped twisting the buffalo hide in his hands and rose knowing the baby had been born. He was ready to stride forward with fatherly pride as his parent instructed. The midwife would give the child to the Clan Mother, and she would transfer the baby to him.

The band was prepared to cheer when the Clan Mother appeared holding the baby high above her head in keeping with tradition. Swift-Feet rushed to the birthing hut door. The older woman came out carrying the child against her chest and shouted, "We have a new brave." She made no attempt to lift it above her head.

Short cheers faded into gasps and startled mumbles. The people stared at a newborn larger than most children of two summers. The father was stunned at the size of his son. He stumbled at the unexpected weight, and struggled to raise the child above his head as a new father was supposed to do. It wasn't easy. He quickly brought the baby back into the woman's arms to return it to the mother for a first feeding.

The Keeper of Memories' jaw hung in awe as his fingers quickly scanned the beads on the memory belt, starting at the oldest part. He didn't pause until reaching the beads he had added. No birth so huge had been recorded during thousands of moons. He rose knowing the Lake-of-Salt Band with parts of four clans of the scattered Utan people waited for him to speak. "We see the largest baby any of the clans has produced. Some may fear this is the rebirth of Tso'apittse, the giant who ate our babies." He looked around making eye contact and saw some cower. "That is not true." He paused to let his words be absorbed as he looked directly at the Chief. He turned to another elder. "The giant would be ten times bigger. Am I not right, Spirit-Sensor?"

The medicine man smiled and rose. He'd seen this child in many visions and thus usurped the Chief's rights to speak and name the infant. "Let us welcome Moose to the Bear Clan and our band. He will be the greatest brave in Utan history." He paused, choosing not to add that the immense child would need to learn to assert himself and his thoughts in non-physical matters for the prediction to come true.

Although the mother died a few hours after the birth, rapid growth in the boy's size was not a surprise to anyone in the tribe. Most figured Moose would be clumsy, cumbersome, and slow minded. The general belief was the boy would become a mighty warrior as predicted. The expectation was he would be an easily led man of bulk who would faithfully follow the Chief's orders in battle, the way a well trained dog did on a hunt. He would overpower potential enemies with his size and ferocious strength. Spirit-Sensor was amused by the many discussions the people had in this regard, never relating what his visions revealed about the future.

Swift-Feet and the close family members were the first to notice indications of quickness in all aspects of the boy's life. He spoke intelligibly in seven moons. His ability to ask for what he wanted was joyously demonstrated by the grandmothers to his father, grandfathers and uncles when they returned from the fall hunt. Winter passed and thirteen moons after birth the large child began walking as if with a purpose, exhibiting unusual physical coordination with his hands as well. The women of the family were delighted by how quickly he emulated older children in going out to the trenches to urinate and defecate. His surprising skills became apparent to the tribe by the end of his second summer when he began wrestling with and defeating boys of six summers.

The father returned to the village with a new mate after a trading trip to Coyote Valley during Moose's third summer. Subtle household competition began between Night-Bird, the paternal grandmother, and Deep-Eyes, the new mate. They each wanted to be the one who gave the boy proper motherly love and he happily responded to both.

Swift-Feet understood the problem and discussed it with Wise-Bear. They decided that with the new spouse pregnant, it was time for the third son to leave the overcrowded family dwelling. The home was the oldest brother's to inherit.

They constructed a new dwelling nearby. There the couple could define the future of the magnificent boy, while Night-Bird would be close enough to contribute. Swift-Feet prayed Deep-Eyes would survive childbirth and fill the new home with many children.

Because of his intimidating size, parents of other children had Moose banned from physical contests among the young in his fourth summer. He became a consistent winner in the dance competitions and dominated the mental quickness and memory games for his age group. Without special encouragement, the boy spent hours quietly listening to the elders around the village campfires. They were impressed the way the boy retained lessons in the Utan ways and the secrets needed to become a great hunter, fisherman and warrior.

The Keeper of Memories believed Moose should be trained to take his place. Others argued that he should be trained to become Chief since Bold-Eagle had not produced a son. Spirit-Sensor tried to convince them Moose should be trained as a medicine man. It was decided his final role would be chosen after proving himself a warrior.

Moose was larger than all the adult braves in his twelfth summer. The Council approved the boy to compete in men's contests. He soon won all of the events. The deposed champions openly resented the quiet large youth.

As the family settled down on woven mats for an evening meal, he asked, "Why don't they like me, father? I never gloat when I win." He was sincere. Somehow he'd expected the teasing remarks about his size to end with his success.

Swift-Feet stared into the eyes of a son noticeably bigger than himself. He felt a twinge of jealousy at no longer being the fastest in foot races, yet proud he was still second best. "I've been champion in the races for many summers, and I don't like being defeated. You are now best in all fifteen events. No man has ever dominated more than five. No one likes being a loser. Your mother helped me learn to lose with respect for the winner before you were born."

Moose looked at the only woman he'd known as mother. He asked,

"How did you do that?"

The father turned to Deep-Eyes knowing he should speak first. His mind relived the joy he'd felt finding the Elk clan woman who'd presented him five children in eight summers.

"Sweet-Girl was my friend when I was trying to become the fastest brave. She saw me reach my goal the summer before Moose was born. You've been mother to Moose since he was three summers. What would you say to him?"

Her expression showed pleasure in being asked by father and son. She smiled and looked at Moose. "You bring us joy watching you develop into a kind and powerful soul. Hold your head high. Ignore the envy of fools, and one day you'll lead our people."

At the beginning of his seventeenth summer, Moose's chin was a full hand's length above the next tallest brave. His oval face was thinned, and his chest had filled out to match very broad shoulders. He'd used youth to hone overwhelming physical and mental skills. The quickest, most agile, biggest and strongest member of the band, he was known among the elders for his kindness, gentleness and memory. Most were sure he would one day be their Chief. Peace had existed well over a generation. He was declared a brave that summer and many wondered if he would ever have the chance to prove his skills in battle.

Spirit-Sensor watched the boy's progress into manhood and was pleased. His visions of the future were being confirmed, yet he was concerned because Moose never ventured an opinion, or questioned whatever was said by an elder. As the medicine man, his opportunities to talk with the boy in private were few because Moose was never injured or ill. He advised the youth to assert the considerable accumulated knowledge. Passivity was not a Chief-like asset.

The Banush Band was an odd warlike group of the Paiutan People who stayed in the north when most of their tribe moved west. Surrounded by Utan People, a tenuous peace existed between the peoples for twenty-two summers. When they suffered from barren crops and the loss of several women in childbirth, thirty-one hunger driven Banush ended the peace. They bypassed the large Utan encampment at Bear Lake to raid the smaller village near the Lake-of-Salt. They expected only women, children and elders at harvest, making it easy to steal food and young females.

Moose and nine other braves returned early from a very successful hunt. They surprised the would-be thieves. Moose grabbed the leader, broke the man's knife arm, and threw the body six feet toppling three other charging raiders. He leaped over the stunned pile and slammed together the heads of the next two, knocking them unconscious. Spurred by his performance, the other Utan braves were controlling one or two each. The battle ended with eleven Banush warriors running north to save themselves as the other twenty were being vanquished. Three died as result of head injuries. Seventeen were fettered and placed in a compound with the animals.

At the campfire a week later, Bold-Eagle asked about the battle. The women, children and elders told a story that made it seem Moose defeated the raiders single handedly. Their story rang with truth supported by the braves Moose led into battle. The Chief pronounced, "Moose is proven a magnificent warrior. He decides what to do with the prisoners. If he chooses to make them slaves, he gets first pick."

Beads were added to immortalize the big man as a memorable hero while the band gathered to celebrate. The victory added to the joy of a good harvest and great hunts. They cheered knowing the storage cave next to the flat rock would be full for winter.

Spirit-Sensor quietly thanked all of the gods and the ancestors for having been given the gift of visions to see the future warrior. He hoped to soon know how Moose would fit into the long term future of the tribe. His chest swelled with pride when the decision was announced to release the prisoners, allow them to stay or leave, and take the remains of their fallen comrades if they left. They would spread the word that it was foolish to attack the Utan people by the Lake-of-Salt.

Trading parties took stories of the giant brave to other bands and tribes living in the big mountains to the north and east, the deserts to the southwest, and the cliff dwellers on southern plateaus. Visitors came from afar.

"We give thanks to Moose, our great warrior," Bold-Eagle told them with pride. "Tell all you meet about his mighty skills so peace will be ours for many cycles to come."

Four relaxed summers passed as many came to see and meet the famous brave. Some in the band were concerned because Moose turned down all of the eligible maidens from within their village, and all those that visited. During the week before the eighth moon, a tall maiden named Happy-Moon came with her family from the Eagle Clan of Utan People in the great desert to the southwest. Moose felt their hearts intertwine when their eyes met.

They both admitted desire to mate. This caused a lot of parental discussion as the families sat on woven reeds to share the noon meal. Moose wasn't willing to follow Utan custom where the brave who accepted a first daughter in another band would leave to join her clan. He struggled to express his deepest feelings. With fear of losing the first woman he was willing to mate with, he haltingly said, "I adore Happy-Moon, but I will not move to the Valley-of-Death."

Proud-Cougar, her father, argued tradition be followed. He'd traveled that far just to see the legendary massive brave. Happy-Moon was with them in hopes she'd find a mate at one of the other stops. After it was clear she wouldn't accept a man from among the clans of their band, he took her on summer trips for four cycles. There hadn't been a brave she was willing to consider on visits to twelve other Utan encampments. Secretly delighted his daughter found an acceptable mate, he was stunned Moose was willing to consider her. Proud-Cougar knew if the giant became part of the Eagle clan, his chances of becoming Chief of their encampment were greatly enhanced.

The unresolved aspect of the family discussions forced a special band Council meeting the next evening around the campfire. Proud-Cougar spoke first. "My daughter is willing to become Moose's mate. He has expressed desire for her. I am pleased. But," he paused to scan the important audience, "do we dare risk bad medicine by not following Utan custom? I ask the brave be instructed to follow that custom and become part of the Eagle Clan."

The Council looked at each other with grim looks. None of them wanted to see Moose depart. The man made what seemed a valid point. Moose's grandfather, Wise-Bear, a long time member of the Council stood and looked at the Chief for permission to speak.

Bold-Eagle nodded.

"Proud-Cougar is a fine man from our cousins in the Valley-of-Death. He has a beautiful daughter. He is not of our Council, and does not have the right to ask us to force Moose to leave. There are two things I would ask before any of us would consider the idea."

"Ask," Bold-Eagle said.

The grandfather nodded. He asked the Keeper of Memories, "Do you have history where the tradition hasn't been followed?"

The elder had already checked his beads. "I do not find a memory where that has happened."

"Thank you. Spirit-Sensor, you told us Moose would be our greatest brave when he was born and that has come true. Will it create bad medicine to not follow custom?"

The medicine man stood and looked at the expectant faces. He wished for a moment it wasn't dark so he could go to the flat rock for a special vision that might truthfully answer the question. That wasn't something he was ready to do. He spoke from his heart, "I don't have a potion to defy custom. I wish I did. I sense Happy-Moon is the right mate for Moose, so I cannot speak against their union. We must choose between the bad medicine I feel would befall us if our greatest warrior goes so far away, and the bad medicine if she stays here. I know we have maidens available within our band which would eliminate the question of bad medicine, but, we all know none of them is acceptable to Moose." He spread his hands.

Wise-Bear smiled. "I will ask one thing more. Can you find a potion to undo bad medicine regarding tradition?" He sat without waiting for an answer.

"I can try."

Silence continued for a few moments. Swift-Feet rose. He was recognized by the Chief. "I do not wish to sorrow my son or Happy-Moon. I am willing to let Spirit-Sensor seek to find a potion, but I'm not willing to let my son leave against his will."

The Chief asked, "Moose, do you truly want this woman, and are you willing to risk bad medicine?"

Moose nodded his head hesitant to speak without rising.

Bold-Eagle scanned the council and spoke in a loud voice. "We don't have an Eagle Clan here. Moose does not want to leave. We don't want him to go. Should we break tradition and accept Happy-Moon into our Bear Clan?"

Spirit-Sensor spoke. "Ask the mother. If she agrees, we should welcome Happy-Moon."

Gentle-Flower began speaking before Proud-Cougar nudged her shoulder. She didn't look to see his expression knowing he'd expect her to back his request. Their strong willed daughter verged on becoming an old maid. Her voice was strong and clear. "I will waive custom provided they visit Eagle Clan with their children every fourth cycle. And, to follow an alternate tradition of our clan that should avoid bad medicine, we will accept their second son to be raised by us from his second summer." She secretly wished she might've had the chance to mate with such a magnificent male.

Bold-Eagle asked Spirit-Sensor. "Do you accept her words as the potion you seek?"

The medicine man nodded.

"Moose. Do you accept the terms?"

"Yes, provided Happy-Moon approves."

The maiden stood and turned her eyes to each Council member saying, "I hope you are willing to accept me in the Bear clan, for I do wish to mate with Moose and make many mighty braves for the band." She paused to smile. "I mean, I will gladly accept and comply with my mother's request."

*   *   *

95

They held commitment ceremonies early the next morning so Happy-Moon's parents could immediately depart for the long trip home. Moose, his father, brothers, cousins, and several others rapidly constructed a new extension of birch wood tied with rawhide strips to the crowded dwelling of the Swift-Feet family. The gaps could be chinked with hard clay mud later. It was finished in time for the evening meal and the celebration which followed.

The elders glanced and smiled at each other, pleased Moose and his tall bride might soon start producing many huge braves. The ceremony ended with secretly voiced community concerns about the sexual capability of Moose. He'd shown no interest in the six maidens who were at least a second cousin and from another maternal clan. Several widows had quietly offered to service his needs, yet he never showed normal interest in women for a man in his twenty-first summer.

Deep-Eyes whispered to Swift-Feet as their son and his mate stood up. "I hope you told him he should be gentle, and what he's supposed to do."

He smiled and put his arm around her. "I explained that years ago when hair appeared around his manhood. He's always been respectful to women. I don't expect that to change."

She chuckled and put her head on his shoulder. "I'm sure the son will be as sweet as the father. I've often felt the way the young girls ridiculed his size in childhood kept him from considering the tribal girls for a bride. I never understood why he didn't accept offers from the widows. Did you?"

"I asked him. He felt it important to be a virgin if he expected a virginal woman. I was surprised. But I'm proud his moral strength is equal to his physical prowess. I give you credit for that."

Moose and Happy-Moon entered the new structure amid cheers from the crowd. The drums, dancing, and flute music would continue well into the night.

Happy-Moon in her twentieth summer lay with her arms around Moose. "I'm pleased I chose to wait for you, and grateful you wanted me for your mate." Her hand encouraged him for a repeat performance as she said, "My mother said this would be too big for a virgin, and to expect a lot of pain when it entered me. She didn't know you hadn't used it before when she said you'd just force it into me." She kissed his ear. "Thank you for telling me it was your first time."

Moose grinned and kissed his mate. As their lips and tongues parted, he said, "I have love for you."

"I know," she said and smiled.

Two moons later the tenth full moon of the annual cycle was due and celebration was joyously anticipated. Cherished supplies that would feed the band through winter and into the next growing season had been carried up the hill in a variety of woven baskets. The women transferred the herbs, pine nuts, beans, corn meal, roots and dried meats into larger baskets, making sure food from the prior season was on top.

The men sat on the flat rock beside the communal storage cave entrance waiting for their mates to exit. They discussed funny moments that occurred during hunting seasons.

Moose grinned. "I think Crooked-Legs gave us a great show grabbing that deer's tail to slow it, so we could easily put an arrow through its heart. I laughed so hard I missed and almost hit Crooked-Legs."

After a burst of uproarious laughter, Moose scanned the group and said, "We had great hunting. Tonight we thank our mates and the Great Spirit. They did all the drying and preparation work for today."

As the women exited, the men joined their mates for the short journey down to the village. The band would finish preparing for winter in huts constructed over the last twelve generations in the wind protected valley. Four men remained when Happy-Moon emerged, inwardly joyous with knowledge her husband's first child was in her womb. She was ready to take Moose's hand for the walk to their lodge. The gentle giant started to rise.

Spirit-Sensor, the medicine man, said in a preemptive voice, "Moose stays with me."

Happy-Moon thinly smiled and wondered why her mate had to stay. She knew it was unwise to argue with a man of mystic power. A glance at the great warrior's eyes told her to leave. She nodded and followed the others.

Soon only Moose and the medicine man remained. "My woman joined the ancestors two falls ago. It is time to see if you can handle the visions I believe you can have."

Spirit-Sensor took a pipe from his bag and filled the bowl with crumbled dry leaves from a small pouch. "Let your eyes relax and see all of the big lake while I light this."

Moose did as he was told. The elders and his father long ago taught him seeing a wide panorama made a better hunter. He wondered what the medicine man wanted him to hunt on the lake.

"Take the pipe. Suck it in and count to ten before releasing. Do it three times."

The odor was different than corn straw, or the precious southeastern tobacco acquired from traders and only used on special occasions. Moose puffed on the pipe. The taste was sweet, like ripe berries.

"Continue seeing all the lake." Spirit-Sensor commanded.

The water seemed to shimmer more. A mist formed to block his view of the lake. Moose heard a roar. A giant silver bird lifted off the ground headed north with fire shooting out from under the wings. Moose blinked his eyes. His jaw dropped.

"What did you see?"

"A huge silver bird with fire under its wings."

"I have seen them." Spirit-Sensor nodded his head. "That was not mine, but a good first vision. I have seen much from here; strange bow-topped vessels rolling on four round things pulled by odd looking creatures, like a cross between buffalo and deer coming through that pass; men riding elk with no horns; a huge village of odd looking structures. They are visions of things to come. That's how I knew you'd be born. I saw your future."

Moose spoke softly. "I see an odd village. On that knoll is

something like the top half of a golden moon. Another silver bird landed by the lake."

"I knew you would have visions when the time came. You have learned to overcome your fear, and to argue for what you know to be right. Now I can go away. You must continue to see the future so you can lead the people as the future comes."

Moose excitedly said, "I see huge canoes being propelled by wind in blankets out on the lake. Do you see them?"

"I have." Spirit-Sensor nodded again. "Once I studied them to see if we could hook blankets to a pole on our fishing canoes, but Bold-Eagle has forbidden me to try it."

"It would make our trading trips to Skull Valley and Bear Lake twice as fast," Moose said. "When will I see the men riding elk with no horns?"

"Be patient. You will see many things after I'm gone."

"Where do you go?" Moose wasn't sure he wanted an answer.

"I cannot tell you. You have the visions, so I can leave. My bag is yours. Take it. Do not discuss what you see. Use the visions as if they are new ideas to help the people. Do not pass on this bag until you are sure the recipient is worthy. The sun sets soon. I will sit here until I leave."

Moose looked at the old man and knew truth had been spoken. He stood and made the motion of peace.

The medicine man returned the gesture saying, "Do not come here for visions after sunset."

The giant man of the band nodded and stepped silently off the flat rock to head for the village, looking forward to telling his mate what he'd seen. Happy-Moon was surely worthy of the knowledge. Many questions came to his mind. The visions didn't fade until he was half way down the hill.

Happy-Moon was concerned why her husband had to stay with the medicine man. "Is Moose sick?" she asked Dark-Eyes as they prepared the family evening meal.

"Why do you ask?"

"He sat so long with Spirit-Sensor on the flat rock."

"I wondered myself," Deep-Eyes said, "but I didn't see them in healing prayer position. I'm sure Moose is fine."

"Then why is the medicine man in the prayer position now?"

Dark-Eyes looked up on the hill and smiled. "He is an old man, well over forty summers. His mate's been gone almost two cycles. He has refused the widows who offered comfort, so he must be speaking with her spirit." She turned back to Happy-Moon. "You are with child. You shouldn't worry."

The evening meal was over and the people gathered around the central fire for the fall celebration. Elders told stories to the young while they waited for the sun to drop below the western horizon. The Chief would signal the drummers to start the song of gratitude to the Great Spirit and the bounty of creation. They eagerly awaited the dancing that would last well into the night. The remaining work to gather wood for the winter fires was not as demanding.

Bold-Eagle, wearing his ceremonial headdress, was relieving himself when the sun dropped below the horizon. The people waited in silence for him to return and start the celebration. He reached the central fire pit and raised his arm.

"Look," one of the children yelled as she pointed to the flat rock. All eyes turned to see a glowing white light in the shape of a standing man. The light became a sparkling mist that seemed to slowly disappear.

Moose knew it was the medicine man. Before babble could break out, he spoke in a deep, authoritative voice. "Spirit-Sensor has joined our ancestors. He told me it would be so, but didn't explain what we would see."

"Those were his words?" The Chief approached him. "Did you share his visions?"

"Yes." Moose was immediately uncomfortable at being honest. Spirit-Sensor said it had been forbidden by the Chief to use what he'd seen.

Bold-Eagle tipped his head back and looked down his nose as if to intimidate the huge sitting warrior. "You will tell us those visions."

Moose spoke slowly. "Spirit-Sensor was a wise man. He showed me things I never dreamed." He was surprised there were no interruptions when he spoke of giant silver birds with fire under the wings. A day prior, he would have asked many questions of such visions.

Before Moose could continue, Bold-Eagle raised his voice to a shout. "I don't know how Spirit-Sensor did that. We will check his lodgings and the rock in the morning to test the magic. I know Moose is crazy for now." He raised his hand. "Celebrate our harvest and successful hunts." His arm snapped down and the drummers began the song of gratitude.

The next night another gathering was held by the central fire. The Chief announced, "The Keeper of Memory told me the history beads say the flat rock has seen others long before our time leave us without a body to bury. I declare it a sacred place. Black-Hawk is now our medicine man. No one shall sit there without his presence."

Moose was disappointed. He expected the best visions would come from the flat rock. It was soon a wonderful discovery to find that whenever he sat alone on any knoll with inner peace, the visions came. He would find a nearby rise to sit on toward the end of each day when his work was done. The visions were never discussed with others.

His odd habit seemed to confirm the Chief's declaration that Moose was in a crazy spell cast by Spirit-Sensor. He was still their best hunter, reigned supreme in the summer contests of speed and skill, and remained kind and attentive to all members of the tribe. None would speak of craziness in his presence. They all hoped the spell would someday end.

The peaceful cycles seemed to rush by with summers full of visitors who wanted to see the giant. Happy-Moon was a beautiful and devoted mother. Her eyes always glowed when she looked at her mate. His eyes always appeared brighter when he looked at her and the children. Early in the fourth summer after the wedding, Moose, Happy-Moon, Little-Moose and Baby-Moon traveled south and west to visit her parents. They wanted to be there and return before the heat became unbearable.

They returned in time for Moose to join the hunting parties. Happy-Moon helped with the harvest and preparation of food for storage. The band sighed with relief that no one had threatened the peace with Moose gone. They knew the trading parties would spread the word that their greatest weapon was away on a visit to the far away Valley-of-Death.

"Our oldest son will be a big man," Happy-Moon said as she snuggled against him under their spring rabbit pelt blanket. "We celebrate Little-Moose's ninth summer tomorrow night when the moon will be full. I don't think he'll be as large as you."

"He is a strong and smart boy. I'm proud of him." Moose wrapped his arm around her. "You have produced six fine children. We are blessed to have five with us."

"I'm pleased you think so." She hugged him and said, "Sometimes I wish Grateful-Spirit didn't have to go to my parents. At least we know he's well and happy."

He returned the hug and used his free hand to clear the fallen hair from her face. "We cannot undo what was done. Our promise was made to fend off bad medicine, and it worked well."

She sighed. "Speaking of bad medicine, I'm grateful you stopped having those odd visions."

He'd chosen to avoid ridicule after the night of Spirit-Sensor's magnificent departure. Visions from the hillside were silently used as ways to help and guide the people. Even Bold-Eagle reluctantly joined the amazed and delighted crowd when he showed how fast a canoe could move using a pole and a blanket. The last six seasonal trading trips had gone faster. All the families expressed gratitude when he showed the band how to improve the quality and life of the stacked log hut seals against winter winds by adding crushed sage mixed into the mud. He led them to the richest hunting grounds and always found abundant crops of the wonderful pine nuts.

"I have only spoken of visions once. I'm sorry our children heard others call me Crazy Moose."

"The people speak of it less." Happy-Moon smiled. "How do you know they called you that?"

Moose laughed. "Each of our little ones asked me why."

She giggled. "I might have spanked them if I knew."

He grinned and gently mussed her hair. "Our babies don't need pain. They need understanding. I told them gossip makes a fool of those who speak it, as well as those who listen. The crazy name didn't make me less a hunter, a trader or a warrior. We've had peace since word of my size spread through the region." Moose put his hand under her chin. "Do the children love me less?"

Happy-Moon took a long moment. "I love you more for not letting me spank the children." She dropped her hand to his crotch. "They're asleep. Let's make a new brave."

The next morning was warm and beautiful after the sun crested the eastern mountains. The time for serious hunting would come soon. Moose stepped outside and decided to talk to Bold-Eagle about the coming trading sessions.

"My Chief, do you recall we've heard about the tribes in the far south having obtained beasts called horses from ones called Spanish?"

Bold-Eagle laughed. "I know those stupid stories. The idea of a beast that men ride is foolish. The idea of a fire stick is idiotic. The Apaches made all that up to scare the rest of us."

"No, my Chief. Spirit-Sensor told me they were coming. The stories confirm it. I guess they will come soon. We must trade for those things this season." Moose did not relay his own visions.

"Forget Spirit-Sensor's visions. I'm glad you stopped having them. Black-Hawk is a better medicine man."

Moose shook his head and walked away knowing his Chief wouldn't listen. He was angry with Bold Eagle's stubbornness and with Spirit-Sensor for placing the visions load on him.

The sun apex meal was eaten with his mate and offspring. His thoughts rumbled over how to teach the benefit of all those visions to the band. They needed to be prepared for the future. He looked at his family. The only one who might have vision talent was Happy-Moon, and he wouldn't curse her with that skill.

The meal was over. Frustrated that he hadn't fully used the visionary capability for proper leadership of the band, he went up near the flat rock and asked the ancestral spirits to tell him how to pass vision skills to one who could use them to lead the people. He focused, ignoring many scenes that tried to reach his consciousness.

Happy-Moon's face kept popping into his mind. About to forget the question because he didn't like the answer, he was surprised by a strong feeling to choose Black-Hawk, only two summers older than himself, and long a detractor.

Moose started back to the village. The feeling grew stronger so he went directly to the medicine man's lodging.

"Come with me to the flat rock. I will give you the bag of Spirit-Sensor."

Disdain showed in Black-Hawk's expression. At length he spoke. "He did have herbs I haven't been able to find, one that eases pain for women in childbirth. I didn't know you had the bag."

The warm afternoon sun baked the men as they silently waited for the women to take evening meal needs from the cave. "When they are gone, we will sit on the rock and talk." Moose said wondering if Black-Hawk could truly accept the visions, and learn about the future in a way that could be taught to the people and their hard-headed Chief.

Happy-Moon came out. Her basket full of cornmeal, beans, berries and jerky. She looked at Moose as if expecting him to help her and their two older daughters. He motioned down the hill to tell her he would be staying with Black-Hawk and saw a fearful shiver flash down her spine. Recalling the day Spirit-Sensor vanished was the last time he'd sat on the sacred flat rock, he decided to ease her obvious fear. "Prepare our celebration meal. I will join you soon."

She smiled. "Come girls. Papa will follow soon." Her posture showed that she trusted him.

The sun was well above the western horizon. Black-Hawk was given the same instructions received from the previous medicine man. He knew the spirits had given the right answer as he watched Black

Hawk's reactions.

"You weren't crazy." Black-Hawk had a stupefied look. "The silver birds are huge. There's a strange village filling the whole valley."

Moose grinned. "You will have other visions. If you are wise, you won't tell the people. Use what you see to prepare them for change. Men unlike us will come on horses using fire sticks to wound us. We must trade for those beasts and fire sticks to protect ourselves. Silver birds and a huge village are a long time off." Moose was pleased.

"The others can't comprehend this. I didn't. I'll never call you crazy again, Moose." Black-Hawk's jaw dropped. "I see men with fire sticks riding elk without horns."

"What do they wear?" Moose wondered if it was the impending Spanish in shields and strange head cover.

"Blue coats with yellow stripes on the arms."

Moose nodded. "I have seen them, but I think they come much later."

"Why do you think that?" Black-Hawk asked with respect.

"I have seen our braves riding the elk with no horns, called horses by the Apache, and using fire sticks in battle with the blue coats. We must trade for those things soon and learn to use them well."

"What else have you seen?"

"Things you will see. They will fill your heart with pain knowing we must never let the silver birds and monstrous village fill this valley. I believe the visions are to help us protect our home." Moose paused. "Bold-Eagle will not hear the truth in your visions."

Black-Hawk took his eyes away from the lake and looked at Moose. "He is old and without sons. I will ask the council to make you Chief at the meeting tonight."

Moose knew it was time to join his family. "The meeting and start of summer celebration is at sundown. Thank you for your confidence."

"Together we can protect our future." The medicine man said and grinned as he rose.

"Spirit-Sensor said not to come here after dark." Moose stood up and offered the deerskin bag. "You came for this."

"Thank you," he said accepting it, "and, I got much more. You are the only one I can talk to about this. When my mate asks why we talked, I'll tell her it was to make sure you'd accept my nomination tonight."

"Gentle-Rain will be shocked," Moose said and grinned, briefly recalling the long period of ridicule.

Black-Hawk grinned. "Not as shocked as I am by what I saw today. There are huge canoes with blankets on the lake now. Is that where you got the idea?"

Moose smiled. "Yes. Perhaps we will find a way to stop those huge rolling vessels from coming through the mountain pass. They are the ones who would make that village on our land and drive us out."

"We will defeat them."

The smell of baking corn-meal-flats filled his nostrils as he approached the family hut. Happy-Moon smiled. "It will cool soon so you should dress."

Moose chose the new buckskin pants and tunic she made for him the week before, knowing it would please her. He added the ceremonial breast plate, necklace and headdress. The children rushed through the meal and went off to play during the short time before dark.

"Are you sick?"

"No," he shook his head.

"Why did you sit so long with Black-Hawk?"

"I gave him the medicine bag, and he wanted permission to ask the council to make me Chief."

"That's a surprise," she laughed. "What was in the bag?"

"Some herbs he hasn't been able to find, one that helps a difficult childbirth." Moose grinned. "That's not a problem for you."

Happy-Moon patted her belly and smiled. "Little-Moose will become a fine young man, and bigger than most, but, I feel we made the brave last night who can fill your footsteps."

"I welcome another child," he said and reached to place his hand on her stomach. "All our sons and daughters are fine. They help each other compete. Brothers and sisters close to my size would have kept me from being so lonely until I met you."

Her broad smile showed delight with his quick response and the beauty of his words. They rose to join the gathering around the central campfire.

Prepared for the celebration, all the hunters wore their tooth necklaces and ribbed chest-pieces to honor the many animals that fed the people. The braves wore eagle feather headdresses to denote their status. The senior elder gave thanks to the Great Spirit and all of creation for the bounty of prior seasons. He asked wisdom be bestowed on the council.

Ready to pronounce the beginning of the seasonal celebration, Bold-Eagle shouted in a feeble voice, "Do we have anything for the council to consider?"

"Yes, my Chief," the medicine man said and stood up.

"Speak."

"You have been a great Chief. I am one of many who believe you are now too old to be effective. I ask the council to remove you. And since you don't have a son, I ask that Moose be chosen our new Chief."

Total silence came to the gathering.

Swift-Feet, a council member, broke the silence. He loved the idea, but knew it was his duty to defend the Chief. "Bold-Eagle is not too old."

Sturdy-Elk said what others were thinking. "Moose's father speaks this way because many have called his son Crazy-Moose for ten cycles. I am pleased Black-Hawk has changed his heart. Moose is our greatest brave, and should be our Chief when Bold-Eagle goes to Mother Earth. This discussion should wait until then. Let us have the spring celebration."

The council unanimously backed Sturdy-Elk. The drums and dancing soon started the celebration.

Moose stood at the edge of the group, clapping and chanting familiar words while he glanced up the hillside and saw a glint of moonlight reflected from the edge of the flat rock. His anger over the quick rejection and curiosity about a night vision of the valley slowly took command of his mind. As frustrated as Spirit-Sensor had been, he slipped in silence behind the outer lodgings and made his way up the hill.

He was sure no one could see him so he stepped up onto the sacred surface.

The valley was lit by lights from things he knew weren't there. The whitish pad near the lake had various red, white and blue colored lights lining the edge and there were many large silver birds sitting next to huge structures he hadn't seen before. One of the silver birds landed and shortly after another lifted off the ground. The noise was loud. He looked to see if the group around the campfire was paying attention. A black ribbon with yellowish lights suspended above it covered the spot where the people were. Things with white lights moving like falling stars went in both directions through where the campfire should be. He was confused. The lights on the hurtling objects turned red when they passed his view point.

Moose knew then why Spirit-Sensor had said not to come there after dark. He'd seen the future village and the strange whitish and dark gray ribbons with fast moving boxes on them, but the night view made them a far greater threat than the flaming silver birds. He had to get to the village and protect the people. Moose rose to his feet.

"Papa," his three year old daughter screamed and pointed to the flat rock. Most eyes turned to follow her finger. The drums stopped.

Tears filled Happy-Moon's eyes. "That's Moose. No other man is that big." She sensed whatever caused it, they would be together again. "You will meet your father little one," she said patting her stomach. "I promise to find a way to go where he is going."

The people stared at the huge glowing man beginning to disintegrate. Black Hawk clutched his throat with fear and curiosity. He knew that would happen if he ever went there after dark. He would need to teach someone else to have visions. He looked at the giant's beautiful wife and wondered at her serenity in the situation. Maybe she would be his choice to learn the visions, and she could disappear instead of him.

Happy-Moon stood tall and took the hand of her two youngest daughters. "Somehow I know we will see your father again."

*   *   *

Moose did not sense any movement, although his vision was briefly blurred by glowing red and white lights streaming in all directions as if passing through a fog. His view of the valley and the lake was cut off by a multilevel structure with lighted rectangular holes. He looked down and knew he was still on the flat rock. The trail to the village was gone. It was covered by a dense carpet of green. He turned and discovered the entrance to the storage cavern was gone, covered with a strange tangled growth. The people needed that food to survive until the next growing and hunting season. His mind began to focus on getting beyond the oddly lit impediment to get down the hill to the campfire.

He barely heard a feminine scream followed by a masculine bellow as he looked for a way out. The area was surrounded by strange walls with spiked tops. There appeared to be a gap on his right. He stepped off the rock and dashed for that space only to find the way blocked by more of the wall that abutted the structure. Glancing back, he decided the best way out was to use the tangled growth over the cave entrance to climb onto the knoll above. There should be a path up there that wound down to a narrow crevice leading into the valley further south. Moose ran back to the flat rock, leaped high into the tangled growth and clambered to the knoll.

A warbling screech rapidly approached and he could see several sets of flashing red and blue lights approaching the area. The path on either side was blocked by more walls unseen from below. There was an explosion from near the back of the structure. He saw the flash and heard the whine of something far louder than that of a flying insect pass near his head and thud into the hill behind him. It had to be a man with one of those fire-sticks he knew the tribe needed to acquire. Two more explosions followed as he dropped prone. He froze there knowing the man could easily kill him with the projectiles if he stood. Several men wearing tan clothing rushed into the area below and a light snapped on hitting his face, and blinded him. There was considerable loud jabber from below, none of which made any sense. Moose knew the commotion regarded him. Visions of a smiling Spirit-Sensor in strange clothing told him to relax. All would be well.

* * *

Davis County Sheriff Chuck Moose arrived at his office shortly after 6 a.m. as usual. The doors wouldn't open to the general public until eight. The jail and emergency entrances were always open. The time would be used to review the night reports, catch up on paperwork, and review the court schedules. He got a cup of coffee and sat at his desk.

There was a buzz on his intercom as he picked up the stack of night reports. He knew it had to be the desk officer on the open side of the building. "Yes, Morton?"

"Hey, boss. Have you read report thirty-three from last night yet?"

"I just picked up the pile. The media would have called me at home if we had a murder or something big. What's special about it?" He couldn't recall if the desk had referred to a night report this early except in major cases. The folder was found about two thirds of the way down the stack.

"Just that we had another Indian show up in Senator Charlton's yard up on Highrise Avenue between Centerville and Bountiful. I'm sure you remember how angry he was the last time. He damned near killed this one just as our guys got there."

"I've got it here," the sheriff said as he flipped the green folder open. "At least it isn't a red folder. I'll read it now." He released the intercom. It buzzed again. "What is it now, Morton?"

"Mr. Sensor from the Urban Indian Center wants to see you. Should I let him through the inside door?"

"What does he want?"

"He was at the scene last night. It's in the report."

"OK," the sheriff shook his head. "Let him through. He knows the way."

The sheriff opened the report and began reading. Moments later a slender man in a perfectly fitted blue suit entered. The tie matched his grey shoulder length hair. Chuck waved to a chair. "When I finish reading, we can talk."

Shaking his head as he read the last sentence, Sheriff Moose looked at Spirit-Sensor. "Didn't you arrive here the same way about ten years ago?"

"I did. I was lucky he didn't have a gun handy then. You remember that night don't you?"

The sheriff laughed. "I remember it well. You were docile and with a smile, trying to explain yourself with sign language. It was a good thing old Buck Wolf was on duty that night."

"I agree. I'm sure my system would've reacted to those strong tranquilizer shots the way Moose did. We weren't used to strong medicines like that."

"The report says this guy is huge. The EMT's guessed him at six nine or ten. I had to chuckle when Sergeant Young wrote the guy has shoulders and a chest that'd make a pro wrestler jealous." He grinned and took a sip of coffee. "What I find even funnier, you said his name is Moose. It'd be great if I'm related to someone that big."

"You are," Spirit-Sensor said. "He was your paternal sire twenty-one generations ago."

"Jeez. How many years ago was that?"

"Not quite four hundred."

Chuck grinned. "You know, I'm beginning to believe all that stuff I heard as a kid. We left the rez and my dad became a sheriff, but my grandparents used to visit and tell all kinds of weird stories about a giant and his family who disappeared not too long before the tribe had to leave the valley and go up into the mountains. Are you telling me that's him?"

"I am," Spirit-Sensor nodded.

"Then how come I'm here if his family came with him?"

"His oldest son chose to stay. And by the way, you need to prepare Senator Charlton. The flat rock in his back yard is a sacred spot not far from the ruins of the village that are under the freeway. A woman and six children, one a babe in arms will show up there in a year. There will be a few others in time to come, but none as significant as Moose and his family. They will be a great help to me in helping protect what's left of the ruins of our people in this magnificent valley."

Thomas Canfield's phobias run to politicians, lawyers and oil company executives. He likes dogs and beer. But be careful where he sends you—and listen to what people say along the way.

The Chamber of Azahn
by Thomas Canfield

Fear shot through the peasant's black eyes. He shook his head, held his hands out in front of him to indicate that he wanted nothing to do with the matter.

"I'm going to ask you again," Reinhart said with forced emphasis. "And I'm going to keep on asking you. I don't intend to go away. If you won't provide me with the information I'm seeking someone else will. Then all this money," Reinhart fanned out a sheaf of twenty dollar bills in U S. currency, "will go to them and not you."

The man passed his tongue over his lips. His eyes darted from the currency to the object Reinhart held in his left hand: a disk of black stone. Inscribed on the stone was a representation of the sun and a series of hieroglyphics depicted in gold.

Johnny Norris leaned forward in the cab of the truck. "Are you sure he can understand you?" he asked. "Perhaps he doesn't speak English."

Reinhart's lip curled in scorn. "He understands well enough. Look at him. He's afraid, is what it is." Reinhart leaned toward him. "My friend just called you a coward," he said. "A man who lives in fear and is held hostage by it. Is that how you wish to be thought of?"

The man's dark eyes stabbed into the interior of the truck. The strange, almost vertical, pupils burned with bitter resentment. But the broad expanse of his face remained impassive, curiously detached from the emotion that resided in his eyes. He said something in a low, guttural voice.

"What is it, what did he say?" Norris demanded.

"I don't know." Reinhart slid one hand under the seat of the truck where he kept a handgun. His movements were casual and unhurried, calculated not to incite suspicion "He spoke in the local Indian dialect. Some still employ it amongst themselves."

There was a long, tense moment of silence. None of the three men moved. The sun beat down from overhead and the chrome grill of the truck reflected the light out across the cracked and buckled ribbon of asphalt that was the road. Finally the man spat into the dirt and began to speak in rapid-fire Spanish.

Reinhart stared off through the glare of the windshield. He nodded several times, his brow furrowed in concentration. Finally he slipped his hand out from under the truck seat, slipped the gear shift into drive.

The man stepped away from the truck, hooked his thumbs over his belt. He had large, work scarred hands that bore testimony to the harshness of his life. He stood watching them now, motionless, his squat form appearing more a part of the arid landscape than a living, breathing entity belonging to the human world. Reinhart began to ease down the road.

"Wait!" Norris swung around. "Don't you intend to give him the money?"

"He doesn't want it." Reinhart flashed Norris a lopsided grin. "Considers it tainted or some such thing. God alone knows that he could use it. That couple of hundred there is probably worth a year's income to him. Maybe more. Only he wouldn't touch it. He made that very plain." Reinhart shook his head with grudging admiration. "You'd never have that trouble back in the States, people refusing to take money."

"No," Norris said. He watched the receding figure out the back window. "I wonder if we aren't making a mistake."

"Are you kidding?" Reinhart thumped the palm of his hand against the steering wheel. "We just found the sweet spot, Johnny. We just hit the ball out of the park. Three or four miles up into these foothills and we tap into the mother lode. The Indian just verified everything that we had been told. What more could we ask for?"

"Plenty. I don't like the way that he acted. I don't like the fact that he wouldn't take our money. What else did he say to you, what was he so insistent about?"

"He said a lot of things. Some of it I didn't understand myself. The important thing, the essential thing, is we're practically there. We don't need to waste time beating around on our own. We hike up there, get what we came for, and get out. Simple as that."

"I don't like this," Norris repeated. "He warned you, didn't he? Warned the two of us. He told us not to go up there."

Reinhart jerked the wheel sharply and the rear end of the truck fishtailed around in a wide arc. They swung onto a rutted dirt track that led up into the foothills.

"So what if he did? What did you think he was going to say? Feel free to go up and plunder ancient artifacts, as many as you like. Just remember to clean up after yourselves."

"Slow down, would you?" Norris said, clutching at the dashboard with both hands. "For Christ's sweet sake, slow down. We aren't on pavement anymore."

Reinhart eased off on the accelerator. "Hell, Johnny, you got to be practical about these sorts of things. The guy was not a welcoming committee."

"I figured as much. And that isn't what I asked you. I asked you what he said."

Reinhart shook his head, as though trying to shed a memory that he had already grown weary of. "He told us not to go up there. He implied that bad things would happen. There was some sort of interdict placed on the area a long time ago, some sort of prohibition. Why exactly, our friend didn't say. One thing is certain, none of the locals would dare to venture up here."

Norris drummed his fingers against the dashboard. "So, we make him for a fool and ignore everything that he said?"

Reinhart swung the steering wheel again, ducked around a large pothole and slid back onto the track without tapping the brakes. "That's right. At least, that's what I plan on doing. You got other ideas, you better tell me now."

"No." Norris spoke with reluctance. "We came all this way, we invested all this time and money, we're committed. If we didn't mean to see it through, we should have decided on that a long time ago."

Reinhart slammed the brakes without warning. Norris lurched forward, banged his head against the windshield. The truck skidded to a halt. A huge boulder rose up in front of them marking the end of the track.

Reinhart hissed an epithet between his teeth. He turned to Norris. "Sorry," he said.

Norris touched his forehead, winced. "I thought I told you to slow down."

"You did. Only I wasn't listening. If that had hit you anywhere but in your head I might be worried."

Norris sat back in the seat. "You know," he said, "if only one of us was to come out of this alive, if it's necessary for one of us to die a horrible, bloody death, I hope to hell that it's you." Both men grinned. They climbed out of the cab, hoisted rucksacks and shovels out of the bed of the truck.

Norris glanced up at the white, molten mass of the sun overhead. He slipped a ball cap on, tugged the brim down low over his eyes. "It's hot out there. I hope we don't have to do any serious digging."

Reinhart flicked a look over his shoulder. "We each got a full canteen. That ought to suffice for one day."

The two men ducked around the boulder and followed a narrow footpath that wound up into the hills. Blasted, broken rock, bleached and scoured by the sun, lay scattered over the landscape. There was scarcely any vegetation at all, only isolated patches of chaparral clinging stubbornly to the parched and barren soil.

Norris saw a lizard basking in the sun. It bore curious markings of yellow and rust and a black diamond-shaped configuration on its head. The diamond seemed to undulate and pulse. The lizard stared at them as they passed, its eyes like those of a prophet who has foretold death. The air was still, the land silent.

The sun began to take on a bronze cast as they climbed higher into the hills. The light became imbued with a hard edge that changed the appearance of everything that it touched—the broken stone, the blade of the shovel, the flesh of Norris' hand. It was as though it bore something tainted, something corrupt, in its essence.

"Chase?"

Reinhart shook his head. "Not now. We're almost there. Only a little further."

"Yeah, but the light," Norris protested.

"What about it?" Reinhart snapped. "What has that to do with anything?"

"Look at the sun!" Norris stopped, pointed at the sky. "Look at it, for God's sake. It looks as though it were hammered out of a sheet of bronze. You don't find that strange?"

"Listen, let's not worry about it. Let's focus on the reason we came."

"Why did we come, Chase? Tell me that. Was it only for the money?"

Reinhart swung around with a savage scowl. "You're god damn right it was for the money. First, last, and every point in between—for the money. It would be a whole lot easier on the both of us if you would keep that fact in mind." Reinhart turned and plunged ahead again. Norris followed reluctantly.

The footpath led them down through a narrow defile, sheer rock walls rising up on either side. The stone was cool to the touch here, impervious to the harsh assault of the sun overhead. The air, too, was cool, laced with the far away scent of the salt sea. Norris suddenly felt afraid.

"We ought to turn back. We ought not to have come."

"Nobody's turning back. Not now." Reinhart pushed ahead at a feverish pace. "Don't you remember? This is exactly how the site was described on the map—ramparts of stone. Look around you, what do you see? It's like the hand of God himself forged this land."

The bronze sky overhead had turned a darker hue still, ominous and menacing. The two men emerged out from between the walls of rock. An enormous blood-red sun hung above the horizon. It flooded the earth with light, painted the stone and the surrounding hills with color.

They stood at the edge of a shallow depression, fifty meters or more across, that might once have held water. In the center was an altar of white stone. It appeared to have been crafted from a single block of stone. Or perhaps from the very bedrock of the earth itself. At each of the four cardinal points of the compass, save one, a device was set into the stone identical to the black disk that Reinhart had in his possession.

Reinhart stalked forward, his face flushed with exultation. "This is it—the portal of fire, the entrance to the Chamber of Azahn." The sun settled heavily toward the horizon. Bands of gold and crimson and violet crisscrossed the sky.

Here, the People believed, the sun resided at night. Here they created a place Azahn might rest and gather his strength for the coming day. Here they brought tribute.

Norris seized Reinhart's arm. "The Indian—what did he say? Tell me!"

Reinhart cocked his head as though listening to a distant voice. He smiled. "He said that the distinction between a fool and a coward"— Reinhart paused, stared off at the incandescent ball of the sun—"the distinction is that a coward at least knows when to be afraid." Reinhart looked at Norris. "Let go of my arm, Johnny."

"For the love of God, why not leave now while we still have the chance?"

"Let go of my arm." Reinhart's voice was flat and cold. "You set too much store by the Indian, Johnny. You give him too much credit. Just because his people believed that some special communion existed between them and the sun, between them and Azahn, what does that prove? Nothing. It's superstition, plain and simple." Reinhart's eyes burned with the rapt look of one lost to reason. Norris dropped his arm.

Reinhart walked down into the depression, into the fierce gale of the setting sun. He moved rapidly at first, with an easy, fluid gait, but as he drew nearer to the altar he appeared to struggle. His shoulders slumped and he lifted his legs with great effort, sinews taut and straining.

The sun had wiped him clean of any identifying feature, any trace of individuality. He seemed a thin, spectral figure, devoid of mass. He cast no shadow.

"Stop!" Norris shouted. "God damn it, Chase, at least listen to what I have to say."

Reinhart staggered, fell to his knees. He crawled the remaining few feet to the altar. He lifted the black disk using both arms. His ribcage heaved. He resembled some archaic priest of long ago, presiding over a ritual of cleansing and absolution. Or perhaps, the thought occurred to Norris, a rite of sacrifice. Reinhart reached forward, fitted the disk into the altar.

Shock waves rumbled through the earth. Dust drifted across the face of the sun. A stone ledge fractured and split, revealing a huge underground chamber concealed beneath the basin. A warm effulgence of gold spilled forth from within. Norris craned forward, stared at an immense collection of treasure: wheels of gold inscribed with symbols and hieroglyphics, platters and vases and goblets chased with silver, exquisite jade carvings of jaguars and snakes. Three hundred years of tribute. A tropical bird sporting brilliant red and gold and green plumage fluttered up into the air and sped away to the east.

Puddles of darkness began to gather in the dips and hollows of the land. The temperature dropped perceptibly. The sun settled into the line of the horizon, a vast all-seeing eye staring across the earth and its inhabitants with little regard and no tenderness. Azahn—ruler of the skies, suzerain over all the globe. From earliest times the People had known that he must be appeased, placated, must be showered with tribute. To do otherwise . . .

Norris lifted his head. There was a sudden rushing noise, as from a distant wind. The sound gathered force and volume, gained momentum, till it filled the air, filled all the earth. A surge of light spilled through the defile, rich and warm and yellow. The light swallowed the two men, consumed their flesh in an instant, left only faint shadows imprinted upon the rock to mark their having ever been. Time resumed its wonted course and the great eye of the sun flickered shut as though it would look no more upon the folly and ingratitude of Man.

Kfir Luzzatto's first novel, Crossing the Meadow, *was published by Echelon Press (October 2003) and was voted "Best Horror Novel" in the 2003 Preditors & Editors Readers Poll. Kfir is an HWA (Horror Writers Association) and ITW (International Thriller Writers) member and also serves on the editorial board of* The Harrow *as Anthology Editor. His new novel,* The Odyssey Gene, *was published by Echelon Press (July 2006) and was a finalist in the Indie Excellence 2007 Book Awards.*

The more we rely on technology the more it becomes a crutch. And when you remove that crutch, well . . .

Maximum Entropy
by Kfir Luzzatto

K*en lifted his head from the plough and wiped the beads of perspiration with the back of his dirty hand. The sun was already low in the sky and he would soon have to head back.*

He watched his field with pride. This year, he knew, the harvest would be much bigger. He had learnt from the mistakes of the previous year. He was contented and at peace with himself—too smug, one might have thought, for a person who had wiped out ninety-five percent of the population of Earth.

But that was not how he saw it. Quite the contrary—he felt pride at having saved at least five percent of it.

It had all begun two years before, when his boss had called him to his office . . .

"Are you making fun of me, Ken?" he had asked, his eyes fixed onto the virtual computer screen that was scrolling statistical data following the movement of his pupils.

121

Morris Kramm was the powerful Head of Research of the United Companies conglomerate, and, in practice, was responsible for global corporate research, which amounted to more than eighty percent of the total world research.

"I don't know what you're talking about," answered Ken.

He was annoyed. Although he considered himself a pretty hard-working person, he had already put in his five hours that week, and was planning to go home soon. Morris could afford to kill himself with work, if he wanted to, and to slave seven or eight hours a week. He didn't have a life anyway, with a wife waiting for him at home. But Ken was different. He had other things on his mind, besides work. He was young—barely twenty-five, and matrimony was not a near option for him.

Morris nodded and a second virtual screen appeared in front of Ken, showing the same data as the one that Morris was inspecting. Ken was sitting in the W-ambu-comfy-seat that had brought him from his office up to Morris'. It was an amazing seat and, as virtually all the appliances he owned, it guessed its owner's wishes and acted accordingly. This was achieved thanks to the innovative Wish-Divining Technology embodied in them. This technology, discovered already back in 2050, had been developed during the last hundred or so years nearly to perfection. Virtually all house appliances now bore the "W-" sign identifying them as perfect machines that operated automatically according to their owner's unspoken wish.

His seat now performed a turn of a few degrees, to better position him in front of the virtual screen, and he looked at the figures that Morris had emphasized for him. Something was indeed very wrong.

"According to these figures, global research has decreased constantly during the last quarter. The number of new research projects initiated during the last three months is miniscule—virtually non-existent. And here," he added, pointing at the map on the screen, "this morning research has come to a sudden standstill in these two areas here. I tried to call their heads of section right now, but couldn't get through to them—it looks like they've disappeared off the face of the earth. This is really weird."

"You're right. I hadn't paid attention to these figures. The computer should have drawn my attention to them, but it didn't. Look here," he added with excitement, enlarging a section of the statistical data. "The decrease in new research projects is uniform all over the world, except for one company here, you see? DMA Inc. has initiated twice as many new research projects as during the previous quarter."

"What does it mean?" asked Morris.

"I have no idea," admitted Ken, "but something strange is afoot."

"Well, in that case, you'll have to find out what's going on."

"But how?" asked Ken in puzzlement.

"You'll have to go there. And I mean now."

"There? Are you out of your mind? I'm going nowhere. I'm on my way home right now."

"Guess again," said Morris quietly.

Ken stepped out of the W-mobile, the vehicle that had taken him to the headquarters of DMA, Inc. The sign painted on the wall said: "DMA—Your Partner for a Better Life."

He walked to the door and stood before it, waiting for it to identify him and open up for him. Nothing happened. For perhaps the thousandth time that day he cursed himself for having taken Morris' orders. Who was he, anyway, to order him about? It wasn't as if Ken was dependent on his job for support. In an era when everyone was well taken care of by law, the job paid only for some extravagances that he didn't really need, and lately the five or so weekly hours of work were taking a heavy toll of Ken's social life. Many people his age didn't bother to work at all, and he had a good mind to go back to Morris and tell him what he could do with his job.

And the damn door wasn't opening. It behaved as if Ken weren't there at all. It was simply ignoring him. A sign near the door attracted his attention. It read: "Please note: this is not a W-door. To open turn the handle."

Ken's curiosity was aroused. He hadn't seen a mechanical door for ages—probably since he was a child. He tried the handle and it turned, allowing the door to slide sideways. In front of it was a W-elevator with an "Out-of-Order" sign on it. An arrow pointed from the sign to ancient stairs. He stood in front of them, unable to decide what to do.

"Come on up," said a voice near his ear.

"Who's that?" asked Ken, peevishly.

"It's me. Bobo Startz."

That was the name of the president of DMA, Inc. that Ken's computer had provided.

"Where are you? Where is 'up'?" asked Ken.

"You see the stairs in front of you? Just climb one flight and you'll see me."

"Don't you have a decent elevator?"

"I deactivated it ages ago," was the reply. "Are you coming up or not? I don't have all day."

Resigned, Ken walked up the stairs. He was starting to feel the unusual exercise, and he was panting. He made a mental note to check his muscular tone on the home fitness machine. He had taken his fitness pills regularly, and his breathing regime shouldn't have been affected by the effort.

The stairs took him to a lighted floor. It was an open space full of benches and equipment. Everything was in terrible disorder, as if the people who worked there didn't own a housekeeping machine. In front of the stairs, a little office, barely large enough to house a desk and a couple of chairs, was the only enclosed space. The door was open and from behind the desk a person was waving to Ken. He walked up to him.

"Good evening," said the person. "I'm Bobo Startz, but you can call me Bob."

"Nice to meet you, Bob," said Ken, shaking his hand. "I am Ken Leming, from the United Companies Research Group. May I take a seat?"

"Please, make yourself at home," said Bob politely. "To what do I owe the honor of your visit? I didn't know that my humble work had attracted the attention of the Research Group."

"I'll tell you in a minute. But first, perhaps you care to explain to me what you do here? What is DMA's line of business?"

"Of course. 'DMA' stands for 'Deactivating Machines Associates.' What we do is to develop new ways to render the myriad of machines that surround us inactive, fully or partially, in a way that permits us to function as human beings."

"You deactivate service machines?" Ken's tone was incredulous.

"Absolutely. But you shouldn't think that it is an easy task. It isn't by any means. I employ highly skilled engineers for this purpose—they have gone home now. They work only an eight-hour shift," he added apologetically.

"Eight hours a week? But this is scandalous." Ken felt strongly that people should not be made to slave more than five hours a week.

"Eight hours a day, Ken. Five days a week. That's how we work here at DMA. And we plan to have a second shift, next month. The demand for our products is tremendous."

"But why would you do that? I mean, our automated factories work very hard, I'm sure, to produce the machines that make our life easier. So why would someone want to deactivate them? I don't understand it. And, by the way, I'm not sure that this is legal."

"Don't worry." Bob soothed him with a smile. "This is a perfectly legitimate business. As long as it is the machine owner who wishes to deactivate it partially or fully, doing so is legal. And we are here to help him do it. Look," he added with excitement, "we have just finished our final working prototype of the W-kitchen taste-chooser deactivator. It's a breakthrough. If you buy one of these, you will be able to cook for yourself again. You'll be allowed to choose the ingredients that go into your dish and to cook it to your liking. Isn't that great?"

"This is quite disgusting," said Ken with a shiver. His W-Gourmet Maker Super, an extravaganza that had cost him a fortune, cooked his preferred dishes exactly as he liked them, without the touch of a human hand and in a completely sterile environment.

He shivered again and inspected Bob's desk with a growing feeling of uneasiness. It was cluttered with papers and crumbles of what seemed to be the remains of a meal eaten a few days before.

"Where is your W-butler?" he asked accusingly.

"Oh, I have dumped it somewhere in the warehouse," Bob answered placidly. "Of course, after I deactivated it. I hated the little nosy machine. Always keeping after me to dress up and be tidy. Much more comfortable this way," he concluded with a spacious movement of his hand meant, no doubt, to point out to his guest the coziness of DMA's quarters.

"But, do people pay for what you do?"

"Have you ever heard of the FOTSON?"

"Isn't that some religious sect or something?"

"It is the 'Fraternity Of The Sons Of Nature'—people who believe that we should live as close to our natural habitat as possible. These are reasonable people who recognize the value of some machines in improving quality of life, but on the other hand wish to live like human beings, and not as some kind of vegetables. They are my best clients and much of my work is done for them."

"This sounds crazy to me. Why would a sane person wish to do menial work that a machine can do for him?"

"If I tell you something, do you promise not to tell anybody?"

Ken nodded, surprised. Bob got up and walked to the head of the stairs. He looked down and, apparently satisfied that nobody was around, walked back to his office and shut the door behind him.

"Have you learnt some thermodynamics in school? Yes? Good. I don't want you to think that I'm crazy," he said. Ken nodded—it seemed all that he was being able to do at this juncture—and Bob went on. "As you know, then, the entropy is a measure of the extent to which the energy of a system is unavailable. It can only increase in all natural processes that are irreversible. Therefore, in an isolated system the entropy is always increasing as the system tends toward equilibrium. Don't look at me like that," he added, evidently noticing that Ken was gaping at him, "it is not my invention. It's the second law of thermodynamics."

"Sorry," said Ken, "but I can't see what this has to do with your company."

"Aha! You soon will. Do you know what happens when your body, which is a system in itself, reaches maximum entropy through its natural processes? You die."

"What?"

"As I said. If all the elements of your body are in perfect equilibrium, no processes can take place, because there is no driving force to make them happen. And if your body stops making things happen, you die. As simple as that."

"I still don't get it."

"I'm coming to it. I believe that the human habitat, as a system, is dangerously approaching equilibrium, because of the harmony that is being achieved between man and machine. And unless we take steps to break this harmony and to cause the equilibrium point to shift, the system consisting of man and machine may simply stop working one day, leaving us impotent in our non-working W-armchair or W-flying vehicle, to die, prisoners to the point of equilibrium of our universe. By deactivating as many machines as we can, I believe that we are saving the world, at least temporarily, by causing the point of equilibrium to move farther away from the present."

Ken stood up. He felt a tight knot in his stomach. He walked to the window behind Bob's desk and looked out. Nothing much was moving in the area. The almost frozen quiet outside brought Morris' words back to him. *Research has come to a sudden standstill in these two areas . . . I tried to call their heads of section right now . . . it looks like they've disappeared off the face of the earth.* Yes, coupled with Bob's simple enunciation of the laws of thermodynamics, that made chilling sense now.

"It may be too late," he said in a low voice.

"What do you mean?" asked Bob in surprise.

"What would you expect to be the herald of the approaching point of equilibrium?"

"Well, certainly you would see that some sub-systems have stopped functioning, at the beginning partially and then fully. Then the whole system would freeze over at once."

"And how long would you think that one would have, once the first signs had manifested themselves, before the whole world reached equilibrium?"

"I believe that it would have to be a matter of days, maybe even hours. But why all these questions?"

"No time for that now," said Ken, walking resolutely to the door. "I just realized the meaning of the figures I saw today on my computer. Come with me, I'll tell you on the way. We must move immediately."

On the W-mobile, Ken told Bob quickly about the data coming in from all over the globe, which indicated that the research and development activity was about to come to a standstill.

"It fits!" exclaimed Bob. "It is exactly as we predicted that it would be—only we didn't know which sub-system would be affected first. It makes sense that research and development is the first to be affected, because no motivation—or driving force—has been left to develop. The machines do everything by themselves anyway. And my company's record is out of the ordinary, because we are swimming against the stream and we still have a lot of creative work to do to dismantle all the machines that are created daily for us."

"You may have saved the world—or, at least, delayed its end," said Ken, "by keeping the first sub-system to be affected ticking. But it can't last long. Not the way the statistics look now."

"But what can we do?" asked Bob in despair. "I thought we were doing the maximum, and I don't think that anybody can do any better. Not in the short time that we have left."

"You're right. There is only one thing to do."

"What?"

"We must shut W-Central down."

"But you can't do that!"

"Why can't I?"

"Because W-Central operates all the W-machines in the world."

"I thought you were against W-machines."

"I am. I have been working for years to stop them. But gradually, and with the full cooperation of the owner. If you deactivate a W-machine suddenly and unexpectedly, any person using it will be injured and will very likely die. If you stop W-Central without prior warning, you may kill ninety-five percent of the people of this planet. You can't do that."

"Can't I? And if I don't and the world reaches maximum entropy, how many will die?"

Bob lowered his gaze and, after a brief silence, murmured, "Everybody."

Ken looked at Bob and knew that they had no choice. Bob also knew it. Ken could tell by looking at his face.

The entrance to W-Central, located in a huge building a few miles outside the city limits, was through a wide gate that was watched by a mechanical attendant.

"Please pass through the wind chamber, gentlemen," said the machine with its synthesized voice.

The sign posted at the door of the wind chamber explained that all particles of dust had to be removed from the visitors' clothes, to avoid malfunctioning of the system due to contamination. It also excused itself graciously for the inconvenience. Ken and Bob stood in the room for fully two minutes while streams of air stripped them of any particle that nestled anywhere on their body.

"The damn machine has no security at all," commented Bob. "It is so full of itself that it doesn't even contemplate the possibility that one of its serfs—yes, that's exactly what we are, don't argue—may want to harm it."

They left the wind room and, using Ken's VIP card, gained access to the core of the building where the huge computer that ran W-Central was located. Ken had visited the building many times before and knew his way around it. They walked along a high bridge from which an assembly line was visible three stories below. It was assembling W-kids—a new line of humanoid robots. He had heard that they were perfect children—they were clean and respectful, and could be turned off when you were fed up with them.

The building was alive with the activity of many maintenance machines that ran in all directions. They hurried along the corridor until they reached the door of the main control room.

"Wait," said Bob. "We can't simply walk in and turn the thing off."

"Why not?" asked Ken. "That's exactly what I was planning to do."

"It has only now hit me that W-Central is built on Wish Technology. It knows exactly what you want to do, and I bet it won't let us do it."

"So how can we stop it?" asked Ken in despair.

"Don't worry," said Bob. "I have an idea. W-machines can be programmed to have some autonomy so that they can continue to serve you even if they lose their contact with W-Central for a while. Commercial machines are distributed with this capability turned off, but I happen to know how to turn it on. The algorithms that run the wish technology in stand-alone mode are not as strong, and therefore the machine is less efficient than when W-Central runs it, but it still can function."

"This is very instructive," said Ken with overt annoyance, "but where does it get us?"

"It gets us a machine that will turn W-Central off for us if we meet with any problem. I've seen a storage room for W-butlers on our way here. Let's go back and find it."

They ran along the corridor until they reached a door marked "Butlers Storage." They opened the door and stepped into a room full of small robots similar to the one Ken had at home. They chose one at random. It was rather ugly, with two pairs of arms equipped with different devices designed to serve its human owner.

"Here," said Bob, fishing a screwdriver of sorts from his pocket. "I'll deactivate its transmitter-receiver before I turn it on. Done," he added a minute later, and pressed the on-off switch.

The robot stirred, made a few clicking and whirring noises, and then stood still.

"Identify yourself," ordered Bob.

"Butler 1-Y-356-F at your service, sir."

"Do you recognize me, butler?"

"Yes sir. From your brain waves I detect that you are Mr. Bobo Startz. At your service, Mr. Startz. May I brush your jacket, sir? Or perhaps you wish me to mix you a refreshing drink from my personal supply?"

"No, Butler," said Bob with a satisfied smirk. "Follow me."

He walked out with the butler in pursuit, and Ken followed them. They retraced their steps to the central room, and stood before the door.

"Try to think of other things," suggested Bob. "Perhaps you can think about your statistics, or your boss, or something. Let's try to fool the damn W-Central."

He opened the door and they walked in. The room was vast, with an impressive control panel housing perhaps a hundred switches and at least as many control lights.

"I sense that you wish me to turn off a switch for you, Mr. Startz. At your service, sir. Which one would you like me to operate, sir?"

"How do you know which one is the right one?" whispered Ken.

"I have no idea," admitted Bob. "One option is to turn them all off, but I think that first I'll try to figure out which one is the main switch." Then turning to the robot he added, "Stand by, Butler, while I make up my mind."

He moved toward the control panel and inspected it from a distance, without touching it. Suddenly a light came from the ceiling and hit him. Bob fell on the floor, coughing and contorting with pain. Ken ran to him, helpless.

"Don't come too close, Ken," whispered Bob. "The damn machine has been too smart for me." He coughed again, spitting blood, and before life left him he managed to say, "You're on your own now. You know what to do."

Ken stepped back and looked at the robot.

"Butler," he called.

"Yes sir, Mr. Leming. It was Mr. Startz's dying wish that I should be of assistance to you. Can I offer you a drink? Or perhaps you will allow me to brush your hair?"

"You know what I want, don't you?"

"Yes sir, Mr. Leming. I'll attend to it right away. May I take the liberty of telling you, in the meantime, that your trousers need pressing. Perhaps you would like me to do it . . . no, I sense that you wish me to proceed with my duties. At your service, sir."

The butler moved quickly to the control board and, with a speed that made Ken blink, ran from one switch to the other and turned them all off in a matter of seconds.

The room became suddenly silent. Nothing impressive had happened, but something in the air told Ken that things were different now. He walked to the door and opened it. The machines that had run to and fro before, servicing the building and tidying it constantly, now stood still. He walked to the bridge and looked at the factory below. He saw no sign of movement. The machines were frozen in different grotesque positions.

A light in the distance attracted his attention and he approached a window. It was a red light coming from far away, in the direction of the city. The city was on fire, as probably was every single city all over the world.

He started to feel a vibration coming from the floor. The energy center of the building was probably about to explode, as must have happened everywhere, because it was not designed to work without control. Ken started to run in the direction of the exit.

A noise behind him caused him to turn and look. The butler was sliding after him.

"I noted that your brain waves were becoming fainter, sir," it said. "Please, don't worry. I am at your constant service."

He didn't answer and kept on running, until he reached the main entrance. The mechanical attendant that had let him in stood motionless at its position. Ken turned around and saw the butler sliding quickly along the corridor that led to the exit. Flames were already advancing behind it. The main W-door of the building, now useless, was partially open. Ken closed it manually and then barricaded it by tilting the heavy body of the mechanical attendant against it.

The butler reached the door and bumped into it, and then simply stood there. Ken looked at it and saw the flames reaching rapidly behind it. He turned his back to the last functioning machine of the world, and started to walk away. From behind the door he could still hear the butler's voice.

"Your shirt is dirty, sir," it was saying. "Please allow me to change it for you. You can't walk around like that, sir. It is not appropriate . . . "

Its words were lost in the noise of the fire from which a new tomorrow was about to be born. And Ken kept on walking.

Born in Kuala Lumpur, Ivan Sun studied in Singapore and Perth and now resides in Melbourne, Australia. His short fiction and poetry have been published in online journals and broadcasted nationally on Australian radio. He has two long fiction works in progress: the first regards a World War II survivor investigating the death of her son in the Australian outback; the other is set in an alternate Venice and is based on the Bluebeard fairy tale. Ivan keeps a website at http://www.ivansun.com.

Sometimes one has to use unusual tactics to avoid being persecuted by large cult organizations . . .

After the Stonehenge Bombing
by Ivan Sun

The day started pretty routinely for Dr. Matthias Berger. He woke up at 6 a.m. to his alarm clock. He drank half a cup of sweet black tea, leaving the remainder behind when he ran out of his house towards the nearby train station.

But then the day started to take a strange turn when Dr. Berger arrived at the security entrance of the City College. While he was waiting for his laptop satchel to pass through the hazard detectors, his gaze hovered absently over the advertisement for Cold Cola on the digital billboard. He tapped on his jacket's side pockets while his mind ran through a complex set of computer algorithms, the subject of a paper he was working on. Then his fingers froze still; his attention riveted to the image of smoldering rubble that filled the billboard. A scrolling banner on the bottom of the screen declared: "Stonehenge bombed!"

A flurry of gasps emanated from the queue of staff and students. Dr. Berger stood dumbfounded for a long moment before his attention was drawn to his satchel. It had traveled through the other side of the xray machine, and was now causing a bank-up of other bags and trays behind it. He grabbed his satchel and walked so quickly to his Department that his feet barely touched the ground. A dozen of his colleagues were already gathered at the departmental staffroom, watching the news on the wall-mounted screen. A symphony of mumbles filled the air. Solemnly, Dr. Berger took a seat amongst his colleagues, as if he was a latecomer to a classical concert.

According to the present news report, the Church of Moral Order (COMO) had claimed responsibility for the Stonehenge bombing. This was ostensibly to stop, once and for all, the unholy rituals performed there by the underground Druidic Order. Next came a broadcast from 10 Downing Street. In delivering the long meandering media statement, the Prime Minister repeated three times the refrain that although the loss of Stonehenge was "regrettable, thankfully no lives were lost in this act."

"You'd think he was talking about a brothel being fire-bombed!" said Dr. Jean Pung (or Dr. J. P., as he preferred to be addressed). The other academics eyed him uncomfortably. This diminutive but brilliant academic from Hong Kong had a tendency to make outbursts of this sort. He also cut a melodramatic figure with his shoulder-length silvery hair and dark uniform of black shirt and suit. He was the most successful among them during the last research grant application round. He was not a well-liked figure in the Department lately.

The Head of Department, Professor Lawrence, then said, "Have you read the editorial in the *Times* today? COMO is the 'religio-political phenomenon of the decade,' the party representing the 'religious majority' of the nation. Even as we speak, the Opposition party is rushing to re-package its key policies. So they fit in line with COMO's values!"

A hush of gloom now surrounded the academics. There were few proponents of the "religious majority" amongst them.

"Spare a thought for the Druidic Order," said Dr. J. P., breaking the silence. "I fear that the Stonehenge bombing marks a new era of intolerance." With this cheery news, he exited the stage like a moping

Hamlet.

"I've heard that Dr. J. P. has some sort of affiliation with the Druidic Order," whispered Dr. Gelding, a junior academic.

"I'm not surprised," replied another professor. "He has contacts in unusual places. You know . . . secret societies . . . I'm not surprised if that's why he is so successful in the grant rounds. Secret friends in influential positions."

The academics started to disband and return to their offices. Dr. Berger, who had sat quietly through his colleagues' discussions, also returned to his office. But he found that he could not settle into his computer algorithms as easily as he normally would. For some unknown reason, he was enthralled by the idea that Dr. J. P. had some special connection to the infamous Druidic Order, which had been driven underground by COMO.

After an hour, Dr. Berger finally gave in to his desire to drop by Dr. J. P.'s office.

"Come in!" cried the shrill voice of Dr. J. P., who had mistaken Dr. Berger's timid knocking as that of an undergraduate student.

"It's only me," said Dr. Berger. "I hope you don't mind. I just wanted to talk to you about . . . "

"Have a seat, Dr. Berger," he said, gesturing to the chair in front of his desk. "It's not about the last grants round, is it? I have already explained that I don't have any interest in your research area . . . "

"No," protested Dr. Berger as he sat down gingerly. "Actually I want to talk to you about the Druidic Order. And how they are going to respond after the Stonehenge bombing. Just curious, you know. And I heard . . . that you might have some acquaintances within the Order."

"The departmental grapevine must be better than I thought," said Dr. J. P. with some amusement.

"Don't worry," said Dr. Berger hurriedly. "It's only conjecture. But such a secret—if it were true—would be safe with me, of course."

"Well, I'm pretty sure you are not a member of COMO. I remember you going out of the way to support those students who were interrogated by the National Religious Squad. That incident last year."

"That's right. The Botswana Quarters incident. The poor boys were accused of conducting satanic rites. As you can see, I support the ideals of free religious expression."

"I see," said Dr. J. P., his brow furrowed as if he were debating whether to impart a delicious piece of information. Finally he seemed to have decided in Dr. Berger's favor. He said cautiously, "I do have some connections with the Druidic Order. I am, in fact, going to see a High Priest of the Druidic Order this afternoon. It's a social call, really. Dave's an old friend. You are welcome to join me. You might even get a chance to ask him a few questions."

"Why, that would be a real treat!" said Dr. Berger.

"You don't really seem surprised that I know an Arch-Druid. You can't have learned this through the departmental grapevine too, or have you?"

"No. But this has been a bizarre morning. I guess I'm not that easily shocked at the moment . . . But don't worry. I will tell no one about this meeting with the Arch-Druid. I don't want COMO or the Religious Squad on our trail."

"Good. I suggest we leave the campus separately. I'll rendezvous with you at 3 p.m., at the Sherlock Holmes monument, Baker Street station."

At two-thirty in the afternoon, Dr. Berger locked up his office and made his way to Baker Street. He walked quickly, flushed with anticipation. As it was a fine day, there were many pedestrians strolling on the pavement. He noticed some familiar faces—students from his last lecture—walking on the other side of the road. They smiled and waved back, friendly. He observed that more and more of his students were now wearing ECCMs, electronic closed-circuit monocles that represented the new frontier in national security. Each wearer's field of vision was recorded and then uploaded to the Central Security Mainframe. *CCTVs now have legs*, according to the latest advertising campaign. Terrorist attacks had noticeably diminished as a result of the popularity of this device. A supercomputer screened the uploaded video data instantaneously, generating emergency calls as required. The video data were also archived so that they could be retrieved later for criminal investigation.

These walking CCTVs had also quickly insinuated their way into pop culture. A number of magazines and websites now reported on the weekly top ten Home Baked Movies, which were homemade video files from electronic monocles made available for download on the Internet.

Dr. Berger had considered buying an electronic monocle, so ubiquitous it had become on the streets and in every form of paper and digital advertising. But what would it record, other than a life of research, administrivia and domestic tedium?

As Dr. Berger approached the gleaming crystal statue of Sherlock Holmes, he squinted his eyes as it reflected glints from the setting sun. He marveled that even after numerous attempts during the last century to destroy this monument, it had been repaired or reconstructed each time. It had even been completely re-designed several times. The current incarnation of the Sherlock Holmes monument wore a rather twentieth century ponytail and a more contemporary electronic monocle as a metallic detail—dating from the recent serialization of the Sherlock Holmes adventures. The monument had also acquired the square jaw and athletic physique of a Superman, quite a world away from the egg-headed, scrawny detective of the original Strand magazine illustrations.

Dr. J. P. stood at the foot of the crystal Sherlock Holmes, waiting. He was paying close attention to the pod-organizer in his hands. Probably looking through a grant proposal or a student thesis, thought Dr. Berger.

"Here you are," Dr. J. P. said amiably, "I was nearly convinced you have changed your mind . . . "

"I wouldn't miss out on meeting the Arch-Druid," replied Dr. Berger excitedly, "for all the Sherlock Holmes re-runs in the world. I hope you have not been waiting long."

"Not too long," he said. "Please hang on a moment while I finish this paragraph . . . " He kept Dr. Berger waiting for what seemed like an inordinately long time. Meanwhile Dr. Berger stood patiently and amused himself by observing the commuters as they stepped through the hazard detectors of the Baker Street station exit.

From time to time, Dr. J. P. threw a glance at his colleague, even as he continued tapping away on the pod-organizer. "Okay, I'm done!" he finally declared. "Come with me, Dr. Berger . . . " Together they walked up Baker Street for a few blocks towards Regent's Park, until Dr. J. P. drew his attention to a drab-looking flat.

"Are you sure it's safe?" Dr. Berger whispered, glancing left and right at the street traffic.

"Sure," replied Dr. J. P., smiling. "Don't worry. As long as you haven't sent an email to Fleet Street or COMO." He then rang the doorbell of the flat.

The door opened, and there stood a plump Indian woman. "Dr. Jean Pung!" she greeted cheerfully, her round face beaming. "How good of you to call! And your friend? So pleased to meet you; I am Pooja, Mr. Dave's housekeeper. Please come in!"

Together the two guests followed the swaying hips of Pooja as she walked up a steep set of stairs leading to the first floor. She knocked and then opened it to reveal a deep and narrow room. Bookcases, neatly stacked with books, lined every available wall space in the room. At the end of the room there was a superb view of Regent's Park.

A small, elderly man sat on a sofa beside the window. He had a head of cropped, silvery hair and a neat trimmed beard. His green pullover had a distinctive home-knitted thick-skeined feel. His eyelashes were remarkably long and copper-colored, and as he gazed down at his book, he looked as if he was dozing.

"Your visitors are here, Mr. Dave," said Pooja reverently.

The Arch-Druid looked up from his book and smiled. He snapped the book shut and put it aside on a coffee table. "Ah! Dr. Jean Pung and Dr. Matthias Berger. I have been looking forward to your visit!" Was there a faint Irish lilt in his greeting? Dr. Berger could not be sure, nor was he sure what was the custom when greeting a senior member of the Druidic Order. One could do worse than to start with a handshake, he guessed. But as he started to walk towards the Druid, he was suddenly asked to stop.

"Please excuse us and stand still for a moment while I request Dr. Pung's assistance in relieving you of your weapon."

"Weapon? I don't know what you are referring to," said Dr. Berger, astonished.

But Dr. J. P. had already started the body search, brisk and clinical, both his hands patting up and down Dr. Berger's body. Pooja stayed and watched with great concern.

"Don't worry," whispered Dr. J. P., "Dave will explain." Then he stuck his hand into Dr. Berger's pocket and brought out a mobile phone.

"But that's not a weapon," said an astonished Dr. Berger. "I've had it for over a year, and never had any trouble getting it past the hazard detectors. Either at the College or at the Tube!"

"Please be so kind as to demonstrate, Dr. Pung," said the Arch-Druid gravely.

Dr. J. P. carefully examined the silver clam-shell phone. He flicked it open and tapped at a few buttons. Then he pointed it for few seconds at a potted plant sitting on the floor beside the room entrance. An electronic melody, comic and jangling, rang out.

Pooja clucked her tongue with great annoyance. "Why on earth would you pick on my poor little fern, Dr. Pung! Now I have to remove it before it goes *kah-boom* and leaves a mess on the ground!" She then picked up the potted plant and left the room with a huff, slamming the door behind her.

"I . . . I . . . definitely did not know," Dr. Berger stammered, "that I had such a weapon in my pocket. Someone must have planted it here!"

"Certainly it was planted there," said the Arch-Druid Dave. "We also know that you are a sleeper agent who has been programmed to seek out and assassinate the last remaining Arch-Druids of our Order."

"That cannot be! I am sympathetic to the ideals of diversity in religion. You can look through my personal blog, interview my students, my colleagues.

"Yes," said the Arch-Druid Dave. "All that you have outlined qualifies you, in fact, as a candidate sleeper agent. But all the same, we know about you. You see, as part of our Druidic tradition, we possess special insight into the future. Warned by a runic oracle and the efforts of our team of Druidic Hackers, we have long expected that you would try to make contact with me through Dr. Pung. Dr. Berger, you have been programmed not to be aware of your deadly mission until triggered off by an implant in your right cortex. In the meantime, however, it sends you signals compelling you to draw closer to anyone associated with the Druidic Order."

"This is rather incredible," Dr. Berger said. "Let's say there is an implant in my brain. Well, I am right in front of you now, and though there was a weapon in my pocket, which you have removed, I am not aware, at any point during our meeting, of the slightest impulse to harm—much less kill—you!"

"That's because we have deactivated your sleeper-agent implant," explained Dr. J. P. "While we were standing beside the statue of Sherlock Holmes, I was in fact calibrating my pod-organizer to hack into the reception frequency of the implant device, and then to disable all its programmed functions."

Dr. Berger started to sway on his legs, seized by vertigo. The Arch-Druid suggested that he take a seat on the sofa beside him.

Dr. Berger sat down and contemplated his situation out loud. "Let's say that you are right. Do you know who instigated this? Who set me up as an assassin?"

"COMO sent you," replied Dave, "under the instructions of their Pro-Vice Chancellor. For a long time now they have been hatching plans to exterminate the last of the Arch-Druids."

"COMO!" Dr. Berger spat out in disgust. "I've had enough of their diabolical schemes. How do you plan to retaliate? Do you have a secret army? Why don't you recruit me to your cause?"

"We, as high priests, are torch-bearers to a spiritual order that stands for peace, love and wisdom. The only army we can recruit you to is our Druidic Peace Corp."

"So you do not plan to avenge this attempt on your life, or the Stonehenge bombing?" Dr. Berger asked.

"Hatred and evil bring about their own destructions," the Arch-Druid said and laughed. "Sometimes it is immediate and sometimes it takes many generations. It is not in the nature of evil and hatred to survive.

"The Henge has been a focus of spiritual devotion since the golden age of our Druidic history. Even when it came to ruin centuries ago, there has always been a legion of Druids and admirers returning to the sacred site to perform rituals, or use it as a focal point to commune with Nature.

"Stonehenge has inspired countless artifacts in art and architecture. Now it may lie in ruins, but its spirit will live on, in these artifacts, and in the hearts of those who follow the Druidic traditions. Our oracle tells us that one day, in the very spot that the Henge once occupied, there will arise a monument that will exceed the splendor of the Great Pyramids . . .

"And now, if you will kindly permit us, you will need to forget our meeting so that when the COMO operative next checks on you, you will not be able to inform them of my hide-out here. Dr. Jean Pung will give you an injection of a memory serum, and all the events of this afternoon will recede to a fragment of a dream. If you will kindly permit . . . "

"I give my consent," Dr. Berger replied earnestly. "But it is a shame that I will forget our conversation."

"In some cases," Dr. J. P. explained, "the feelings and imprints of the events are left behind. But no more."

There was a knock on the door. Pooja re-entered the room and handed over to Dr. J. P. the steel air-syringe held in her hand. He wasted no time in applying it to the left side of Dr. Berger's neck. It took no more than a few seconds for the serum to take effect. Suddenly Dr. Berger was acutely aware of the light that streamed through the window. He looked out into the view of Regent's Park, mesmerized by the foliage of giant trees, gently undulating against a clear blue sky.

"Farewell and sweet dreams," said the Arch-Druid, as Dr. Berger drifted out of consciousness.

Dr. Berger woke up with a splitting headache as if he were having a hangover. He found himself back in his office, lying on the floor; his eyes opening to the life-size poster of Sherlock Holmes—played by Jeremy Brett in the 1990s TV series. He stood up unsteadily, still dazed. As he took a few deep breaths to quell the throbbing in his head, he was surprised to realize that he retained a clear recollection of his meeting with the Arch-Druid Dave and his flat on Baker Street.

He headed to Dr. J. P.'s office. The office lights were still on. He knocked on the door and entered.

Dr. J. P. sat at his desk with a pen in his hand and a messy spread of papers before him. He looked startled to see Dr. Berger.

"What do you want?"

"I . . . remember our meeting. With you and . . . Dave. After the Stonehenge bombing."

"Dave? Which Dave?" asked Dr. J. P. sharply. "I know a number of Daves."

"We were all watching the Stonehenge news in the staffroom. Shocked. And then you went back to your office, and I came to speak to you . . . "

"Yes, very shocking, the news about Stonehenge. But I came back to my office to do some paperwork, where I have remained all day. Two of my research students dropped in, but definitely not you. I haven't seen you since this morning at the staffroom!"

"And Dave? Dave, the Druid on Baker Street?"

Dr. J. P. stared at his colleague as if he were a madman. Then he laughed loudly. "I think you need to go home and rest, Dr. Berger. I know you have been working very hard on your grant applications. I'm sorry you haven't been successful in spite of all the work you have put in. But seriously. Take my advice. Go home and rest. Watch your Sherlock Holmes or something to get your mind off your work."

Dr. Berger stammered an apology, red-faced, and fled the office. He ran back to his own office where he grabbed his coat and then ran out of the building towards the College's exit. He was surprised to see only wrought iron gates. The security entrance and hazard detectors were gone. No digital billboard, either.

Racing towards Baker Street Station, he saw a group of two young women and a man walking on the other side of the road. Their faces looked familiar. Students he recognized from his last lecture. He smiled at them and waved his hand, friendly. They ignored him and looked faintly annoyed to receive such attention from their lecturer.

He approached the statue of Sherlock Holmes. To his surprise it was the bronze nine-foot version of the statue. But for some reason he was expecting a crystal, shining sculpture. With a ponytail, the strong physique of an action-hero, and an electronic monocle. In fact, he could not remember anyone wearing the electronic monocle at all since racing out of the College.

Dr. Berger ran up Baker Street and knocked on the door of the flat he felt sure was the one that Dr. J. P. had brought him to.

A diminutive lady opened the door and he recognized Pooja's round face although she was wearing her hair much shorter. She had a crying baby in her arm. The baby was crowned with flaming red hair and had remarkably long eyelashes.

"Oh, excuse me, Pooja. I am here to see Mr. Dave."

"I beg your pardon," she said as she jiggled the crying baby about. "My name is not Pooja. I think you got the wrong house."

They argued for nearly ten minutes, as he insisted that earlier that day he was most certainly upstairs in the flat.

"But you were not here," she repeated again and again. "I live here with my husband and my children. Please go away. My husband is at work."

Finally however, after Dr. Berger showed his university staff card, she decided that he was probably harmless: an absent-minded professor who genuinely made a mistake with the house number.

With great reluctance, the lady allowed him in and took him up the familiar staircase to the first floor. His heart pounded with anticipation. The door opened to a deep and narrow room, densely furnished with Indian decorations and furniture. The large window was partially covered by heavy drapes. A small toddler sat on the floor playing with wooden building blocks, creating a miniature version of Stonehenge.

Through the window, Dr. Berger could see the leaves of the trees undulating against the dark evening sky.

"I'm sorry. So sorry," he muttered to the lady and then quickly ran out of the house.

A week after the Stonehenge bombing, COMO went on to detonate a bomb outside the United Nations New York headquarters. Through their website, they claimed responsibility. Within a few months, the world was witness to the destructive force of the United Nations coalition army. COMO's organizational hub and key sites of worship were raided and destroyed using intelligent missiles. These buildings were laid as flat as the smoldering rubble that Stonehenge was reduced to.

Dr. Berger was not comfortable with the idea of the United Nations acting as an agent of retribution. However, he could not deny that the effect was the same, as predicted by the Arch-Druid Dave . . . if he had recalled correctly what happened that afternoon after the Stonehenge bombing.

Joel Arnold's work has appeared in over three dozen publications, including Weird Tales, Chizine *and* Gothic.net.

Games have rules, but sometimes you don't know which rules. And there are consequence for not following the correct ones . . .

Burrow
by Joel Arnold

It was dark and hot, and the smells were those of rot and perspiration. Clay moved with a mechanical precision through the tunnel, the light on his hard hat moving from the bottom of the wall to the top in a sweeping zigzag pattern. If a chunk of glass or metal winked at him, he'd take his dulled pick and dislodge it as best he could. Sometimes, if he was careful, he could remove an entire glass bottle that way without it shattering. He'd place it, along with the plastic containers, aluminum cans, bullets, and other items of value, in his cart. He thought it was best to have a method, best to focus on one's work. It made it all the easier to get through the day that way. Made it possible not to lose his sanity and try digging his way out to the top like others had. He'd come across more than one miner who had tried desperately to dig their way out, all the old bones and debris crushing them in a suffocating avalanche.

He had spent his first fourteen years on the surface. The waters had receded, but what good had that been? There was still not enough room. And the Game had been going on for the last fifty years.

The Game.

The rules were simple. You're placed deep in the mines, and you have to find your way out. This could take years, and you had to work for your food. You had to mine the precious remnants of past generations.

Aluminum. Plastic. Steel.

They called it a game, but it really wasn't a game at all. How many people had Clay known to make it out alive when he had been above? Had he known any? Even his father never made it out. His father had been a strong man, level-headed—if anyone could make it out, he could.

Yet he hadn't. Clay had not seen his father in five years.

Sometimes, when the oxygen was low, Clay imagined his father down there next to him, watching him work. Was it possible he was still alive? Could he have survived all these years in the tunnels? Did he make it out in the year and a half that Clay had been down here?

He remembered watching his father being hauled into the tunnel's entrance on a mining cart, arms and legs manacled. His father looked up at him and smiled just before the entrance of the tunnel swallowed him in one pitch black gulp.

Maybe that was the worst. The fact that he remembered the surface. Remembered feeling the fresh air on his skin, the sun like a kiss on his face. Fresh water, the sound it made lapping at the shores of old crushed rock and bone.

Best not to think too much. Best not to let fading memories instill too much hope.

Some of the men sang to keep from thinking too much. But Clay didn't believe in that. To him, their voices sounded pitiful and lonely ricocheting through the tunnels, and whenever he tried to sing, his voice returning to him unheeded in diminishing echoes, it reminded him of how much of his life had been wasted in the mines.

No. It was best to concentrate on the swing of the pick, the connection of metal to bone. Keep the senses tuned to the rhythm, the *chink* an accent to every fourth beat of the heart. Even though it made a crude clock, a cruel reminder of the glacial passage of time below the surface—at least it denoted progress. Momentum. At least each strike at a tunnel wall was a strike toward freedom.

Clay struck.

Two cubic meters of compacted bone and dirt loosened and tumbled around his work boots. He held his breath a moment, listening for signs of instability, the tell-tale rumblings of a potential cave-in. But the debris settled around his ankles and the tunnel's walls held tight. He leaned over, kicking apart the remnants of a not-too-distant past. There was a femur. A jaw-bone. Half of a skull. A set of ribs.

Amidst the rubble, something winked at him in the weak cone of his helmet's light. He reached down, but stopped short. It was a copper penny. He looked behind him into the tunnel's dark throat. He waited, straining to listen above the sound of his own breathing.

You can never be too careful. That's what his grandmother always told him. *They're always watching, Clay. Always listening.* And she was right. How else could they know where to find you, to dole out their pitiful ration of food, have it delivered to within a few meters of where you toiled? Their little rusty-can robots on squeaky wheels, the food tray balanced on top of their short squat bodies, and if the food spills on its way to you, that's your own tough luck. Another good reason not to dig at too sharp of an angle. If the damn things have to find you on a steep upsweep, half your food's going to be soaking into the ground, soaking into the upturned bony mouths of the hundreds of skulls that lined the tunnel floors.

He squatted over the penny, pretending to dig at a phantom stone in his boot, then quickly slid the penny between the boot's hard leather, and his own callused skin. He stood.

You can never be too careful.

He filled his cart with the bony detritus hewn from the tunnel. Pressed a button on the cart that signaled another worker, another Player-of-the-Game, to bring an emptied cart and haul the full one away.

There's always someone lower than you, he thought. Always someone worth less no matter how worthless you are.

He heard steps coming toward him, the dull crunch of hard boot rubber on old bone. He didn't turn around to look. What if it was one of them, one of the enforcers sent to terminate his play? Had they seen him take the penny?

The light from another helmet threw Clay's shadow flat against the tunnel wall. If he had been caught, if it was time to leave the game, he didn't want to see it coming.

He felt a presence behind him, waiting. Clay stared straight ahead. Lifted his dull pick and swung at his own shadow. It struck weakly against solid bone.

Get it over with, he thought, the back of his neck hot in the glare of the other light. But there was only the receding squeak of the cart's wheels as it was hauled away.

His shoulders sagged. The smell of his own sweat, the feel of heat prickling his face, overwhelmed him. He wanted to drop to the ground and sleep until the game was over. Sleep until the sun engulfed the planet. The sleep of eternity. He often envied the previous owners of the bones he picked through.

But he heard his grandmother's voice again. The last words she said to him before he was swallowed up in the tunnel's maw.

"We're not quitters, Clay. Don't you ever give up."

He rolled his shoulders back. Let the tears flow down his dirt caked cheeks. He took a deep breath, the dust-filled oxygen like glass shards in his lungs. He swung his arm, the pick bouncing impotently off the mass of bone in front of him. But he forced himself to keep swinging.

"Did you hear it? Eddie made it out."

Rumors.

"Hey, did you know—Frank broke through."

The miners thrived on them.

"They're sending people down from above to show us the way out. They're going to help us. They're actually going to help us out of this goddam mess!"

Rumors of the sunlight above, of how far they had come, of how close they were to the surface. The rumors gave them hope. Yet the rumors could kill. There were times they stirred a man's heart past the point of acceptance, shook it up until he couldn't take it anymore, and he had to get to the surface *right the hell now*. He'd dig like a madman, burrowing up through the dirt at a dangerous angle, not paying attention to the intricacies, the textures of the earth. More often than not he'd become trapped. The earth, the bones, would cave in around him, crushing him, jamming his fingernails, his teeth, his eyes full of countless generations of the dead.

Clay ignored the rumors as best he could. What good were they? If he was near the surface, he'd find out soon enough, rumor or not. Best not to let glimmers of false hope lead to pain and agony further down the line.

He believed that the only way out was to work methodically. Dig slowly, carefully, consistently. Eventually, his pick would break through the surface and the fresh air would fill his lungs, the sun fill his heart.

"I know your father."

The voice arrived at Clay's ear like one of the many insects that scurried about down here. Clay continued to face the wall of bone and dirt, his heart quickening.

The stranger was only inches away, his breath painful in Clay's ear. "He made it out. I saw him on the outside."

Clay struck his pick hard in the conglomerate before him, hard enough to make his hands go numb and his wrists scream with pain. He let go of the pick and stepped back, the metal tip deeply embedded, the wooden handle vibrating with the force of the blow. He wiped the sweat from his face, tried to keep his breathing under control.

"Who are you?" he asked, his voice quiet and hoarse from disuse. He knew they sent spies down here to gather information and tempt the miners to lose their cool. "How do you know who I am?"

"He sent me down to find you."

"You're full of shit."

"No. It's true. He made it out."

"You didn't answer my question. How do you know who I am?"

The man took a step back, looking Clay up and down. "You think I wanted to come back down here? You think I'm enjoying this?"

"You're not a miner?"

"Don't you get it? He made it out. He won."

Clay studied the man. A light tan, a lack of calluses. The dirt on his face was only surface dirt, not deeply ingrained in the wrinkles and pores.

"Shit, kid. What's your problem? I thought you'd be pissing yourself with joy right now."

Clay turned away from him.

You can never be too careful.

"Wait." The man pulled a small gray envelope from his shirt pocket. He opened it and slid out a photograph. "Here. Take it."

Clay turned. His fingers trembled when he touched it. He slumped forward, grabbing onto the handle of the pick, still protruding from the mine's wall, for support. It was a picture of his father. Standing on the surface. Squinting from the sun. Even though Clay hadn't seen his father for five years, he knew the picture was recent, knew it couldn't have been taken before his father was sent into the mines. He looked older. Deep wrinkles. Hair gray and balding.

"Why didn't he come himself?"

"Are you kidding? It took him four years to get out. You think he'd want to come back here, risk getting lost? Maybe he thinks I'm full of shit when I tell him I know where you are. Maybe he thinks it's a trick to get him back into the mines."

Clay couldn't take his eyes off the photograph. Tears made pink slash marks through the dirt on his face. "How do I know this isn't a trick?"

"Can't help you with that, kid. That's up to you to decide." He pulled a piece of paper from his pocket. On it was drawn a map. "Here's where we are now," he said, pointing. "And here's where you wanna go." He traced his finger through a convoluted maze of tunnels, criss-crossing and switching back on each other, all rising steadily to the surface. "Once you're in this area, you can dig your way out. That's the main thing, kid. You still gotta dig yourself out. Otherwise, if you follow me on up to the main entrance, they'll cry foul and toss your skinny ass back down to the bottom."

Clay took the map. Studied it. Used his fingernail to mark his current location.

The man gently pried the photograph from Clay's hand and pocketed it.

"Can't I keep it?" Clay asked.

"That's not the way it works." The man turned, looking up the dark maw of the tunnel from which he'd come. "I have to go now."

Clay nodded. His eyes went back to the map.

"What should I tell him?" the man asked.

"What do you mean?"

"Should I tell him you're coming?"

Clay didn't answer. He stared at the map, the narrow hand-drawn lines like thin dark worms on the paper, the trembling light of his helmet making them dance.

He'd been in the tunnels for so long now, kept to himself so much he didn't know whom to trust, wondered if trust was merely a commodity of the past, discarded like so many glass bottles and cans and bullet shells. The inside of his mouth tasted of bitter bone dust.

He didn't know what to do.

Ten hours later, he had traversed most of the map. At least he thought he had. He couldn't be sure. The map was hard to follow, the proportions off. He'd passed only a handful of other miners, most of them resting against the tunnel walls, their eyes glazed over, the pupils wide and hungry for light. He passed a fresh corpse, only the feet sticking out of a collapsed wall, as if the remains of the long ago dead had devoured him.

He trudged forward, his body aching, his heart racing. It was hard not to let the excitement eat him alive, hard not to sprint ahead. What if this was a trap? Just one more twist in the game?

The map ended. He looked ahead, following the dim cone of his helmet's light. Had he made a wrong turn? He saw nothing beyond the light. He stood still. Tried to quiet his own breathing. There were no other sounds. Not even the far-off echo of the other miners' picks connecting with the tunnel walls. Not even the drip of moisture as gravity sucked it hungrily from above.

Where do I go? he wondered. What's left?

He stepped forward. Stopped. Turned around. There was nothing. Nothing. He looked at the tunnel wall. Reached out and touched it. Felt the debris crumble beneath his fingertips.

He closed his eyes. Thought of his father waiting on the surface. Is he standing over me? An earthly angel above this dehumanizing crust?

He made up his mind. Stepped back. Hoped his father would be proud. Lifted his pick in the air. Took aim at the tunnel wall, his cage, his prison, and swung.

Over and over again, he swung. The earth crumbled around him. He kicked it away. Kept swinging. The earth fell in great clumps. The air was thick with dust. He quickened his pace. Clink! Clink! One swing after the other until his muscles burned, his head spun with the lack of oxygen, yet still he kept swinging.

He struck higher. His father, the one he'd glimpsed in that picture, filled his mind. Beckoning him. Urging him forward. Swing! Clink!

And the earth caved in around him.

The earth swallowed him whole.

He was encased in it, like a caveman frozen in ice.

He pushed his hand forward, the only part of his body that could still move. He sucked in the stale, rancid air, bits of dirt and decaying bone entering painfully into his lungs. Don't panic, he told himself. Don't panic.

Think. Take it one step at a time. Slowly. Methodically.

He forced his left hand forward, the only appendage he could move, through the putrid soil. A shard of glass from a broken bottle cut into the base of his palm. Coarse dirt embedded itself deep beneath his fingernails. The pain was intense and he wanted to scream, but he couldn't even do that.

He remembered the copper penny he had found. Would some miner in the future pry it from his rotting bones?

Find a penny, pick it up . . .

He struggled once more for breath, inched his hand forward, feeling the skin peel back, exposing raw nerves.

Father, he tried to whisper, but could not.

When he inhaled for the last time, dirt filled his mouth, and his bloody fingertips felt the sting of fresh air.

He had won.

Jenny Blackford has had children's stories published in Australian markets including Random House's 30 Australian Ghost Stories for Children *and the* NSW School Magazine. *More recently Jack Dann accepted a story of hers for an anthology to be published by HarperCollins. She also writes and reviews for the science magazine* Cosmos, *the ecological magazine G, and for the* New York Review of Science Fiction, *as well as assessing manuscripts for Driftwood Manuscripts.*

Here she follows Pausanias around an ancient Greek shrine, ancient even in Pausanias' time, where an unexpected encounter has him decide whether or not to include this place in the guide book.

Python
by Jenny Blackford

People say many different things about Delphi, and even more so about the oracle of Apollo. For they say that in the earliest times the oracle belonged to Gaia . . .

—Pausanias: *A Guide to Greece*, second century AD

Pausanias led his mule higher and higher up the steep, slippery limestone track, looking for the ancient shrine to Lady Gaia. Holy Delphi, sacred to Lord Apollo and Lady Athene, was well below him now, hidden by the slope.

The late spring sun hadn't emerged yet over the peak that he was climbing, but the day was already warm, and he was starting to sweat uncomfortably under his woolen tunic. Travelers from all over the Roman Empire would already be poking through the old temples and treasuries of Delphi below. When he looked back, he saw pale, rocky mountainside dropping sharply down to a flat valley covered in a green

155

river of trees. At the other side of the valley, another pale, rocky mountain spur rose up. Along to the right, the rocks opposite gradually diminished in height, and the narrow valley sloped to a far-away green and brown plain. A thin line of blue intruded there, coming from a body of water at the plain's far edge—the Gulf of Itea. The gods were indeed wise; they had chosen the loveliest of places for their sacred site.

Pausanias had carefully written up everything he could find in Delphi—notes for inclusion in his long-planned guidebook. *That* was what the public was interested in: the great temples and statues from six hundred years ago or more, before the war between the Athenians and the Spartans had ruined the economy of Greece, and the Macedonians had conquered them all. Now, the Romans tried patiently to keep the peace between the ever-squabbling city-states of the Greece they so admired for its intellectual glories. All the same, the traveler was itching to see the shrine that the old women had told him about, high on the mountain.

An image of the goddess Gaia had fallen from the sky in a great fireball many, many years ago, they'd said, before Menelaus had left his city of Sparta and sailed to Troy. The locals had built a shrine in a nearby cave to house her and her Python, a supernaturally large snake. Much later, they'd decided to build a flashy new shrine lower down the mountain, and, later still, Apollo had taken it over. But even now, centuries upon centuries later, the old women of the town still went to the little shrine high on the mountain to offer their thanks, or their pleas, to the Goddess.

Finally, Pausanias spotted what he was looking for, to the left of the track, just where fat old Chrysippe had said. There wasn't much to see: a few pale rocks stacked up on either side of an opening into the mountainside. He bent over and traced the curving markings on the rocks with his finger and smiled, then tied the mule to one of the gloomy cypress trees by the path. This was what he lived for: the carvings in the rocks were very, very old. The women were right. Gaia had been worshipped here long before the bronze-greaved Achaean heroes had built their monumental works.

Pausanias walked back to the rocks, carrying a leather pouch. Touching the rocks again, he couldn't suppress his grin. This shrine must already have been old when Lord Dionysus had first brought wine to Greece from his holy mountain of Nysa: wine would not be the correct offering, here. Ancient shrines needed ancient offerings. He rummaged in the pouch and took out a honey cake—barley meal pounded with honey and cooked on a hot rock—and a flask of sheep's milk. They were old-fashioned enough for an ancient goddess to be content with them.

"I bring you gifts, Lady Gaia," he said, standing next to the rocks that marked the entrance to the shrine, with the offerings in his outstretched hands. You couldn't be too careful. "I pray that you might find them appropriate. May I approach your altar?"

Nothing happened—at least, nothing visible or audible. After a minute or two, Pausanias concluded that the goddess's silence could be taken for consent. He placed the offerings on the ground, then got down on his knees to crawl through the low entrance to the cave, watching nervously for snakes, spiders and unpleasant creatures with even more legs. His knees and hips creaked ominously. He was a medical doctor by training, even if he preferred to travel; he'd seen many patients crippled by arthritis. Soon, he knew, he'd be too old for this.

Once inside the entrance of the cave, he stood up slowly and carefully and waited for his eyes to adjust to the dusty gloom. There was something interesting at the back of the small shrine, past the rough stone altar: a big, lumpy object, up against the cave's grayish limestone wall. As he'd hoped, it wasn't a modern marble statue, pretty though they could be once they were painted brightly and clothed in expensive garments. He'd seen so many of *them* already, on this tour of Greece, that each one had made him feel a little more like screaming. But, thank all the gods, this wasn't yet another bad copy of a Pheidias statue. The dark, squat shape wasn't even recognizably human in form. If he was really lucky, it might even be a *xoanon*, an old wooden image, carved or found by the locals here unimaginably long ago.

Excited now, Pausanias displayed the gifts in his outstretched hands. "Lady Gaia," he said, "may I approach your sacred altar?"

"Come on then," a hissing voice said. "Put your gifts on the altar. Don't be shy."

Pausanias squinted into the dark to see the owner of the voice. He could have sworn there wasn't anyone else in the small, dark cave.

"Excuse me?" he said. "Who are you? I didn't think there was a priest here."

"You are Pausanias, aren't you?" the voice said from a particularly dark corner. "Writing a guide-book, Chrysippe told me. I asked her to send you up here."

"Um, yes, oh," Pausanias said, then trailed off into incoherence. Who was he speaking to? And why couldn't he see him?

"You wouldn't be able to pronounce my name," the voice hissed. "You might as well call me Python. The locals always have." With those words, a snake as thick as Pausanias' upper arm slithered from behind the altar.

Everything looked a bit too pale, and Pausanias' legs felt wobbly.

"Holy Python," he said.

The snake snorted. "Just 'Python' will be sufficient from you, Pausanias. You're a learned man, unlike most of the locals—though that Chrysippe's not stupid. She thought I'd like a chat with you. We don't get many real scholars here these days. Standards are slipping."

Pausanias had some difficulty getting his mouth under control. It wanted to make useless gibbering noises, rather than talk properly. "Standards," he said carefully. "Slipping. Scholars. What? What do you want with me?" Then he couldn't stand it any longer. In a rush, he blurted it out: "Are you going to eat me?"

"Just give me that nice honey-cake and the milk, and I'll be happy. My metabolism's slow, and I'm not really a carnivore, though I know I look like one to you. Beggars can't be choosers. I've come to like those honey-cakes quite a lot, actually, since my ship was wrecked."

Every month, ships were wrecked on the rocky shores of Greece. A storm at sea was a serious danger, even with modern Roman shipbuilding technology. But where had the snake's ship come from? And when? Pausanias was terrified, but antiquities fascinated him. He wanted to know how the cave had looked when the snake had first come here, and how much it had changed with occupation. "So how long have you been here, um, Python?"

"Longer than you can imagine," it said. Was there sadness in its hissing voice? "But enough of that. No need for me to bore you with my little problems. How about that snack you were offering me? For the benefit of the goddess, of course."

Pausanias crept forward, one tiny step at a time, until he could put the cake and the milk-flask an arm's-length from the snake. It opened its mouth unimaginably wide, and swallowed the honey-cake whole. "Could you pour the milk into my bowl there on the altar, do you think?" it said. "That would be the least messy all around."

Pausanias hesitated. "It won't offend the Goddess?" he asked.

"No," the snake said, "I don't think you need to have any fear of that."

Pausanias took a deep breath, and gripped the flask tightly. He stepped forward. At least it would get him closer to the wonderful *xoanon* behind the altar. After the snake drank, it looked deep into Pausanias' eyes. Soon, without any sense of time having passed, the traveler found himself sitting cross-legged on his cloak, staring at the strange, misshapen dark lump that was the body of the goddess, telling the snake his life story.

"So, that brings me up to this morning," he said, much later. "I climbed the hill, found the cave, and you know the rest."

"Thank you, Pausanias," the snake said. "Your travels will make a good book, I think. But it's close to noon now, and Chrysippe tells me there's a very fine shrine to Pan and the nymphs in a cave a bit further along the path. It's time you were on your way."

No! "But I have so many questions for you, Python. You must be Gaia's Python, I think, but they say that Apollo killed you long ago."

The snake laughed. "I'm not as easy to kill as all that. Even you could have outrun Apollo's gaggle of plump priests, my traveling friend, and my kind can move very quickly, when we need to."

"Where do you come from? When was your ship wrecked? Who

made the image of the goddess here?" Pausanias gestured at the fascinating lump, all protuberances and crevices.

"Trust me," the snake said. "You don't want to know about it."

"Oh, but I do, really . . . "

"I'd love to tell you," the snake said, "but then you would die. Don't be alarmed, Pausanias, I don't really mean it. It's just an old saying in my department back home, so very far away. But I'll do the right thing. I'll follow all the rules and regulations, even if my colleagues are taking forever to rescue me from this alien place." The snake sighed again.

What could the Python possibly mean?

The snake said, "It's been a delight talking to you. I used to see everyone who was anyone, until those priests came. But times have changed now. The Romans would probably want to take me to their Emperor to display in his park, with his other exotic animals." The Python looked deep into Pausanias' eyes again, and went on: "In a moment, you will have forgotten all about me. You'll be standing by the altar looking at my poor crumpled escape pod. You will remember her as a wonderful piece of carving, but you won't want to tell anyone about her. And good luck with your book."

Soon, Pausanias was untying his mule. Gaia's *xoanon* here was unique, but it was probably best left to the locals. He didn't like the thought of tourists trampling through the ancient cave. He tugged hard at the leather strap, and the mule grudgingly started to walk with him, up the slippery limestone track towards the shrine of Pan and the nymphs.

Adele Cosgrove-Bray began writing poetry at the age of fourteen. She went on to write and illustrate a monthly dream analysis column for Your Future *magazine before becoming more interested in Dark Fantasy fiction. She was elected Chair for Riverside Writers in 2003, a post she still holds. She is also a member of Wirral Writers Inc. Adele has worked as an editor, a library assistant, a photographer and a potter. She has lived on the Wirral peninsula in Cheshire, England, since June 2000 where she writes full-time and shares life with her husband Richard, two cats and two dogs. Visit her website: www.adelecosgrove-bray.com.*

If you see a ruined inn across the way don't be surprised how easy it is to imagine voices echoing off the bluffs. But take care not to disturb them.

Seagull Inn
by Adele Cosgrove-Bray

"Where will you site your easel, Aunt Lydia?"

"I thought I'd place Telegraph House in the lower third of the canvas, and have the sea above that, looking towards the beach edging the mainland."

"I'll be wandering around." Rowan's slender hand caressed the heavy SLR camera bag worn around his waist like a holster.

"Watch your footing along the cliffs, won't you. I can do without having to pay for rescue helicopters."

Rowan smiled and gazed across the short, tough grass towards the small ruined building at the far end of Hilbre Island. "It looks like we have the place to ourselves. How long have we got?"

Lydia nodded towards the somber grey waters of the Irish Sea which had already flooded the bay between the three small islands and West Kirby beach. "It'll be around five hours before the tide goes out and we can safely cross the sands again."

When folded away, her portable easel looked like a wooden attaché case. Lydia now carefully extended its thin, telescopic legs. "How about we meet here in two hours for lunch?"

Rowan nodded, the soft breeze tugging at his sandy ginger hair. The crown was streaked blond by the sun. "Sounds good to me."

Lydia removed her blue backpack, unzipped it and began extracting plastic tubs crammed with tubes of oil paint. A thicket of assorted brushes were held together with an elastic band. Rowan could also see the tops of two large thermos flasks.

Lydia asked, "Shall we have coffee before we begin working?"

"Sounds even better! It's quite a distance over the sand and rocks."

"Two miles. But did you enjoy it?" Lydia produced plastic cups and began unscrewing the lid of one thermos.

"Yes, actually. The sense of space feels like a weight pressing down. The vast sky, the low roar of the ocean in the distance; seabirds calling overhead; the wind constantly moving over mile upon mile of exposed sand . . . . It's far from silent, and yet it's intensely peaceful here."

Lydia handed him a coffee then quickly poured her own. "Hilbre Island was a religious site for centuries. Its name comes from St. Hildeburgh. There was a shrine dedicated to her here, before the Norman Conquest, but nobody seems to know anything about her now."

Rowan crouched down on the short grass. Lydia had previously offered to patch the threadbare knee of his badly faded jeans but he had just smiled enigmatically and politely declined. "Whereabouts was the shrine?"

Lydia smoothed a lock of silver-white hair beneath her lilac woolen hat that matched the jumper she wore under her cream waterproof jacket. "I'm not sure. Nothing of the shrine survives, and the foundations of the monks' buildings are thought to lie beneath the Buoymaster's House."

Rowan sipped his coffee appreciatively. "Monks?"

Lydia smiled at her nephew's insatiable fascination with antiquity.

"Monks were here for over four hundred years, until the dissolution of the monasteries."

"So it's all saints and seagulls, hmm?"

Lydia laughed warmly. "Hardly. Hilbre Island was notorious in the 1700s. But I'll tell you more later, when we eat. Right now I want to make a start on that canvas."

Rowan drained the last of his coffee. He recognized Lydia's intense, introspective expression and knew her mind was already on her painting. "I'll have a look around the island."

Lydia smiled and nodded as she entwined her slender fingers around a charcoal stick. She began analyzing the composition of the small huddle of Victorian buildings. She paid little attention to Rowan as he walked away.

Lydia began whisking light strokes of charcoal onto the primed linen canvas. She liked working with this textile, as it offered an interesting surface texture while remaining springy under the brush. She had intended to paint Hilbre Island more frequently but time kept slipping through her hands. And, in all truth, she had felt vulnerable walking out here by herself. A person could easily slip on the kelp-plastered rocks and break an ankle.

Reaching for her wooden palette board, she wondered how long Rowan might stay with her. He was charming. Her heart bled, knowing how his mother had recoiled from his disclosure of his bisexuality. He had been living on the streets when Lydia found him and gave him a home. Now he was attending college. Lydia could not fathom her sister's attitude. Dismissing this train of thought, Lydia tightly clasped a 2" hog's hair brush and began creating pools of shadow on the canvas.

Rowan carefully tested his footing before he moved his weight forwards onto his extended leg. The rock pool lapping his boot looked knee-deep and he didn't want to plunge into freezing water, and the rounded ledge he was attempting to navigate was proving a little tricky. But the photographic opportunities presented by this gloriously rugged cliff of red Bunter sandstone demanded his attention. Deposited here some time during the Triassic period, it had been part of mainland

Wirral until the end of the last Ice Age, some 10,000 years ago. Now the three islands, Little Eye, Middle Eye and Hilbre, were part of a protected nature reserve and classified as being of international scientific importance.

Rowan used a small shelf of jutting rock as a seat. The rust-colored rock was covered in a fine layer of gritty sand. Dark olive-green kelp draped over much of the rock, its tangled clusters spiked with glistening black cockle shells. Oceanic breezes carried the honking cries of Common and Atlantic Grey seals, which were visible only as lozenge-shaped silhouettes on distant West Hoyle sandbank.

Rowan leaned forwards to peer into the calm pool by his feet. A small grey crab scuttled away from his shadow and towards rusty-brown fronds of lacy seaweed. An almost-transparent shrimp slowly combed the sandy bed for microscopic food. The pale sun felt warm on the back of Rowan's neck. This island could be a real sun-trap, he guessed, and yet the evidence of ferocious storms was all around in splintered, tumbled rocks and high tide lines.

Rowan slowly explored further along the cliff face, taking photographs of light bouncing off the calm sea, or of the chattering clouds of birds which billowed beside the tide's rippling edge. He recognized Dunlin, Curlew, Rock Pipit and Sanderlings, though there were many other species.

Scooped into the cliff face was a small cave. Rowan smiled instinctively as he stood within its shelter. It had a rough ledge running around part of its walls. A shallow pool of water covered most of the floor.

Gazing across the tranquil steel-grey sea, Rowan noticed how the horizon was impossible to distinguish. It was like looking into a dull, silver-grey mirror which reflected nothing but itself. He dismissed this illogical thought with a shake of his head, and left the cave.

The route forwards seemed too dangerous, so he doubled-back on himself, though taking a slightly different track along the treacherous rocks until he found a sheltered spot. He sat down and pulled out a notebook. The faint scratch of his faux tortoise-shell ink pen felt meditative as he recorded his impressions of the rugged beauty of this fascinating small island.

Algid tendrils of fog had crept over the languid ocean and stealthily fingered the shoreline. Rowan wisely closed his notebook and carefully made his way back to the grassy summit. As he trudged along the gritty access path beside the Heligoland bird trap, he could see Lydia standing by her easel. She waved when she saw him approach.

"Look at this fog! I can't see the mainland to finish my painting," she said. "And I was beginning to worry about you."

Rowan casually ran a hand through his tousled, floppy hair. "I was exploring the rocks."

"That's what I was worried about," said Lydia, shaking her head but smiling anyway. "Lunch?"

"I'm starving!"

Her mild anxiety dissipated instantly at her nephew's smile. From within her backpack, she produced a flask of piping hot tomato soup and two plastic lunch boxes filled with chicken sandwiches and chocolate bars.

Rowan sat down on the grass and looked at Lydia's canvas. "Will you be able to finish the painting at home?"

"Oh, yes; I usually tinker with my work for months before I call it finished. And even then I find faults that had escaped me before. I'm not a great artist; I just enjoy painting. If someone else likes my work, that's fine. If they don't, it doesn't trouble me."

"I wish I had your self-belief. Anyway, I think you're selling yourself short. You do have talent, Aunt Lydia."

She handed him an open lunch box and joined him on the wind-scorched grass. "Many people have talent. It's how a person develops and uses talent that counts."

"At least you know what you want to do with your life. I haven't a clue." He delicately slipped a piece of straying chicken into his mouth.

Lydia smiled tightly. "I wish I'd found my interest in art when I was still young enough to make a career of it. I didn't even begin painting until I was fifty-two. But never mind about that now. This fog is rolling in very heavily."

"It's hardly possible to see the ruined building at the far edge of the island."

Lydia nodded her agreement as she took another bite of her sandwich. "That's the old lifeboat station, built in 1839 and used for the next hundred years. There's a steep ramp beyond it, leading into the water, where the lifeboat used to be launched from. Now it's used as a bird-watching hide, and it also houses what is arguably the most important tidal gauge in Britain."

Rowan leaned back on one elbow. "That's quite some history for a small, plain building. I might take a look down there later."

"In this thick fog? I'm not sure that's wise. Some of the ground around there is rather awkward."

Rowan took a drink of his soup. "The light's useless for photography now, anyway. Everything would come out looking flat."

Lydia pulled her scarf a little tighter to her throat. "I'd like to finish this painting but the coastline is obscured by fog."

"Did you hear voices?" Rowan looked towards the lifeboat station. "I thought we were alone here."

Lydia followed his gaze. "I didn't hear anything, but perhaps some of the island's residents are at home. The Mersey Canoe Club and the Hilbre Bird Observatory own two of the bungalows. The third is privately owned. There's an old slipway leading to the brick and stone boatshed; maybe someone's working there. During the seventeenth and eighteenth centuries, there was a salt boiling works at the base of the slipway. Maybe someone has been studying that, though only the seawater channels remain now."

Rowan grinned. "You're a mine of information about this place!"

Lydia sipped her soup and smiled. "I love the atmosphere here. There's a very real sense of history. Hilbre Island used to be a landing place for passengers traveling to and from Ireland. Rowing boats reached the ships anchored in the bay. Now everything sails from Liverpool, of course, because the River Dee gradually silted up too much for ships to enter. But at one time, Chester was by far the more important port of the two. In fact, in 130 AD, Ptolemy wrote about Chester's port but made no mention of the River Mersey at all because, at that time, it was just a tiny inlet."

Rowan smiled. "Wow, so much history for one tiny island! No wonder this place has such a strong atmosphere. Has anyone done a dig here?"

Lydia finished her soup. "Not as far as I know. There have been some archaeological finds, though. Roman coins, a Roman buckle and broach were found. Some ancient pottery and jewelry fragments, and a Bronze Age axe head and burial urn were found, too, and several Neolithic flint scrapers and arrowheads. A Saxon/Norse cross head carved in the local red sandstone was unearthed by the innkeeper's daughter. And four skeletons were found under a ninth century stone burial slab."

"There! I definitely heard voices that time." Rowan stared towards the ruined lifeboat station, but dense fog had shrouded the far end of the island with an opaque veil.

Lydia frowned. "I heard nothing, but then my hearing isn't what it once was. I hope this fog clears before we leave Hilbre. Walking back to West Kirby with such poor vision could be dangerous, even using the safe route."

Rowan tried to distract his aunt from her worries. "Why do walkers need to stick to the route from West Kirby to Little Eye, then trek to Middle Eye then Hilbre? Why can't people just walk straight across?"

"Quicksand," said Lydia. "And the tides can be deceptive. With the bay being so flat and wide, the tide comes in swiftly along channels that cut people off before they realize it."

"I can definitely hear voices. Look, there're some people moving around down by the ruined lifeboat station."

Lydia followed his gaze. "I think you're right. Are they carrying lamps?"

"It looks like it. I can just about make out their silhouettes." Rowan leaned forwards slightly to reach for the flask of soup.

Lydia held out her white plastic cup. "I wonder what they're doing down there? Perhaps it's a canoe party who've sought shelter from the weather."

"I don't know; they seem to be dressed wrongly for that. Their clothes seem too bulky."

"It's hard to see, the fog's so thick now," said Lydia.

Lydia and Rowan gazed at the dark grey silhouettes moving around the jagged rocks in front of the humble lifeboat station. The figures seemed to be wearing big coats and heavy Wellington boots. Each carried a small storm lamp. They worked as a team, seemingly in silence, their movements purposeful. Their attention was focused on the sea beyond the boat ramp, as if they were waiting for something. Certainly they had paid no attention to Lydia and Rowan.

"Maybe it's some kind of military maneuvers?"

Rowan shrugged. "I've no idea. But it's kind of creepy." The tiny hairs on the nape of his neck were crawling.

Lydia chuckled, but she too felt uncomfortable. Perhaps the cold of this ancient rock was seeping through her protective clothing. She drank her refilled cup of tomato soup, glad of its warmth on her hands.

The figures had settled down behind the ruined building, their attention still fixed towards the boat ramp. Their lights dimmed, as if they had placed them largely out of sight, possibly using the rectangular troughs cut into the sandstone, which some people erroneously believed to have been monks' graves.

"Did you hear that?" asked Rowan, a chicken sandwich in one hand. "It sounded like 'Ahoy there!'"

Lydia raised her eyebrows a little. "Do sailors still use that phrase?"

"Can you see that lamp someone's holding up? It looks like they're guiding a small ship in to land."

"Land here? But they can't! The rocks will . . . . "

Grinding, splintering shrieks of wood shredding on merciless rocks fractured the cold, moist air. The men had waited in stealth for the vessel to impale itself. Now they sprang from their discrete posts and swarmed through the ruined lifeboat station and towards the ramp.

Lydia shivered with realization. "Those men shouldn't be here. I don't know what's going on but it doesn't look legal. I think we should get out of here fast, before they see us through the fog."

Crouching down, Lydia quickly began gathering their things together.

"But people could be drowning!"

"We'll be joining them if we don't get out of here. Those men won't want any witnesses to whatever they're up to."

"But Aunt Lydia, we can't get off the island! We have to wait for the tide. You said so yourself."

Lydia swiftly lowered her easel to the ground and began folding it back into its attaché case state. She hissed, "Hurry! Let's just get behind a building or something. Somewhere out of sight."

Keeping low to the ground, Rowan quickly stuffed the remains of their picnic back into Lydia's blue backpack and flung the straps over one shoulder. Lydia held her folded easel in one hand, and her damp canvas in the other. Running at a crouch, they were soon behind the bay-windowed Telegraph Station, facing the sea.

Rowan carefully looked back on their route. "Some of the men are walking out of the lifeboat station. They're carrying stuff. Barrels, boxes; I don't know for sure."

"For goodness sakes don't let them see you!" Lydia pressed her back tightly against the whitewashed wall. Her legs felt like rubber. "They could be importing drugs!"

Rowan scowled. "It seems a weird way of doing that. Not that I know anything about it, really. Move back! They're heading this way!"

Keeping their backs tightly to the wall, Lydia and Rowan scurried sideways along the length of the Telegraph Station. Rowan's t-shirt clamped to the cold perspiration trickling down his spine.

The men's voices could be heard clearly now. They were laughing about rich pickings and the plight of the drowning crew. Their colleagues were making sure that no one survived the deliberately wrecked ship while they carried the salvaged cargo to Seagull Inn.

Lydia's eyes flew wider when she heard this. She leaned close to

Rowan's ear and whispered, "Seagull Inn? But it doesn't exist anymore! Its remains make up part of the Ranger's home of Telegraph House. It was notorious for piracy and smuggling in the seventeenth century!"

"But it must exist," said Rowan. "They're talking about it!"

But nothing could be heard beyond the piercing cries of seagulls circling the clear blue sky, and the quiet swell of lapping water against the rocky sunlit shore.

Rowan tentatively peered around the corner of Telegraph House. Not one tendril of fog lingered around Hilbre Island. And of the lamping gang, there was no trace.

*After winning the 1973 Nobel Prize in quantum astrology, **Doug Van Belle** was abducted by aliens posing as hyper-intelligent buffalo and he spent several years leaking just enough information about Area 51 to keep people from realizing that it was Area 57 that they should be worrying about. Nothing happened in 1986, absolutely nothing, so quit asking. Doug denies any responsibility for many unfortunate things including: ABBA, sweater vests, dogs that are smaller than cats,* Baywatch, *the way the British cook things, Australia and El Nino.*

But sometimes Doug gets frustrated when dealing with politicians . . .

Clonehenge
by Douglas A. Van Belle

Yes Senator, I have been hard to get a hold of.

No, I have been working on it. I have spent far more time on it than I really should, but I'm afraid I haven't found much that I can do.

I know cloning is absolutely, totally and completely outlawed in Texas, but I looked into it and there wasn't actually any cloning done in Texas.

Taiwan, sir.

They have Made in Taiwan stamped across their asses, right above the company name and the dates of manufacture. That made it pretty easy to figure out.

No law against that. Hell, if it was illegal to bring cloned material into Texas we would have to stop you at the state line and ship your liver back to that Swiss clinic now wouldn't we?

I know it's not funny, but when you pushed the amendment so you could go get your liver fixed, you set the rules that made this legal.

I can't just take them down. They were put there with one of those art in the park permits.

On the permit? Clonewall Jackson.

I know it's not a real name, but that doesn't invalidate the permit.

Yes, I checked. The permit was paid for and approved by the committee. That's all it takes.

I said I checked into it. A lot of artists don't use their real names.

Well, then I would have to decide if I have to charge you with vandalism, theft, public mischief, or destruction of public property.

They aren't yours.

I know they look exactly like you all blown up double-sized, but that doesn't make them yours.

Well, first off. They aren't clones of you. They have a significant portion of DNA that is almost certainly yours but it is only for the parts that show. The guys at the lab say that most of it is manufactured, engineered or generic off the shelf kind of stuff. Second, they aren't really clones at all. No functioning nervous system, no reproductive organs, no internal organs really to speak of—they fall well within the legal definition of non-clonal biological reproduction and manufacture that is legal in most places other than Texas. Third, even if they were exact duplicates of you, you signed away the rights to the use of your genetic material as a base for engineering and production.

Yes, you did.

At the clinic. For a discount of twenty-three hundred euros. I have a copy of the paperwork right here.

You will have to take that up with them.

I have been through every imaginable law and statute from animal cruelty, to the transport of livestock, to the storage of biomedicals. I can't even write'm up for littering.

Obscene. It is ugly but . . .

You know damn well that it does not fit the legal definition of obscene. You were the chair of the committee that rewrote the Texas obscenity statutes. The clones have no genitals and no anus. Every definition of what bits of skin are obscene is based upon distances from or simulating actions with, to or at genitals or the anus. Five centimeters from this, two centimeters from that, this bit of hair but not that hair.

It doesn't really matter if they get pointy when it gets cold at night. Before you can even talk about obscenity statutes you have to be able to prove that they are female nipples and that puts us back on the no genitals thing. Besides, I thought you said they were copies of you.

Copyright? Copyright on Stonehenge?

Well, OK, but even if it is registered as a historic treasure and even if you can call that a copyright, it wouldn't do a damn bit of good.

Satire, Senator. Someone built a perfectly proportioned copy of an ancient druidic monument out of oversized clones of a pale, fat, balding Texas politician that has made his career by bitching to bible thumpers about cloning. If that is not satire I don't know what is.

I know it is an affront to everything you consider decent and civilized. I would guess that is why it is there.

I can't just put a tent over it. I can't censor art on public display unless it fits the legal definition of obscene.

No, not even in Texas.

That won't help. You can't target a law at an individual and even if your friends pushed it through tomorrow, you can't make that kind of regulation retroactive.

Look, no matter what you do with the law, if somebody really wants to they will find their way around it and the more you bitch and scream on TV, the more they are going to want to do it just to piss you off.

Well, I suspect that they keep targeting you because you are such a bombastic hypocrite. You call cloning the soul of the most insidious evil to ever threaten God's grand plan and lead a holy crusade to ban everything from vaccines to spinal repair procedures, but you are not at all unreasonable. You can make exceptions if it makes good Texas steaks cheaper or lets someone who can afford it fly off to Switzerland or Canada to get spare parts.

I would rather defend my respect for the laws as written than have to explain why you would treat reproductive difficulties by enlarging your...

It's right here in the paperwork, pictures and all the details.

The Swiss are nothing if not fastidious in their paperwork.

That's what fastidious means.

There is nothing anyone can legally do about it until the permit runs out.

The day after Summer Solstice.

June. The longest day of the year. It's also the day the guy on the news said the sunrise will shine up the ass of the clone in the middle.

Gareth Owens has previously been published in Odyssey: Adventures in Science, *as well as* Nature. *He has a degree in Paleolinguistics.*

Ruins are judged by the cultural mores of the discoverer. A building for which the purpose is unclear becomes a temple. New finds are labeled as ritual artifacts. How will a future culture judge us?

It's a Temple
by Gareth Owens

FAO Prof Dolly Roxette

Professor of Pre-Federal Studies, Angel Cody Institute, University of Sangelese.

Serra Pedagogica bich

Introductio, Nathan Cody-Smith. Editorio the *Sangeles Journal of Imaginative Archaeology*. Ina inglisi dansa Sangelese publicatea ab 103FR.

Traveyoi ina "Tales from B4" Vidio, en per.....nd was impressed not just by the obvious scholarship, but also by the quality of the storytelling. From what I saw, you have a gift for a phrase.

Whilst not peer reviewed, the *Sangelese Journal of Imaginative Archaeology* has become the foremost archaeological digest of the inner system, and has a circulation that now stretches to the most distant outworlds. The further that humanity travels from home, the greater is its desire to know about the place where we all came from.

To that end I would like to invite you to submit a piece on your specialized area of the late pre-federal period. What I'm looking for is a vignette, perhaps a dramatization that creates a picture of what it would have been like to live before the Time of Troubles. A snapshot of a decadent culture at its height.

I look forward to your reply

Steamy Loving

Nathan Cody-Smith, Editor

FAO Nathan Cody-Smith, Editor
Sangelese Journal of Imaginative Archaeology
13^b Street of Shame, Canton of Clan Smith
Sangelese

Most esteemed editor fellow

As a professor of pre-federal history, and a field archaeologist with the University of Sangelese, the period immediately prior to the war, stretching from about 90B4 up until first contact with the iL'Kizz, is for me, without a doubt, the most fascinating of all human eras. It was a time of technological sophistication, coupled with fearsome naivety. Even the most cursory tour of the Broken Cities makes such a conclusion tragically obvious.

I received your request for a contribution to your august organ with a certain amount of trepidation. I am often asked to provide a layman's picture of what life in the latter days of the land of La might have been like, and I think we have now reconstructed and retrieved enough to create a reasonable image of the whole.

"Buster's Big Day Out" is my attempt to catch the ethos of an average day for an average inhabitant of La in about 73B4. I have included full annotated footnotes for the more academic of your readership, but should also caution that subscribers of a delicate disposition may be shocked by the barbaric practices that our ancestors considered as everyday and commonplace.

It was my intention to create both a compelling narrative and a historically accurate picture and hope that the academic correctness of the piece does not overpower the story. Your comments on this point would be appreciated.

With Hot Love
    Dolly Roxette
        Professor of pre-Federal Studies, Angel Cody Institute,
        University of Sangelese

Buster's Big Day Out
by Dolly Roxette

Buster lifted his gaze from his Personal Computulator, heaved himself with some effort from the couch and walked over to the televizualisor, or Telly V., as it was also known. This was the spring of 73B4 and "I Love Lucy" was having its first run. Buster turned the noise up.

In common with most of his compatriots at the time, he found the irritating voice of the famous redhead hysterically funny. Life was simple then, and the ill-fated United States of America was a young country with a population that had been drawn from many different ethnic, linguistic, and cultural backgrounds. It was a time that only unsophisticated things could become successful, because of the need to be transcultural in appeal.

Buster's room was L-shaped, and covered with a thin layer of woven material that had been gathered from the back of a domesticated ruminant.[1] He hardly noticed its rough texture at all, as he had two pieces of hardened dried animal skin strapped to his feet for protection.

Reluctantly he turned the huge knob on the front of the Telly V, stopping the electricity that coursed down the wires lining the walls of his dwelling. The Telly V issued a huge mechanical "Clunk" and the great glass valves cooled. The laughter that accompanied the deliberately moronic tellyplay, faded to silence.

It was time for Buster to "go out."

He went upstairs to his room to put on his outside clothing.

---

[1] See Harris and Beccles "Carpet: The Final Mystery," New Vegas University Press, FR150, p 138.

Atmospheric corrosives were unknown in those days, so keeping warm and dry were his only concerns.

It was a happy age, those last few years before the war, and everywhere, in everything, colors were bright and garish. Buster chose a garment of hooped corduroy in bright green and vivid blue.[2] To compliment the effect he topped the outfit off with a blouse, or chemise, of yellow "silk" (a material derived from boiled insect carcasses.)[3]

He was ready to leave now. He picked up his juju trinkets, a small collection of almost bladelike metallic pieces that were all threaded together onto a shiny steel ring. He raised it to his lips and kissed the blessed items, one by one. It was widely believed by all his friends and family that such juju trinkets would ward off the evil spirits that the new machines were bringing to the world. President James Kennedy, the leader of the United States of America, the country that Buster lived in, had recently been killed riding in the back of such a machine.[4]

He left the house by its front entrance and with his head bowed. He shuffled as if in a religious procession, around the side of the building and went into the attached temple. This was the place where he stalled his sacred mechanism.

It was with some trepidation and a great deal of reverence, that Buster approached this machine, a conveyance called an autocar. A simple wheeled affair powered by exploding hydrocarbons, the autocar had become the ubiquitous expression of the religion of the culture.

Automotivism was, before the Time of Troubles, a worldwide cult. The remains of autocars are found wherever there are human settlements, and are the major type-fossil of the age. His own autocar was

---

[2] A reconstruction of the Sausalito Pantaloon is on permanent display at the Unity Museum of Human History in Sangelese.

[3] See "Sericulture: A Guide for the Squeamish," Frossette and McNeal, Ancorp Academic Publishing 189 FR.

[4] On nearly every skeleton excavated from within The Broken Cities, one of these small rings of metallic amulets has been found, their use was obviously ritual. For a discussion of the ubiquitous juju trinket phenomenon and its cult see Winter Twist et al. "Spirit Charms of the Pre-Federal Era," New Moon Publishing, New Moon 4, 186 FR.

a fearsomely powerful vehicle called a Jord and it was capable of velocitude in excess of eighty kilometers per hour over the ground.

After his house the autocar was the biggest thing in Buster's life, it was his pride and joy,[5] and he gained much kudos in his peer group from its conspicuous expense. To pilot an autocar was called driving, so Buster drove his autocar from its temple, onto the metal of the road, and by dextrous use of his feet he made it go to its max fastness. The sky was a dazzling and irrational blue, without even the slightest hint of yellow, and the clouds were sparse and high. He told the car that he wanted it to drive by the ocean.

Buster lived on the outskirts of an unimaginably vast settlement called East La, and the tragedy that loomed over the great cities of the west was still far beyond the horizon. He was heading north to meet his woman friend. She was a popular entertainer of the day called Madonna.[6] They were off to Hollywood to see a pictures called Star Wars, but before that, they had arranged to meet and have a ritual meal together in one of the many popular eating establishments that had sprung up to take advantage of the abundance of cheap food on the America continent.

Buster pulled into the burgering and went inside the gaily painted eating-place. Doris was waiting for him at one of the many small round tables.

The burgering made and sold a flat pancake called patty. Patty was made from reconstituted flesh of eviscerated domestic animals, although probably not cats or dogs . . .

*　　*　　*

---

[5] Status in the pre-federal era was based on possession and income rather than more valuable cultural and scientific attainment, a situation that would eventually be perceived as one of the root causes of "Dumbing Down" and indirectly of CivWar II. See "Morons with Money: Death of a culture," Dino Velasquez's seminal work.

[6] The real name of the singer known as Madonna is an area of contention but this author thinks that the most likely candidate is probably Doris Day, although compelling cases have also been made for, amongst others, Louise Armstrong and Gladys Schwarzenegger.

Serra bich . . .

I'm sorry but I'm going to have to pass on "Buster's Big Day Out," Professor Lady but I seem to have given you the wrong impression of exactly what it was that I was after. I enclose a copy of the Journal, as you seem not to have taken into account the house style of the publication.

Essentially the Buster narrative is a little too dry for our readership. We are catering for a society of humans that span light-years. The purpose of our magazine is to remind that isolated population what it means to be civilized, to be part of humanity. The lone terraforming specialist, two years from the nearest civilized system could not care less about Buster's hooped corduroy pants, or his meat eating habits, or even his argument with his girlfriend. (The choice of Madonna was probably not a wise one btw, as it is common knowledge that she was a fictitious character like Sherlock Holmes or Dorothy Lamore).

What the readers of the *Sangelese Journal of Imaginative Archaeology* want, is the juice, the scurrilous details of a culture based on personal indulgence. We live in a time of widespread privation, and the wild history of the pre-federal era is an escape fantasy.

From the deepie camps of the Indiana radlands to the scumling communities of New Moon 4, a few minutes reading about the fleshpots of the last century B4 can take trapped souls out of their own existence, and let them into a world where they can daydream about wealth and safety.

You know this period better than anyone else in Sangelese, and I have read your work in other publications. So it is with regret that I pass on Buster, please do not regard this as a rejection, as we would very much like a piece from you, but it just needs to be more in line with the spirit of our publication.

Hot Love Nati

Most Esteemed Editor Fella

I have now had a chance to peruse your sad excuse for a magazine, and find it to be an extruded piece of filth of amongst the worst kind. I feel absolutely no shame in the fact that Buster was rejected, and I'm staggered that the likes of Prof Toklis and Dr. Twist have allowed themselves to become prostituted into providing the soft-core pornographic stories that appeared in the issue that you sent me.

As for the graphical representations that accompanied the stories, well, no wonder your "*Journal*" is popular with the lonely of the galaxy.

I shall in future limit myself to academic publishing, safe in the knowledge that my ideas and my words are not heading out to sully minds across all of inhabited space. You might as well have sections like Orgies of the Ottomans, or the Revels of Rome.

I consider myself to be a well-adjusted member of Ancorp corporate culture, and not easily shocked, but the trivialization of the destruction of our last high civilization, and the pornographication of anything remotely serious in order to sell more units, is a symptom of the decadence of our own society.

You are part of that "bottom line," a concept that cheapens us as a species, and as a society. I will have nothing more to do with you.

Peace on you

Prof Roxette

Serra Bich

It is with great regret that I read your previous communication (although your idea about the history of revels and orgies is definitely worth following up), and whilst I understand that an academic of your standing would be loath to contribute to a populist platform such as this one, I feel it would not be unfair to point out that we have already had contributions from some of the leaders in all the main fields of current archaeological work, including Prof Narbandian head of the Ancorp Institute of Paleoxenology and Prof van Broekinhetwaterland chief of the Unity Emergency Xenolinguistics Squad.

Prof van Broekinhetwaterland allowed us to use a very seductive image of herself at the masthead of her piece, "The Tongues of Teshub," and since that article appeared, she has gone on to be nominated for the Tanhauser Prize. So it is with confidence that I can assure you that an association with the *Sangelese Journal of Imaginative Archaeology* is in no way detrimental to your academic career.

    Hot Love

        Nati

Slime in Chief

    I have no idea why you continue to communicate with me. I would have thought that I had made both my position and my disgust perfectly plain. I'm only sending this because there is one point in your last diarrheic outpouring of verbiage that needs to be countered.

    To me it would matter not one jot if Kharis Pwall himself were to come down from New Moon 4 and contribute to your magazine, it would not affect my opinion of you, only of him. So you can take all your Toklis's, Twists and benighted Broekinhetwaterlands, and crawl back under whatever rock you emerged from, and I hope that you're all very happy together

    Peace and Love

        Prof Roxette

Serra Bich

    The sharpness of your tongue is very definitely a marketable commodity, and also strangely exciting. Did I mention that the *Journal* pays 500 Kilobills for every published article?

    Hot Love

        Nati

Licentious in Lycra—Sensuous in Spandex

Prof Dolly Roxette explores the sensual world of Pre-federal fibers and materials. A scratch and sniff series in ten parts.

Part one:

Leather and Rubber, their uses in the recreation dungeons of the last century B4.

Stoney M. Setzer is a middle school teacher, residing with his wife and two children in Griffin, Georgia. He has had stories published in lulu.com's Southern Comfort *anthology and* Dragons, Knights, and Angels *magazine, as well as a story in the upcoming* Strange Stories of Sand and Sea *from Fine Tooth Press.*

When you've seized complete control, make sure you know your way around and that you are knowledgeable of those from whom you take . . .

The Guardians of Llarazan
by Stoney M. Setzer

"You're mad!" Buzek cried. "What have you done?"

Except for Buzek and Ulf, all of the other Guardians were bound and hanging by their wrists from the rafters. Heavily armed men had their weapons trained on their captives. Buzek had just entered, but one of the armed men covered him with his automatic weapon immediately upon his arrival. As for Ulf, he was free because he commanded the invaders.

With a shrug, Ulf replied, "Call it progress. For all these centuries, you and your friends have been content to sit on the greatest power this world has ever seen. I, for one, am *not* so easily contented."

Buzek's eyes widened. "You can't mean . . . !"

"I can, and I do," Ulf interrupted. "Why do you think I became a Guardian in the first place?"

"You putrid traitor!" spat Bergeron, the Elder Guardian. "You've lied to us all this time!"

"And you idiots bought it. Now, Buzek, you are going to take me to the ruins of Malizonus' castle."

Buzek's jaw dropped, making his long white beard stretch almost to his waist. "I can't do that!" he exclaimed. "The whole reason for our Council is to protect the secrets of Llarazan from all who would abuse them!"

"People like me?" Ulf sneered. "Sorry, Buzek, but I think I'm holding all the cards here."

"Stand your ground, Buzek!" cried Campeau from the other side of the chamber. "I would rather he kill us all than get his hands on any of Malizonus' belongings!"

Ulf threw his head back and laughed, making Buzek's blood run cold. "Have you forgotten that my specialty is Llarazan torture techniques? If Buzek doesn't take me to the ruins, you'll force me to provide a demonstration. I've taught my associates here everything I know. Is that what you want for your comrades, Buzek?"

Involuntarily Buzek shuddered. He was not as well-schooled in the ancient tortures as his captor, but he knew enough to realize that death would be a relief slow in coming.

"Go ahead, Buzek," Bergeron said, drawing gasps from the other Guardians. "Take him to the ruins. Show him *everything*."

After a moment, Buzek comprehended, nodding slowly. "All right, Ulf, you win. Let's go."

The heyday of the Llarazan Empire had come before the rise of Babylon, in the opposite hemisphere. Malizonus, a man shrouded in mystery, had seemingly come out of nowhere and established the Empire from nothing and had made it the dominant power in that half of the globe until his death some twenty years later.

Most of the mystery centered on exactly how he had been able to accomplish such a monumental feat. A number of accounts maintained that he had been an unparalleled military genius, while others portrayed him as a scientist whose knowledge eclipsed even that currently held by modern minds. Still other, stranger accounts presented Malizonus as a sorcerer who had built his kingdom through the dark arts.

Perhaps the only certainty pertained to Malizonus' character. By all accounts, he was a ruthless tyrant who cared for human beings only as subjects for him to control. One particular legend concerned his Golden Gauntlet, which symbolized his absolute power as well as his absolute cruelty. It was written that "Malizonus ruled his empire with a golden hand," referring to the Gauntlet, and most legends imbued the item as either his most powerful technological tool or the channel of his magic, depending upon which version of events one followed.

Whatever his methods, his chief lieutenants decided after his death that his secrets should disappear from this world along with him. Their reasoning was simple: Since no man could match the skill and cunning of Malizonus, no one could be trusted to utilize his knowledge without disastrous results. Upon their unanimous agreement, the Guardians of Llarazan were established with a self-assigned mission of protecting the secrets of Malizonus from the world and vice versa. All of the hard evidence that could have proven the existence of Malizonus or the Llarazan Empire was spirited away, and a number of spurious stories concerning both were circulated, thus accounting for the mystery. Only the Guardians themselves knew the truth.

Because there was no hard evidence available, mainstream historians readily dismissed Malizonus and his empire as myth, which suited the Guardians perfectly. As the years progressed, public knowledge of Llarazan diminished, until finally the most challenging portion of the Guardians' task was for each generation to correctly identify and train men who could be trusted to guard the secrets after their own passing.

Obviously, in the case of Ulf, the Guardians had failed.

"No tricks," Ulf warned, "or else your friends back in the Chamber . . . ."

"I know!" Buzek interrupted. "You needn't remind me."

Ulf laughed as he stroked his curly dark beard. "My, aren't we touchy?"

Buzek merely grunted in the passenger seat. The helicopter, of course, had been the Guardians' property, for it was the only viable means of reaching the ruins of Malizonus' castle. Now Ulf piloted the craft over seemingly endless kilometers of wilderness according to Buzek's navigation. Initially the older man had given fleeting consideration to leading his captor on a wild goose chase, or perhaps even grabbing the controls and crashing the copter. After all, his own life would be a small price for keeping Malizonus' secrets, especially the Gauntlet, out of Ulf's hands. However, he knew the consequences for his fellow Guardians if he tried either stunt, and fear for their safety made him cooperative.

Of course, Ulf had given no guarantee that either he or his comrades would be spared even if he did cooperate. Then again, maybe they wouldn't need any such assurance from him.

"About another forty kilometers northwest," Buzek said, his voice devoid of emotion. "We're almost there."

"Excellent, excellent," Ulf replied. "You're cooperation means more than you realize, Buzek. Maybe there will be a place for you in my empire. Tell me, how are you with a mop and a broom?"

Buzek held his tongue while Ulf chortled. If he didn't, he was afraid of having Ulf cut it out for him. Such was standard Llarazan torture procedure, so as to deny the victim the catharsis of screaming.

His silence did nothing to discourage Ulf. "It will be glorious, my empire. So glorious that it will eclipse any empire the world has ever seen, even that of Malizonus himself. All the world leaders will be my servants. Every last cent of the world's riches will be mine to command. My men back at the Chamber will be the captains of my army, enforcing my every whim. And then I will have my harem, such a harem . . . ."

Deplorable, Buzek thought in disgust. *No better than the real Malizonus.* From that point he tuned out his captor's monologue for fear he would be able to hold his peace no longer.

He's right, though, he thought soberly. *This fool will have all of that and then some if he succeeds, especially if he gets the Gauntlet. I can't let that happen!*

"Incredible," Ulf breathed as he stood beside the copter, his helmet tucked under his arm. "I thought the day would never come!"

They had arrived at the correct locale, a deep valley tucked away in the midst of the wilderness. Before them sprawled the ancient remains of a castle, the one that had been the center of the Llarazan Empire. Although Buzek's duties had brought him here more than once, he still could not help a sense of awe as he surveyed the ruins. To think that this structure was thousands of years old, and still stood at all! His appreciation was not so much for the majesty of the palace as for the countless generations of his Guardian predecessors who had labored so diligently to keep this hidden.

Back when he was but an apprentice, he had asked one of his mentors—Bergeron himself, in fact—why the Guardians had not simply destroyed the castle and all that was inside if they were so adamant about concealing it from the outside world. Even as he had asked, he had thought the question childish and ignorant, and he distinctly remembered fearing that his mentor would laugh in his face. Buzek also recalled the relief that had washed over him when that did not happen.

"A common question, and a natural one," Bergeron had replied. "You see, we could raze the castle itself easily enough, but I'm not so sure we could eradicate its contents. Without the castle, there would be no containing them, so the castle serves a purpose. That is why it must be preserved."

Buzek swallowed hard as the sweat accumulated on his brow. The weight of the world, everything for which every Guardian in history had worked, now rested squarely upon his frail, aged shoulders.

If Ulf sensed his tension, he gave no sign. The exhilaration of basking in his moment of triumph consumed him, leaving him oblivious to everything else. He looked directly at the walls covered with ivy and moss, but he seemed to gaze straight through them, seeing instead what the castle had been before and would become again under his hand: rebuilt crumbling parapets, dingy walls gleaming in splendor, and majestic flags—his flags—fluttering proudly in the breeze.

"Take a moment, Buzek," he said pompously. "You stand at the brink of history. Today, all the skeptics shall dine on crow! Llarazan is reborn!"

Clearing his throat, Buzek replied, "You know, absolute power may not be all you expect. It's not too late to turn around."

Ulf turned around, but only to slap the face of his guide. "Bite your idiotic tongue! Do you really think that I would stop now, after all the time and effort I've invested?"

Gingerly Buzek touched his stinging lip, feeling a tiny trickle of blood. "I've always heard that a wise investor knows when to sell."

Immediately he flinched, expecting to be struck again, but instead Ulf laughed. "Honestly, I thought you knew me better than that. How would the Americans put it? 'Relentless' is my middle name. You only think that Malizonus was ruthless! My little finger shall be thicker than his waist!"

"Hasn't somebody already used that one?"

Ulf ignored the jab. "We're here," he said into his cell phone. "So far, so good. No, don't harm them. Every king needs slaves, right?" With a chortle he closed the phone and looked at his escort with cold eyes.

"Enough small talk. We're going in."

So single-minded was Ulf that he didn't notice Buzek's furtive glance at one of the castle's gargoyles as they walked beneath it.

Buzek had never seen so many cobwebs in his life.

The main hall of the castle must have been glorious in its day, especially given the architectural standards of its era, but time had been unkind. While prioritizing the external structure, the Guardians obviously had been indifferent toward the interior. The walls and floors were festooned not only with cobwebs but also with dust and mildew. Despite relatively strong lungs for a man his age, Buzek found breathing the stale air difficult.

Predictably, the decay did not faze Ulf. He had already assumed the self-assured manner of ownership, as if the castle had always belonged to him. For one who had been so awestruck outside, he now took determined strides, as a man on a mission with no time for diversions. Now he concerned himself only with the acquisition of the

Gauntlet.

Apparently Ulf's preparations had included a study of the Guardians' floor plans. Without hesitation he turned to the right at the end of the main hallway and began to stride down the corridor. If he knew the correct way to turn here, Buzek reasoned, then surely he knew the rest of the route as well . . . .

It's now or never.

"You're going the wrong way," Buzek called, just before Ulf took a left at the next junction.

Ulf froze in his tracks and remained still for a moment. He seemed to move in slow motion as he pivoted to face Buzek. "I've seen the floor plans," he retorted coldly. "Do you really think I would do this without memorizing them first? The throne room is this way."

"True, but I thought you were after the Gauntlet and all the rest of Malizonus' tools."

For the first time, the armor of Ulf's self-assurance showed a chink. That only lasted a second as he quickly recovered. "And are they not all locked in the throne room?"

Buzek laughed as if it were the most ridiculous thing he had ever heard. "Why would you think that?"

Now Ulf's brow began to tighten in anger. "Because," he fired back in clipped tones, "that's what is posted in the floor plans! Have you not seen them for yourself, or perhaps you're going senile?"

Ignoring the insult, Buzek shrugged. "So you think that everything on those floor plans is the absolute truth? That we would just leave the real location of the Gauntlet lying about for anyone to see?"

Ulf faltered momentarily, and Buzek pressed forward. "What if our headquarters were invaded? What if one of our Guardians turned rogue on us, or was a rogue from the start who somehow managed to worm his way into the fold? Have you not proven yourself that all of those things are possible?"

For seemingly an eternity, Ulf stood speechless, mulling the argument. *Touché,* Buzek thought in self-congratulation. The mere act of making his captor think, of disrupting his rhythm, constituted a moral victory if nothing else. The elder man's satisfaction deepened when at last Ulf said, "I see your point. But if that is a ruse, then what makes you so sure that you know the real location? How do you know you haven't been misled too?"

"Ulf, Ulf, Ulf," Buzek chided, "so cunning, so powerful, and yet so much to learn!" He prayed that he wasn't pushing it too far with his petty insolence, but he felt fairly safe for the moment. "What is my rank in the Council?"

"You're a member of the Five?" Ulf knew that as well as he knew his own name, but the disequilibrium that Buzek had created caused him to ask cautiously rather than answer boldly.

"Correct. I'm in the inner circle of the Council. As such, I possess levels of knowledge that you do not. All of the truth is made known to the Five, even things of which the rest of you have no inkling. So doesn't it stand to reason that I would know the true location of the Gauntlet?"

After a moment of mulling, Ulf drew his pistol and aimed it squarely at Buzek's chest. "Lead the way," he commanded.

Obediently, Buzek turned and went the opposite direction of the one that Ulf had chosen.

Buzek had never actually set foot down this corridor before; for that matter, he knew of few Guardians who ever had. Fortunately, he had memorized every detail of the floor plan, which was now proving itself to be impressively accurate. Every niche was precisely where the plan indicated, allowing Buzek to navigate the corridors as easily as if he had been in his own home.

The real test came when they rounded a corner to find themselves at an apparent dead end. Ulf grunted with irritation behind him, the simple guttural noise packed with ominous meaning. Only too aware of the firearm trained at his back, Buzek hurriedly searched for the switch that was supposed to be somewhere on the wall. "There's a secret passage," Buzek explained as he probed the walls with both hands, trying to ignore their slimy, grotesque texture. "The switch is around here somewhere...."

"You'd better hope so."

Just as Buzek was beginning to panic, his left hand brushed against a loose brick. He pushed it tentatively and it slid backwards, deep into the wall. A loud rumbling ensued as a portion of the back wall swung inward on unseen hinges, unveiling a staircase leading downward. Buzek had expected the passage to be pitch black, but dim illumination emanated from an unknown source. A noxious stench assaulted their noses, and Buzek had to fight an impulse to vomit.

By the sounds behind him, Ulf was having a similar struggle, which Buzek found gratifying. "Egad!" Ulf cried after a moment. "Why would the Gauntlet be down *there*?"

"Don't you want to go down into that smell?"

"No! It's nauseating!"

"Then that's why it makes such a perfect hiding place. Assuming anyone makes it this far, the stench turns most of them away."

"Most, but not all," Ulf retorted, jabbing his pistol into Buzek's back. "I didn't come this far to turn back. We'll get used to the smell."

"Suit yourself," Buzek shrugged as he slowly made his way down the stairs. Each step was coated with moss and mildew, rendering the stairs treacherously slick. A misstep would certainly expedite one's descent, but Buzek hated to think of the consequences of such acceleration. Broken limbs, most likely, but a broken neck would not be out of the question. For all his impatience, Ulf understood the safety risks as well. At no point in the descent did he order Buzek to hurry up, and by the end he was actually lagging behind the older man.

Once they reached the bottom, they found themselves confronted by a huge wooden door. The door was chained shut, and an ancient, rudimentary combination lock held the chains in place. Ulf stared at the mechanism blankly. "Whatever the history books may tell you," Buzek said, "it was actually Malizonus who invented the first combination lock. Only the members of the Five know the correct combination."

"All right, then," Ulf snapped, brandishing his pistol once more. "Open it!"

Buzek began to see an opportunity. "Suppose I don't?"

"Do you not see this pistol?"

"But if you shoot me, how do you open the door? That lock may look old, but it's plenty sturdy, and you'd never break through *this* door."

Ulf rolled his eyes. "Name your price."

"Release the other Guardians."

"Never!" cried Ulf. "Didn't you hear what I told my men, that every kingdom needs its slaves?"

Buzek shrugged. "If the Gauntlet is in here, then what are you worried about? You'll take over anyway, and then you can enslave them along with the rest of the world. Their freedom will be a short-lived fancy, a small price for getting what you want, wouldn't you say?"

Glaring at him, Ulf pulled out the cell phone and flipped it open. "I can barely get a signal down here," he growled. "All right, let the rest of the Guardians go. Yes, I'm serious. They're a bunch of old men, what will they do to you?" He then hung up without listening to any further argument. "Go on," he ordered.

"How do I know your men followed through?" Buzek countered.

Impatiently Ulf called back and then paced the floor irritably while Buzek insisted on speaking to each one of the Guardians individually to confirm their release. Buzek showed no consideration for Ulf's battery strength or minutes; he spoke at length to each man, shrugging off any implied threats that Ulf made in an attempt to rush him. After all, the older man had an advantage now.

So intense was Ulf's exasperation that he paid little attention to anything that Buzek said to any of his comrades. He did catch something said to Bergeron, the leader, about a "red event," but he thought nothing of it, especially when it was not repeated to anyone else. Maybe the old geezer meant to say "red letter date," referring to Ulf's eminent triumph, but got the semantics confused. Sometimes old people did that.

"Phone's dead," Buzek said when he finally handed the device back to Ulf.

"No wonder!" Ulf snapped after examining it. "You completely drained my battery! Now how am I supposed to contact my men?"

Buzek chuckled. "With all the tools that Malizonus had, I'm sure you can figure out something."

Not amused, Ulf waved the pistol. "Open that door, now!"

Obediently Buzek manipulated the old lock. As his fingers played over the combination, he commented, "So, you think you're ready for all of Malizonus' secrets."

"Fool! Why else would I be here?"

Again Buzek chuckled, but this time he was glad that his back was turned to his captor. "I guess you know that not everything is recorded in writing. Some of his secrets are only known to the Five, passed down from generation to . . . . "

"What of it? I'll know all of it as soon as you get that door open!"

"Here we go," Buzek replied, removing the lock and pulling the door open on squeaky hinges. "Perhaps I had better lead the way . . . . "

Ulf pushed him aside and rushed in, just as Buzek expected.

The old man slammed the door shut and replaced the lock, closing it with a flourish.

Have mercy on me . . . . Buzek began mentally before the pounding started.

"Open this door!" Ulf bellowed.

"No."

"Do it now, I say!"

Wincing, Buzek said, "You're in the right room. If you get his Gauntlet, you'll have the power anyway."

The beam of Ulf's flashlight moved away from the bottom of the door, signaling that he had taken Buzek's suggestion. Grimly Buzek looked down at the floor, awaiting the inevitable . . . .

A blood-curdling scream emanated from behind the door. Then Buzek heard an animalistic growling, followed by a roar of fury. Ulf screamed once more, then fell silent forever. The rest of the noises induced sickness in Buzek, as he imagined what sights must accompany them. Despite his nausea, however, he stayed until the room fell silent again.

He didn't lie, not really, he told himself as he ascended the stairs.

The door did hold Malizonus' secrets, including the fabled Golden Gauntlet. It also held the descendent of the creature that Malizonus had cultivated as his favorite method of capital punishment, the one that his men eventually fed him to when they grew tired of his tyranny—the one that bore an uncanny resemblance to the gargoyle outside.

Those men were the founding members of the Guardians. In a way, however, the original creature and its descendants were the founding Guardians, for Ulf was not the first usurper who had been delivered into its lair.

Soon the Guardians' other helicopters would arrive, bearing the rest of Malizonus' men. Buzek's colleagues would bring them here on the pretense of reuniting them with their master, which again would not be a lie.

They would join him as soon as they arrived.

Angeline Hawkes has publication credits dating from 1981 with works appearing in over thirty anthologies. She received a B.A. in Composite English Language Arts in 1991 from Texas A&M, Commerce, and was recently named Alumni Ambassador for the Literature & Languages Department. Her horror collection, The Commandments, *published in 2006 (Nocturne Press), was nominated for the Bram Stoker Award. "The Bloody Spear of Nineveh" and "The Sword of the Silver Tongues," from her fantasy series* Tales of the Barbarian Kabar of El Hazzar, *are available as Amazon Shorts. She co-authored the horror novella,* Blood Coven, *with husband and writer, Christopher Fulbright, in June 2007 (Dead Letter Press). She serves as editor of the* HWA Internet Mailer. *Visit her websites at www.angelinehawkes.com and www.fulbrightandhawkes.com.*

Tour the ruins and feel the past deeply within yourself. Sometimes, literally . . . (Caution: some scenes may be a bit intense for some, particularly younger, readers.)

The Tour Guide
by Angeline Hawkes

Hearing a girlish giggle, James turned to look around. The group of foreign tourists had moved to the next structural ruin, but standing next to a door-like crevice he saw a young woman, one of the natives, clad in traditional Mayan garb, smiling as they often did. The ruins were further enhanced with the employment of natives dressed in traditional clothing serving as guides. Many spoke English quite well. Impressed at the quality of his Mayan tour so far, James was astounded with the authenticity of the tour's "extras."

The young woman beckoned him to follow with her dark brown

eyes. James smiled, laughed and complied. She led him here and there, weaving in and out of the ancient buildings and crumbling, foliage-infested ruins, and finally ascended a flight of steep, chipped, stone stairs. He decided that the tourism industry must scour the locality for girls demonstrating stronger Mayan characteristics because this gorgeous woman looked like she could have been King 18 Rabbit's own sister. James had an eerie sense that she'd just stepped out of time. Really packed a punch to his sightseeing. She couldn't have been more than sixteen, but she walked gracefully and self-assured. She was a tiny thing, but looked very impressive in her traditional Mayan dress. He followed her up the stairs to a square indention that was a door. She looked back at him still smiling, and disappeared inside.

"Hey! Senorita? Senora? Miss? Uh, I'm not sure that I'm allowed in there. Is it okay? I don't remember being told about this part of the tour." He called toward nowhere as he followed her, not sure if she understood. She had simply walked right through the low entranceway; he had to bend over at the waist to follow through to a long, narrow tunnel that plunged into complete darkness. Moving further through the corridor, he looked back to the door, and saw that it was now a tiny square of sunlight streaming into the blackness. Unsure of his footing, he hoped that the foundation of the hall was secure.

"Miss? Senorita?" James groped his way along the dark wall. "Uh, I'm not sure that I'm supposed to be in here. I'm going back, okay? I'm going back now." He was pretty sure that if the tourist agency had wanted him in this part of the ruins that there would've been some sort of lighting available, that this part of the temple was off limits to tourists. Maybe the pretty guide was new and in her zeal didn't follow the rules, or didn't know all of them. He was about to feel his way back, when suddenly she was standing before him, holding a torch with a handle covered in gold, ornately engraved with animal motifs. He would've liked to examine the artistry of the torch, but in the dark it was hard to see the finer nuances. Maybe she'd let him bring it into the sunlight to examine after the tour.

She waved for him to follow her again. James shrugged. "Okay. I guess. You're the guide, but I hope this doesn't take too long because I don't want to get separated from the rest of the group and miss the bus or something stupid."

She smiled, saying nothing; even in the flicker of the fire's light she was beautiful. Through the narrow corridor she led him until they reached another low doorway. She waited for him to enter and then pushed or twisted, he couldn't see which, something deep in the carved decorations on the stone wall. A stone door slid shut with a *boom* that echoed through the corridor and reverberated through the chamber. James jumped in surprise. What was with all of the secret, hidden door controls? That was cool. He didn't remember reading about that aspect of Mayan technology. He was certain that archeologists still had a lot to discover about these ruins.

"Uh, is this part of the regular tour? Because this isn't on my map or in my itinerary and I don't remember anyone mentioning it. I don't really want to pay extra. I'm on a pretty tight budget." James rattled on as he rummaged awkwardly through his green backpack looking for his tour brochures. He was sure one of them would have information about the natives re-enacting Mayan ceremonies.

She walked on, her glossy black hair shimmering in the torchlight. They stopped abruptly in front of a large door. This one required no stooping, as it was massive. Again, she triggered a lever hidden in the intricate décor of the stone and the door slid open. Crossing the threshold, she beckoned him with her radiant smile and sensuous waving hand. Entering, still digging deep in his pack, the door shut behind him. He didn't like all the doors closing, but decided it must be a requirement to keep local animals or reptiles out. *Just would make it hard to exit in case of an emergency.*

The room was illuminated with the dancing fire of a multitude of torches. Mayan men, more re-enactors, placed torches in the jade encrusted, golden sconces on the walls. The sconces were formed of twisted gold in similar patterns to the swirls and geometric patterns carved into the walls, and peppered with intricately cut pieces of polished jade. In the center of the fire-lit room was a stone dais carved like the other elaborate patterns.

An old man, wrinkled and stooped, draped in a red cape trimmed in feathers of various colors, wearing a headdress of more feathers, jade and still more gold, walked to the dais, his hands outstretched in revered supplication, his mouth uttering a chant. James was close enough to see the man's missing teeth. He looked every bit his age. The realism of this re-enactment was incredible. So far, the actors were scoring high points on the entertainment scale and James hoped that everyone in his group got to participate in such a demonstration.

"Wow. This is really impressive!" James whispered to the guide. She stood quietly beside him, bowing in reverence to the high priest. James wasn't completely sure she'd heard him. Maybe she wasn't supposed to break character. She was doing a fantastic job and James certainly didn't want to be the one to jeopardize her job performance.

Two strong men, wearing feathers and chest plates of jade, seized James by both arms, propelling him forward. He dropped his backpack; it *thumped* on the stone floor as he stumbled in the clutches of the men. They were a little taller than most of the native men and looked very much the part of the high priest's enforcers. James mentally chuckled.

"Hey. Wait a sec. I dropped my bag." James looked behind at his backpack and turned to retrieve it. He found the men holding his arms to be immovable. It would only take a second to pick up the bag. His money was inside and he didn't want to risk someone walking off with it. James looked at the men. They said nothing, continuing to pull him toward the dais.

"Really, I need to get my bag." James laughed nervously, trying to resist the men in order to reach for it. The men didn't let go, instead intensified their hold, dragging him to the center of the room. He began to try to shake off their grip. The demonstration was really great, but if the tourists felt they needed to stop, the re-enactors ought to be more accommodating. James struggled. The men refused to budge. *What in the hell did they think they were doing?*

The two Mayans heaved him to the top of the dais, plunking him down hard, and secured his limbs in cuffs of gold that clanked shut with snapping noises.

"Okay." James laughed apprehensively, growing angry as he was continually ignored. "Show over. This is really amazing, but I think it's crossed the line and is now leaving the world of entertainment!" He squirmed in the unyielding cuffs. "Hey. These damn things are *real*!" He was shocked when the cuffs didn't pop open. He looked at the shadows dancing about the faces in the torch-lit room. The beautiful guide was bowing, smiling her dazzling smile not seeming to mind that he was loudly interrupting their role-playing with his shouts and curses.

The high priest picked up the tempo of his chanting, his whole body swaying with the rhythm of his sing-songy words, and the others in the room joined in the foreign chant. The eerie ancient words rolled from their tongues with such force that James found them hypnotizing. The mounting crescendo of the chorus buzzed and hummed in James's ears. The words repeated over and over in his mind, confusing him, dazzling him, making him dizzy and sleepy.

A flash of polished black glittered in the orange light of the torches. Shadows danced in an undulating motion against the engraved walls. The room held more people than James could see. The shadows were full of people chanting, bowing, pressing in, filling the room with the warmth of their bodies and the air with the sounds of their melodic, frenzied chant. The high priest with his bobbing feathered headdress held a jagged, obsidian knife high above James.

James stared at it. *What sort of a prop was that? What were they doing trying to scare the crap out of him? History be damned, this show was reaching the freaky dimension.* Two hands appeared, savagely ripping open his blue oxford, buttons popping into the air, baring his chest.

"Hey! Okay! Damn it! That's *enough*. I *demand* to be let up. This is *it*. This isn't fun anymore! You people are *lunatics*! What in the hell made you think this would be a good tourist attraction, scaring the shit out of people like this! *God damn it*! Someone better let me the hell up, or I'm reporting this bullshit! Let's see how much you people like strapping paying customers to stone tables when you're all out of your god-damned jobs!" James hollered until hoarse as the people continued to chant. The repetition of the words grew into an emotional frenzy. They chanted at such a rapid pace that James could no longer make out individual words. Just tones, one solid tone, *chanting, chanting, chanting.*

The obsidian knife glinted above him. James heard his own shrill scream echoing against the stone, filling the room. His eyes grew wide in terror as the blade hit his chest. Gasping, he felt a gathering pool of blackness swirling around him, fogging his mind.

Pain, searing, jarring. The priest rammed the knife deeper. James's head lulled to one side. He opened his mouth to scream, but no sound came. He gagged. Blood splattered his face, covering his eyes, filling his mouth. The monotone chanting continued in a solitary drone of words, endless words. The words beat like a drum. Over and over again. The feather-bedecked priest reached under James's sternum, grasping his heart. With a mighty rip he yanked the pulsating organ from James's chest, holding it—spurting crimson blood over his sun-bronzed body.

The priest reveled in the blood. It renewed him, refreshed him. James blinked, stared in disbelieving horror—then all went black.

The heart pumped in the priest's hand high above the dais as his chanting died, and serenity filled the chamber. Two Mayans came from the crowd and released James's body from the shackles, dangling it between them, carrying it into the darkness. The priest was gone; only a trail of bloody footprints led into the dark as evidence of his having been there.

With her foot, the lovely young woman pushed the green backpack into a narrow ventilation shaft recessed in the floor, sending the pack sliding down a chute to land on a deep pile of totes, packs and bags. She watched it disappear and listened for the telltale *thud* of it having landed.

She took her flaming torch from the sconce on the wall and made her ascent to the surface of the temple, back into the glorious sun, back down the ancient stone stairs, and back to the bustling tourists eagerly surveying the magnificent Mayan ruins.

Leila Eadie wanders around a lot but is currently based in London, UK. She loves strolling through ruins, her imagination giving life to the old stones . . . She has sold her horror and dark fantasy stories to various print and online venues, and her website is www.scarystories.org.uk for those who would like to know more.

And there's no reason to think she won't bring us one of her visions in this story . . .

The Tomb
by Leila Eadie

"Okay, gather round now. Settle down," Professor Hill told the excited group. "I think we're ready to open the tomb." He removed his wide-brimmed panama hat and wiped the sweat from his pink forehead. The white-hot sun was blazing, despite having risen less than an hour ago; the bleached land surrounding the dig site reflected the heat like a mirror. Replacing the hat, Hill turned to face the steps leading down to the shadowed passageway. A quick stroke of his ever-growing belly did nothing to quell the fluttering therein. "Steve?"

The research assistant stepped forward, camera at the ready. "Now rolling, Prof," he said, watching the glowing screen, keeping everything in the frame.

"Let's go, then." Hill started down the stone steps, his heavy boots crunching on the perpetual layer of gritty dust. Steve followed, with the small troupe of students not far behind.

After the bright sunlight above it was dark when they reached the door, and Hill switched on the flashlight. He licked his lips, tasting dust.

201

The workers had done the difficult part earlier, and now only minimal effort was needed to open the door. He pushed it, and cool air caressed his weathered skin as he stepped inside. A side to side sweep of the high-lux light revealed only a bare corridor. There wasn't even any of the damned desert grit underfoot. Yet.

It could have been disappointing, but Hill still felt like a jittery teenager. This was what the job was all about! Discovery; he was the first person to set foot in this corridor for a thousand years. Maybe more.

After checking the air quality, he walked onward, following the corridor around a ninety-degree turn where he found another door with a protruding wheel.

"Make sure you capture this interesting opening mechanism," Hill told Steve, pointing at the door. "Looks like a manual entry system. Could even be a pressure door."

"It's amazing how well preserved it is," Steve said, training the camera on the floodlit area.

"This corridor has been sealed—airtight—until we got here. It has stood undisturbed for at least a thousand years. Of course, we'll only be able to accurately date it when we see what's inside."

Making sure Steve was still filming, Hill grabbed the cool wheel and tried to turn it. His muscles strained and he worried that he'd have to ask one of the students, with their younger, fresher bodies to help him. But it grated and slowly, so slowly, it began to turn.

Would the mechanism still work? Despite his confident words, it was possible that the door might not unlock, delaying the dig until the workers could break through. The wheel continued to turn.

A hiss filled the air, and everyone, even the professor, ducked, bending double and covering their heads. The susurrus of sound died away, and Hill opened his eyes. He brought the air monitor up, testing for poison gas, and relaxed as it again blinked green; safe.

"It's okay. More CO_2 than we're used to, but it's breathable."

An audible sigh of relief echoed the escaping gas, and the crowd shifted, embarrassed at the scare. A girl giggled nervously, and was shushed.

"Ready, Steve?" Hill asked.

"Ready."

Hill pulled the door open. It was heavy, and the unseen hinges were stiff, but it moved, revealing only darkness beyond.

"Onward," Hill said, his voice barely audible. He swung the flashlight around, trying to get a first look at the room the geo-survey had revealed from the surface. He would have a better view later when the workers brought proper lighting in, but he always preferred to get the first experience of a tomb by the single unsteady beam of a flashlight.

The room was large and mainly empty. A ceiling lower than Hill was used to gave a feeling of oppression. He took a few more steps forward and Steve joined him.

"So, any more clues as to what this place was?" he said.

"I have a funny feeling . . . " Hill trailed off. He glanced around at the walls and ceiling, at the places where the room would have been lit. "I think it might be a tomb like the one found in the Far Northern Quarter."

"A Gardiner's Tomb?"

"That's the one." Hill trained the beam on an open door directly across from them. "Her discovery was controversial, but if this is the same, why then it must be seen as compelling proof. Proof of the social behavior and beliefs of the ancient inhabitants of this land."

"You agree with Gardiner's theories, then?"

"She drew the only sensible conclusions from the evidence."

Hill walked on, and Steve followed.

"Notice the undecorated walls, the bare floor underfoot. This was merely an entrance room. Through *here*, however, I hope we will find more evidence of their culture."

Peering through the doorway, Steve saw that Hill was right. Pictures adorned the walls, showing strange-looking buildings, groups of people, even a map of the land as it was.

"Do you expect to find any—" Steve swallowed, took a deep breath, "remains?"

"I shouldn't think so. Not after all this time. They're probably dust by now. Preservation techniques were poor, when they bothered at all."

Steve nodded, thankful.

Textiles were heaped on the floor in small piles.

"It's very sad, really," Hill said as he walked over to one such mound of material. "They brought all this down here, perhaps to take with them to the afterlife."

"They were alive when they came down here?"

"Oh yes. The big question posed by Gardiner's findings, for me at least, is *why* they did so. They lived in chaotic times, rife with war and power struggles. Was this a form of escape, or was it punishment? Was it a prison, in which to be tortured to death? Or was it a religious matter, entirely voluntary?"

"Or a mixture of the two: religious torture?" Steve said, smiling.

Hill frowned at him, and the grin fell from his face. Steve studied the camera's screen to avoid the professor's glare.

"I'm talking about *beliefs*, Steve. It's a serious and important matter. There is one uncorroborated clue, though. Gardiner said she found some written communications. Only fragments of the paper were left. She could only read bits of the ancient writing, but she said those buried here believed they could be saved by being locked up in these rooms. They wanted immortality."

"Madness."

"Possibly. But who knows how many more of these tombs are out there? Or how widespread this belief was?" Hill shrugged and turned away. "Look out for any writing, but if you do find some, don't touch it, whatever you do." He raised his voice to make sure the whole group heard. "Nobody is to touch *anything*, do you understand?"

They moved on. The burial complex was extensive, with rooms disappearing off in all directions. Most of the contents of the rooms had dissolved into dust thanks to the effects of time, though some funerary furniture and tubular food containers still remained. It was puzzling.

In one room Hill found a heap of bones, extremely fragile, but essentially intact.

"Wonderful," he said, and called Steve over to document the find.

"Gardiner never found anything like this!"

"There's at least six skulls there," Steve commented. "Is this a known burial practice?"

"No remains have ever been found in this sort of tomb. Perhaps the conditions in this room were different, allowing for longer preservation of the bodies."

"Some form of refrigeration?"

"Maybe. We'll check over the rooms—all the rooms—much more closely in the next few weeks. But for now, I think we need to get some lighting in here. I need to make notes and document the site in detail. The world needs to know about this. Wait till Gardiner hears what I've found!"

The two men walked back through the complex, herding the students out in front of them. Just as they were passing through the outer door with the wheel mechanism, Hill paused.

"Hold on a moment, Steve," he said. Bringing out a tiny compressed air device, he held it up to a section of wall and fired small jets of air. As the dust flew away, markings were revealed.

"I don't believe it. We've got an identification plate." Hill continued to clear the area of the centuries' accumulation of dust. "Get that camera going again."

It read: "Downing Street Defence Shelter: Nuclear Bunker N° 3."

"I'll look into it properly when we get back to the base, but this confirms it. We've got a Gardiner's Tomb all right. I can't wait to tell her!"

Jacqueline Seewald has taught writing courses, including Creative Writing at the high school, middle school and college level, and has also worked as an academic librarian and educational media specialist. Seven of her books of fiction have been published. Her short stories, poems, essays, reviews and articles have appeared in numerous publications such as: Sasee, Affaire de Coeur, Lost Treasure, The Christian Science Monitor, Pedestal, Surreal, After Dark, The Dana Literary Society Journal, Palace of Reason, Library Journal, The Erickson Tribune *and* Publishers Weekly. *A new romantic suspense/mystery thriller,* The Inferno Collection, *was published in hardcover June 2007 by Five Star/Thomson Gale, available in libraries and on Amazon.com.*

In this story Jacqueline shows younger readers, and adults, that one should develop one's strengths no matter what the odds.

The Boy Who Found Atlantis
by Jacqueline Seewald

In his village, Mehmet listened to the myths and legends told by the elders. His father's mother related the story of Atlantis, about how one day this great, ancient city sank beneath the sea. No one knew why. Maybe there was an earthquake: the ground cracked and swallowed the great city. Grandmother insisted this story was true.

Mehmet's village was very old with Egyptian, Greek and Roman ruins scattered throughout the countryside. In the town square was a mosaic floor of marble tiles with pictures of soldiers and horses fighting a battle. Mehmet studied it, wondering what it would have been like to live in those times.

His father called him a dreamer. His older brother, Ali, called him a dreamer too, but he was scornful.

"Our father spoils you because you are crippled," Ali said. "You don't have to do your share of the work."

The pistachio grove was important to the family. Because Mehmet was disabled, he could not climb and help care for or harvest the nut trees. He felt badly that he could not help more. And he could not run and play the way other boys did. Sometimes they made fun of him because he had an awkward limp and could not keep up with them. When he was not in school, he kept to himself. But he always tried to think of ways in which he could be useful to his parents.

He loved the sea. He found he was a good fisherman and often walked down the beach to the water, baited his fishing pole and waited for the fish to bite. Sometimes he fished from the rocks. He tried different kinds of bait until he found just the right worms. Mehmet knew how to be patient. He never gave up, always looking to do things better than he had before.

His mother was very pleased with the fish he brought home. It gave her more to serve for meals. Mehmet was pleased, too. He was happy to have found a way to help his family.

When it was hot, he not only fished but also splashed around in the water. Then one day, a wonderful thing happened. An older boy named Yakup joined him.

"You must learn to swim," Yakup said, watching him in the water.

"How can I swim when I can't run and can barely walk?" Mehmet asked.

Yakup, a tall boy, gave him a wide smile. "It is easier to swim than walk or run. Trust me to teach you." And he did.

With Yakup's help, Mehmet became a good swimmer. And best of all, Yakup became his friend. Yakup even taught him how to dive.

"You're a natural diver," Yakup said, more than a little surprised. "You are not afraid and you have strong lungs."

"It's more difficult for me to walk than it is for others," Mehmet said. "And so my lungs work harder because I must breathe more deeply."

"Well, it's good for diving," Yakup assured him.

Mehmet found that he loved diving into the Mediterranean Sea. There was so much beauty beneath the waves. Fish glowed in red, green, yellow and blue.

Mehmet worked hard to improve his diving skills so that he could hold his breath longer. Each time he dived, he went a little deeper, and he explored a little further and held his breath a little longer. He was patient in diving as he was with fishing. He could feel his lungs expand and grow stronger with each dive.

One day he found a small statue in the shape of a man half hidden in the sand. It was a magnificent treasure, left behind by some long forgotten civilization. He cleaned it and gave it to his mother as a gift, and she was very pleased.

For his birthday, his parents gave him a special gift, diving equipment so that he could stay underwater for a much longer time. There was an air tank, snorkel tube for breathing, mask, fins and wetsuit. Mehmet could not believe how kind and generous his parents were.

"What does he need all that for?" his brother asked, his eyes growing narrow.

"To find Atlantis," Mehmet answered.

Ali laughed at him. "How stupid," he said in his scornful way. "Our parents have wasted their money."

In the past, Mehmet would have felt hurt at his brother's words, but as his lungs grew stronger, so did his self-esteem. "The old ones say a great city was destroyed and buried under the sea long ago. I want to find it."

"How can a crippled boy like you do such a thing?" Ali said. "You waste your time with such foolish dreams."

Mehmet would not accept what his brother said. He began to use his new equipment to search many nearby places in the Mediterranean. At first, he found nothing, yet he was not discouraged. He believed that if he kept looking for Atlantis, someday he would locate it.

One day, after plunging into the sea and swimming out a good distance underwater, he discovered a small crevasse, a hole in a barricade of rocks. It was nearly hidden. Only a patient observer would have noticed it. What was beyond these rocks? He really wanted to explore further. But the opening was too narrow to allow him to continue with his diving equipment. So Mehmet made a decision.

After taking in as much oxygen as he could, Mehmet removed his air tank and snorkel tube and placed them with care against an outcropped rock ledge. His legs might not have been strong but his lungs were powerful. He was slender, allowing him to fit through the narrow opening, flashlight focused on what lay ahead. He knew he was taking a dangerous risk, but he only intended to leave his equipment for a few moments, just to glimpse at what lay hidden beyond the rocks.

Mehmet saw a red granite statue that was about twenty feet high, tall pillars with carvings of birds and fish, and a road paved with stones. Some buildings looked as if they were once houses and he saw a great central building where people must have gathered. There could be no question. He had discovered a city beneath the sea. Surely, he had found Atlantis!

Mehmet could hardly wait to tell his parents. Soon scientists would come to study this great place, but for the moment, it belonged only to him.

Adrienne J. Odasso currently lives in England, where she is pursuing a Ph.D. in late medieval English literature. Her poetry has appeared on Strong Verse, *as well as in the UK magazines* Aesthetica *and* Hum-Drum. *Her short fiction has appeared on* Behind the Wainscot, *and her poetry will also be appearing in the next issues of* Farrago's Wainscot *and* Sybil's Garage.

Sometimes it pays to take the right things with you . . .

In Every Place that I Am
by Adrienne J. Odasso

When Sefret died, they masked her in silver.

For vision, said the priest as he pried out her eyes. The embalmers glared at him as he left, watching him fold the scrap of bloody linen over on itself. This was not normal practice, but where Sefret was going, she would not need her mortal sight. Resigned, one of the embalmers chanted and swabbed out the empty sockets with oil, and then packed the damp darkness with natron-caked linen. He closed Sefret's eyelids, but one would not stay. His assistant sealed it with melted resin. For good measure, he added some wax.

For courage, said the warrior, weighing the bloody heart in his hands. He crept away through the darkness, leaving the sculpted jar empty. He had not bothered to seal it shut, but the embalmers would not open it again.

For nothing, said the embalmers' apprentice, his face greyer than the scrambled mass that he had drawn through Sefret's small nostrils and into the alabaster dish. He stirred the contents of the dish contemplatively before setting it aside and covering it with a heap of linen scraps. His mother had sent something sweet and curdled with him

211

for lunch, but he would not be able to eat it. He returned to his work with a scowl.

For wealth, said the bandit, slipping the ring from Sefret's withered finger. It glimmered fine carnelian in the light of his lamp as he dashed off into the twilight. At dawn, his brothers found him slain and knew that he had fallen prey to a night-stalking demon. They slipped the ring on his little finger and buried him in the sand.

For love, said the ancient king, no longer a prince. He turned the embalmed tongue over against his palm, sighing. He remembered the day that he had first heard Sefret's voice and knew that the magic had not come from her throat or from the plumes of incense that she swung. The tongue was wrapped in linen and painted with the feather of Truth, and, in silence, it whispered other memories that only his heart knew. In the wake of the funeral procession, he had found her last word on the temple floor and taken it without a sound. It said that his death was not far off, and he would go gladly.

When Sefret woke, her silver mask *saw*, and sang.

Lisa Fortuner was born in the Pocono Mountains area of Pennsylvania, and lived there until she joined the military. She hopes to get a pension so that she can afford to write professionally. But it doesn't hurt to get an early start on writing.

At times we can find enlightenment—even from the past.

Amazon Library
by Lisa Fortuner

"Come down now, sweetheart, the dangerous work is over." John smiled at his wife from the bottom of the shaft.

"Are you sure this won't collapse?" Catherine answered. That little twitch in her cheek made him chuckle and proclaim that she worried too much. With some gentle teasing, she made her way down the rope into John's open arms.

She pursed her lips and fumbled for her flashlight. She shined its beam randomly around the chamber. *So this is an ancient Amazon dwelling.* It looked much like the other dwellings of the period. She'd seen many of them. She wasn't the expert in archaeology John was and never claimed to be, but he valued her domestic and linguistic skills enough to take her on each trip. Though he could never afford to admit it, language wasn't his strong suit.

"Are you sure this is an *Amazon* dwelling?"

"Yeah, of course it is. They mingled with the greater population at the time, actually. There was a head of state, I forget his name, who was married to one even, and I believe some served in the legislature."

She gave him a skeptical look. She loved ancient writing, but was convinced the Amazons were fiction. In the most generous accounts they forced their way into masculine career fields, making their husbands stay

213

at home and treating the men at work like slaves. In the worst accounts they cut off their breasts and slaughtered male children. It all seemed like a race of boogeywomen dreamed up as a cautionary tale for their children.

"Anyway, Buttercup, here's why I wanted you to come down here." John pointed his light towards the far wall of the chamber and illuminated a shelf of books. "You know how time-consuming translation and transcription is, and how dull it can be. As Chief Archaeologist I'm so much busier here than on the earlier digs, and we're shorthanded so I can't spare any of my men to do it. I know you have a lot of spare time, so could you help me out?"

"I'm not sure." She mentally went over the list of chores she had waiting back at the cottage.

"Oh, come on, darling, I'm sure there's something interesting here for you." He walked over to the bookshelf and, after a quick study, pulled out a book. "Here's a book on women! Women's Mysteries. Must be some sort of Amazon ritual manual."

"Maybe."

"It's by a Fry-eh-den." He squinted at the book.

"I think that's pronounced free-dan, dear."

"Oh? Oh yes, Teutonic." He handed her the book. "Try it darling, for me?"

John pecked his wife on the cheek and walked away. She frowned after him, and ran her fingers over the cover of the book. She could translate *one* book between chores. Surely that would get John to leave her alone. With a resigned sigh, she opened it and shined her light on the title page. As usual, her husband had mistranslated the title.

The Feminine Mystique.

Lance Kind grew up on a farm in Montana where he learned to ride a horse at the age of five and shoot varmints by the age of twelve. In the nineties he lived north of Denver where he studied big city life and ski areas while working for a large high tech firm. Today, Lancer writes stories from his headquarters in the Pacific Northwest. He shares his yard with a healthy stretch of moss and his home with his lovely wife Shelli. He considers it a good day when he stays on the good side of both.

But as we continue to indiscriminately bulldoze in the name of progress we'll have to face the consequences—the obvious as well as the not so obvious . . .

Moss Memoirs
by Lancer Kind

When it was very damp, oh so long ago, when you had crawled out of the ocean, we watched and hoped. While you slid over us then learned to go high, we watched and wondered. You were gentle and you pressed down on us when you rested, and we thought we had finally become friends. We, only taking what you left. You and the others, taking from each other, forcing the others to the dirt to root into them and drink; what you left became delicious, and we would root and eat.

But after a while, our friendship withered. You sought to root further than you should and pushed yourselves deep into the dirt. It changed you, and you became ungentle and tore at us, ripping and hurting. The rock hunger drove you to root deeper and take more rock, create makings, and use makings to root more. You became rooted to the roundness of hurting and taking, making, then using makings to hurt and taking more.

Why? It hurts and we do nothing to you. More and more you kept taking, and we stayed gentle while you hurt us. And we did what we always have done, in the damp we spread. Only because we spread, we survived and kept hiding, drinking from the air and eating through our roots.

We stayed simple.

No matter how you tore us, we found places to live. We stayed in gentle dark places and waited. We drank from the air, ate through our roots and sexed in the dampness, while you created makings from what you found under the dirt. We watched your makings spread, dwellings rooting deep and sprouting into the high. You not minding places where the bright presses. Though the dwellings spread and hurt us, where you didn't watch, we spread onto your makings and rooted. Like always, there were places beneath your makings or rooted high where you rarely look because of your obsession with the dirt. Always we rooting beneath or behind, away from the pressing of brightness. But where we coated much and deep, your kind would notice and rip at us with your limbs and rock that was sharp through your makings.

Patient and slow are we, we remembered and watched. We were here first, and grew deep and soft next to our ancestors and soaked and drank. Softly and quietly we spread, taking only what was left for us, only clinging to the dirt and other gentle things. Never hurting. Only using what was left behind. You always take.

But then you started taking from each other and digging for more rock madness and used it to rip each other's markings. You put things together that should not be and crushed all with withering brightness. Everywhere, the damp was pressed away. Spreads of us sickened and died in the dry. You brought the dry and we could only wilt, we who never take.

Old, old ancestors from the damp and cold places survived. It took a long, long time, but we are patient. Now we root everywhere, even in the places you once spread. We did not think we would see you again so soon. We were very lucky the dryness was pressed away by damp. We are lucky that you, man, didn't ruin another place.

Your species never remembers, you withered almost all. But you survived. The taste of dirt is in the air that you exhale, you must have rooted deep instead of dying. You are back, not remembering. You never change because you never remember . . . Refuse to evolve . . . Restart the taking . . . No more! Now we evolve! We unroot . . . and mound together. You don't like the shape we borrow from you? You try to leave because we look like you—we look like takers. You fear other takers.

You won't leave. You are surrounded with our taking limbs that are shaped like yours. You can watch the world that is now damp while we heap upon you and root, gently taking.

You are delicious.

George Page is a born-and-raised Texan. He has had many jobs ranging from nightclub manager, to surgical sales representative, to head of operations for a trucking company. Currently he is the editor of the national medical newspaper, Blue H News. *George began writing during his two years of college at New Mexico Military Institute and continued while finishing his education at Baylor University. He has written many works in the science fiction, fantasy and literary fiction genres. This is his first published story.*

"Airholes" shows us that unexpected parallel events can be frightening.

Airholes
by George Page

Hix wiped the sweat from his brow with a napkin. *It's too hot,* he thought. He glanced at the grime that came off, wadded it up, and tossed it into the trashcan behind the bar. *Too hot for me that's for sure.* He took a swig of beer and tried to look over his notes. The excavations were going well, but he was too long from his wife, too far to get luxuries and too stinking hot to do anything but sit in a dingy, dark bar and drink his perspiring beer.

He knew Penfield should be out at the site, coaxing and coercing the work crews, interns, students and volunteers to persevere despite the radiant sun and biting insects. The spirit of that man was contagious, inspiring . . . and annoying as hell to Hix. It was his first time working with the man from England, but even so, Penfield was one of the top site managers in the world and knew what he was doing. *I should feel lucky I was able to hire him,* Hix thought, *if for nothing but his experience, knowledge and the fact he can be out there in the heat instead of me.*

Loud, jovial laughter jolted Hix from his reverie as Penfield stomped into the bar, throwing a good-natured insult to the bartender and ordering a beer in the same breath. He threw himself into the chair next to Hix, clapping him on the shoulder.

"We're making some real progress! Very exciting! I'm sure we'll be getting down to the meat in the next day or so!"

"That's real good, Pen. I mean it, that's great." Hix was visibly fatigued by Penfield's seemingly limitless exuberance.

"Amazing your radar, it really is! It's making huge strides in archeology! I don't doubt that many mysteries will be explained much more quickly . . . almost as fast as the new mysteries are revealed that need to be solved. The historians have become hard pressed to keep up!"

"Well, it wasn't that dynamic of a field before," said Hix. *That may be the next frontier for me,* he thought. *I could reengineer the whole process of acquiring, analyzing and disseminating all the new—well, old really— information about the past. Could be good.*

"Ah, just what I needed," Penfield said as he reached for the beer placed before him. "Would you turn on the TV so we can see what's happening in the world?" he asked, and began chugging.

The bartender simply nodded and turned on the large, but dusty TV. There were other channels in South Africa, but only *CNN Headline News* ever played in "The Sand Trap." That was Penfield's name for the little bar in Tzunmajini, a remote roadside village prospering with the major archaeological dig on its outskirts.

Discovering a buried city so close to civilization was both a blessing and a curse. The location allowed easy access to laborers and supplies, but there were the problems of keeping traffic and sightseers away, always a nuisance. *All in all,* Hix thought, *we could have been farther in the desert wasteland, but I'm glad we're close to the bar . . . all things considered.*

"Well, the politicians are at it again," mused Penfield eyeing the TV.

"Yes, I suppose," said Hix, clearly bored.

When politics had reached its time limit, the view switched to a panoramic shot of the Mars landscape.

"Well, still no life. Another, please." Penfield gestured toward the bartender.

"I don't know what they were expecting to find," Hix said. "They've been able to see the surface for years. Maybe they were hoping for some mold spores or something."

"It doesn't matter anyway, there's going to be life there now."

"What do you mean?" Hix asked. "Are they finally going to send a manned mission?"

"No. Well, maybe some day. You haven't been following this current mission?" asked Penfield.

"Not really. It's just another robotic exploration, right?"

"Partially, but they also brought along some Terra fauna to see if it can survive in that environment."

"What! What did they send?"

"Ants. Specifically some Alaskan types used to cold temperatures and lower oxygen levels. They started with those and bred some that should be quite comfortable on Mars."

"That's crazy! What's the point?" Hix exclaimed. "Hey look everybody! We've got ants on Mars!"

"Well, I'm sure it will have great scientific value," Penfield deadpanned and tried to hide his growing smile behind a gulp of beer.

Hix chuckled. "So, how goes the project?"

"Wonderful! I still can't believe how much better you've made things."

"Well, thanks, Pen."

An outsider to the science world, Hix had been drawn in by a nephew who managed archaeological digs for a living. He had once visited his relative in Palestine and watched him work. That day, Hix was inspired by thoughts of a modern version to this very old process. He teamed up with other like-minded technophiles who brought to the table a conglomerate of technology used in vastly different areas of commerce. Technology like the penetrator radar, once used to measure the innards of ships and airplanes for terrorist bombs, guns, etc., now worked to detect buried objects. Mounting the penetrator radar on a low-flying airplane was Hix's best idea and yielded vast results including the current excavation.

Hix had filled the site with modern machinery and technology, mixed with time-tested old-fashioned methods. Knowing exactly where things were—even the smallest artifacts—made it feasible to use the biggest earthmovers at one point, and the smallest brushes and sieves at another. A dig was not only completed months or even years faster, but it was vastly more thorough.

Conversion of archaeologists had been slow at first, but Hix's little business quickly picked up. His ten teams were now all over the world with a backlog forty-five deep. They were manufacturing new machines and self-supporting teams organized and outfitted as quickly as possible. Hix and his technologically-driven site management of the modern archaeological dig made his company sought out for almost every exploration in the world.

"The project is on schedule then?" Hix asked.

"Like a London train! I must admit, at first I was extremely doubtful of the timeline you created, but I'm happy to eat my humble pie. Here, take a look for yourself!"

Penfield reached into the knapsack he had hung on his chair and pulled out a rugged laptop. Hix opened it up and began flipping through the aerial photographs, penetrator radar shots, data sets and video streams, all updating live from the site. Penfield shook his head. Even though he had managed the site for two months, he still marveled at how far his once dusty specialty had come.

The Tzunmajini site had been discovered by aerial P.R. a few months ago and was the most promising find in the region. Early data revealed a large village surrounding a central building of some sort. Several weeks worth of dedicated work had revealed a very ancient city. Theories ranged from little known or short-lived civilizations to previously unknown cultures. Carbon dating, laser resonance and other modern tech showed that these were either the oldest buildings in the world to date or—as Hix secretly dreaded—the equipment needed calibration.

On the main overlook map, the laptop showed the computer-generated boundaries of the site and what was yet to be dug up. In the beginning, all of the buildings were simple renderings superimposed on a desolate plain. After two months, Hix looked upon an oblong circle cut fifty feet deep into the ground, peppered with buildings that were enjoying the sunlight for the first time in millennia.

Like all the other times he looked at the data, Hix's eyes were drawn to the hill in the middle of the village, towering over everything in the site. All of the modern technology had only been able to reveal a simple structure underneath all that dirt and sand. Hix knew everything they had already discovered was a priceless find, but he was only truly interested in the contents of that hill. Fortunately, the very technology that allowed him to be curious made it possible for a speedy process to satiate that same curiosity.

The TV began to show still-shots and video of the ants in a clear Plexiglas cube about the size of a small moving box. *Headlines News* ran a loop every couple minutes of the *Opportunity II* robot placing the ant box on the Martian soil, decoupling the air-filters, and backing away. They were scurrying and surviving despite being exposed to the atmosphere of Mars and seemed unaffected by the cold and strange air composition.

"With this particular species," Penfield said, "they are all drones. When they begin to build their anthill or whatever, they will select a Queen and feed her certain hormones that change her body for reproduction."

"How do they choose a Queen?"

"Well, I guess it's whoever does the best in the swimsuit competition!"

Hix almost spat out his beer as laughing overtook him. "You're a funny guy, Pen."

"Well, Hix, I'm disappointed. I timed that comment precisely and I feel stymied that you didn't spray your beer. Oh well, I'll try again later."

"Why don't the ants just crawl out by way of the roof? Through

223

those, whaddya call 'em, airholes?"

"Life support kept them inside during the trip to Mars and they also put some polymer coating on the walls, I believe," replied Penfield. "Wouldn't do to have ants all willy-nilly, now would it!"

The CNN talking heads were working themselves into a froth; it was time to release the new colonists of Mars. *Opportunity II* moved a robotic arm to the cube and pulled out a retaining pin. Slower than expected due to the lower gravity field of Mars, the door fell open and almost immediately the ants poured out to spread across the red plain. *Opportunity II* rolled back quickly and zoomed in on individual ants as they began their new life in their new home.

"You know, I'm glad they didn't use cockroaches," said Hix.

"Yeah, that would have been really creepy," replied Penfield with a shudder.

"You think they'll do well?"

"They made it this far. If we don't watch ourselves, the red planet called Mars may become the black planet of the Ants."

"They could reproduce enough to cover the planet? That's kind of farfetched."

"Not really. They have no predators and nothing to hinder them. In fact, that's probably how we'll counter the ants. We'll introduce a predator to kill them off."

"Once the ants are gone, what stops the predators?"

"Well, Hix, the predators will be taken care of when they run out of ants and we show up to play."

Hix looked at the laptop again. Work had stopped all over the site as the earthmovers carried away the last of the dirt that surrounded the center hill. It was time.

"Well, Pen. You ready to take a walk?" Hix asked with a gleam in his eye.

After leaving the bar and hopping into their respective jeeps, it took only a bumpy ten minutes to reach the site. They had gotten into the crater created by the excavation team by way of slopes and cutbacks and walked down the ancient streets to the center of the site. Hix knew he should have been more excited about the empty doorways and windows they passed, but finally his expected moment was at hand.

Everyone and their equipment were gathered in the center and though the sun was setting, it was still warm. Hix's hand-held version of the penetrator radar showed that this middle structure took up most of the interior of the hill.

"What do you think it is?" Penfield asked Hix.

"Temple? Maybe a palace? Could be like an old medieval castle. You know, large main structure for protection, but with a growing population that mainly lives and works outside the walls."

"That's one idea," Penfield said, "but you know what it is really going to turn out to be, don't you?"

"What?" asked Hix.

"A Starbucks." replied Penfield.

"You're a funny guy, Pen. Enough chit-chat! It's go time."

Machines went to work scraping away large loads of dirt under the careful eyes of engineers with radar displays. When they got close to the walls the machines were moved back and spades and brushes were put to use. Soon they found a large structure with smooth walls on three sides. Machines were put to work again to clear out the inside, radar having previously shown that it was empty except for the dirt. During this process it was discovered that there was a fourth wall that had fallen and they cleared the dirt from on top of it as well.

Hix walked up and wiped a swath of grime from the wall. He got excited and sent Penfield around to the other side to have him do the same. Startled, he stared a moment then spun around.

"HOSES!" he called out.

Giant fire hoses were rolled out and turned on the building. The high pressure of the water and the work of the entire crew soon cleaned the building. What stood before them was a giant cube with translucent walls. Although clear, the surfaces were scratched, pitted, corroded, and yellowed with age.

"What material is this?" Hix muttered to himself.

Confused, he circled the cube. He looked around at the crude buildings surrounding the center. It just didn't add up.

"Hix, come here," he heard Penfield call from inside the cube.

"Pen, I'm starting to get a weird feeling here."

"Hix come here and look up," Penfield said, strangely calm. "Look up at the airholes."

Lyn McConchie has had over 200 stories professionally published since 1991 and her books include The Key of the Keplian *in 1995 and* Ciara's Song *in 1998 (both from Warner Aspect).* Beastmaster's Ark *appeared in 2002 (Tor) and the sequel,* Beastmaster's Circus *in 2004 (Tor), both winning New Zealand's Sir Julius Vogel Award (2003 and 2005).* The Duke's Ballad *(Tor), a sequel to* Ciara's Song *and a Vogel winner, and* Silver May Tarnish *(Tor), appeared in 2005.* Beast Master's Quest *(Tor) appeared in 2006. Her most recently published short story appears in* Trails 2.

Rats in the Walls
by Lyn McConchie

All civilizations have rats of some type. Sometimes the economy collapses because of them. All cities have rats. The older the city the more likely it is that under the floors and through the walls run their tunnels. And that just when you think yourself most alone, small wicked eyes are upon you. Sometimes the rats have two legs . . .

Terra is an old planet. So old that no one in the Empire could find records of a time when it had not been populated. Over the centuries it had fallen out of touch with the old Federation and had been left to survive on its own. During that time on the huge island continent in the Southern Hemisphere, a new megalopolis had arisen, built on the bones of an earlier city.

All the while the Federation had ruled on earth there had been predators. Some of them were even human. Now the city was a sprawling warren full of nooks and crannies. Secret passages ran under the ruins, some of them tunnels dug to facilitate long-forgotten intrigues, others simply dug for convenience in travel or for storage.

Underground cells existed, often built for purposes better left unmentioned. Whole areas of the newer buildings were grounded on previous foundations, many of which had in turn been grounded on foundations that stretched deep into a forgotten past.

The port was referred to as Milbin after that earlier ancient city. But the locals called it Dreamtime for something they claimed to be even older. Here at the port you could buy anything, from a long life to a quick death, your own or someone else's. But after centuries of solitude the Empire arrived.

Terra began a new existence with Milbin full of the murderous arrogant Empire troops who paid for nothing and took whatever they wished from anyone who had it. In the offices of the Governor, Cer Mora ruled and the people of Terra lived or died by his whim. And in the ancient walls ran the rats, hating, watching, and always waiting.

Three men sat with a woman in a bar. One of the men said, "There's only a couple of hundred troops. The rebels here can raise almost as many as that. If we could get into the Governor's Palace we could kill all his murderers before they knew what hit them. The Empire's so busy with other-world uprisings they couldn't send help here for months. And every new uprising sparks half a dozen more. Out on the rim there's the Federation still. If the people rise, Terra could be free again."

"The people here don't have the guts anymore," the woman said, keeping her voice low. "Cer Mora crushed the last two uprisings so savagely they're too terrified to breathe, let alone rebel. We've got weapons certainly—and a hundred and fifty rebels who jump at shadows. We'd be going against trained troops, all of whom have state of the art equipment. Face it. Unless you can find someone with battle experience, a fighter the people will follow, the Empire would take back this city as soon as they arrived. And that's even supposing we could take it in the first place."

The man glared angrily. "You're a rebel liaison and you won't even try. Maybe it's *your* guts that are running short."

She looked at him and laughed harshly. "That sort of comment won't work on me. You can't shame me into a fight my people can't win. I've been off-planet too long, fought too many wars. My people will listen to me but I won't lead them into hell for no chance at all. Find an angle, something I can use and I'll try."

One of the other men leaned over. His face was sardonic. The eyebrows black wings over almost colorless eyes that looked through the others like a ghost wind.

"Cer Mora is more than ruthless. He's clever. Ten to one he already has spies within the rebels. You may not value your hide but I don't plan to face his interrogators. Let's break this meeting up right now. We've been talking here too long. We can meet at the next place tomorrow evening. Arguments?"

There were none. But the following evening Gerand had an idea. "What if we could lay our hands on Mora. What if he just vanished and couldn't be found? His disappearance might produce enough confusion for the rebels to take over without a pitched battle."

The woman snorted. "Mora is surrounded by the best troops the Empire has. What are you going to use to take him, spitballs? If we could get into the Palace unseen so we could make a surprise attack, we'd have hope. As it is, the minute his troops hit us we'd be finished."

"Candera, if Mora's taken he can't order them to fight."

"Don't be a fool, there's chain of command that would kick in. And how do you plan to take Mora anyhow?"

Gerand nodded slowly. "Leaving that for the moment, do you agree that if we got him first there would be enough confusion for us to break into the central armory?"

"Maybe. I do have something. This city's *old*. One of my people accessed some ancient records about Mora's complex. The records claim that there are all sorts of tunnels underneath, but I can't get anyone to go down and investigate. They say no one who's found a way beneath the city ever comes back."

Jonton studied their faces. Candara, thin, as if her beliefs burned up any excess weight she might have had. She was dark-skinned, with black eyes and bushy hair and had once in his hearing claimed to be descended from the original owners of this land. Gerand was small and wiry, with a hawk-face and hazel-eyes. Both had the competent look of people who know their job.

"So if I go down and break a leg no one will come looking?" Jonton asked.

Candara smiled sweetly. "I think I could muster my people for that."

Jonton scowled. "Thank you. I've always wanted to lie in stinking mud a kilometer underground with a broken leg, awaiting the possible non-arrival of incompetent cowards. It's been a life-long dream."

"I'll do my best to see it fulfilled then." Her smile broadened. "Are you sure about this?"

His look was withering. "I'm like you. I don't take risks just for a dare or to save face. If your revolt succeeds my ship gets first cargo rights. You complain about how little I'm prepared to do but you can't come up with anything but a lousy old map. I ask for guides and help to explore, then get rubbish about haunted tunnels. I ask for troops and they're scared of the dark. Fat lot of use they'll be storming Mora's building."

"I don't notice you rushing off to explore down there."

"I'm not risking my neck for your rebellion. If things go wrong all I'll have are empty promises and maybe a fast burial."

Candara nodded. "If we win you can have your pick of all Mora has for your first cargo out; everything but weapons and food. Just find out how we can get into the Palace communications room to shut it down."

Jonton stared thoughtfully at the scarred and filthy tabletop. "I have something in mind. If I could get into the communications room I could re-program. That way I could open a path through to the main doors while blocking off the guards. If there is a way up into the complex from underneath you could bring fighters through there to take Mora's people by surprise."

"It sounds simple."

"In which case your people should have no trouble understanding the plan. Tomorrow night I'll try getting into these underground ways."

He stood up as he spoke the last words, heading unobtrusively for the rear door. Candara looked after him. He was the best the rebels had attracted. There wasn't a lot of hope no matter what she tried to believe. The people were spiritless after years of mismanagement and abuse so that it would take a miracle to rouse them. She took a slow deep breath. But if only they could.

Gerand's latest information had listed all six planets in the Omega system as being in revolt. The Empire was falling, as on the rim the Federation grew stronger, beginning to expand again. If her rebels could take Mora, kill the garrison that was kept here and cut communications to the Empire there was a chance the Empire would be too busy elsewhere to do anything for a long time—if ever.

She'd read the city's old records and she knew the legends of her people. Once this had been a continent called Australia. A series of great quakes had sunk a portion of the northern lands, before flooding through to the heart, making a huge Inland Sea that still teemed with fish. This city was about all that was left of the dreaming times before space.

Her people had been warriors once and all these desert lands had been theirs. Where had they gone—the warriors, the pride, and the dreaming? She sighed. Maybe Jonton could find better weapons and she could reach the pride which slept in the people. She prayed it might be so as she shadowed her way down the back alley into the night.

A day later they met again, picking their place with care since the bar was close to where the map placed a possible entrance to the underground tunnels. Candara waited with Gerand until Jonton met them, his arrival so unobtrusive even those at the bar paid him no attention. Candara kept her voice low as she greeted him, holding out a small parcel.

"Good luck, Jonton. We've brought spare energy pellets for your flashlight and here's a copy of the map. We'll watch for you in case you come out at one of the other entrances it shows. Our people will all keep their eyes open."

"It's news to me they have the wits to open their eyes," Jonton remarked sourly as he accepted the energy pellets and headed for the underground entrance.

Candara and Gerand looked at each other. "I hope he's as good as he thinks he is," the man commented.

"That's the irritating thing. He is."

"If that's the only thing you find irritating about him you must have the disposition of a saint."

Candara grinned. "Never mind. If we can pull this off it'll be worth the aggravation."

"Humph! I'll let you know if or when that happens." They split. There was work to be done.

Below ground Jonton moved deeper into ways that were old before the Empire came. He rounded a corner and glared. Dead end. He started to turn back and remembered nothing for some time. It was hours later that he stirred carefully. It was pitch dark and his head ached. He was bound. Fingers explored within their limitations and he received a nasty shock. He'd been bound with Empire restraints, although somehow he didn't think it had been troopers who'd sneaked up on him. Even if they had, they wouldn't have left him here, or would they?

He settled himself back, glaring at nothing as he felt the filth that grimed his clothes and skin. Someone was going to be sorry for all this, he just hoped it wasn't going to be him. He'd expected to be buried eventually, but he'd preferred it to be after he'd died—and in another couple of hundred years.

A long interval followed in which he became more and more uncomfortable. His throat was leather and his bladder full to bursting. Suddenly the tiny slither of steps came and a hand touched his shoulder. It slid down to place a metal canteen in his restrained hands. He drank gratefully and sudden lava scorched his throat. Whatever drink it was had the alcohol content of high-octane hover-fuel—and a similar taste, he thought ruefully. He cleared his throat, took another sip, then spoke.

"Who are you?"

There was a small stirring in the dark. "One of the rats. That's what them outside calls us. The rats from the dens."

"How old are you?" There'd been something very young in the thin voice.

"Dunno."

"How long have you been here?"

"Dunno. Always, I think. I gotta go now. Jarra said to tell her when you wakes. She wants to talk to you. 'Sides. I'm dens, we don't talk much to outers."

He heard the faint sounds fade. Jonton lay considering what he'd heard. There had been something dangerous down here after all. Who was this Jarra, and what did she want of him? Soon enough a faint glow outlined a square hole in the wall. He watched avidly as they padded in through the confusion of rubble.

There were six of them, none older than fourteen he judged. They were under-fed but not starving, their thinness more the shape of a moderately successful but overworked predator. Their clothing was a mixture of everything, even cut-down bits of Empire uniforms. He wondered where they had come by those—then thought he could guess as he noticed that the two oldest carried Empire sidearms. Two others had long knives while the last two moved with the casual confidence of the armed, even if no weapons were to be seen.

"Get up and come with us." That was one of the ones with an Empire weapon.

"Why?" Jonton questioned,

"Because I tell you to and I speak for Jarra."

Jonton opened his mouth to say he didn't care if they spoke for God, and then reconsidered. There was a feral look in the leader's eyes he didn't like.

"I can't get up unless you free my hands."

The girl took one light pace forward and a foot drove wickedly into his ribs. "If you ain't up and moving in ten seconds you can lie and scream a while."

The look Jonton gave her would have stripped perma-paint from a hover. But he forced himself to his feet and followed. If his years had taught him anything it was when to be stubborn and when not to be. That kid meant exactly what she said and he was damned if he was going to get himself killed by a child.

The tunnels wound on for a long time until at last the small group halted before a wall. A boy touched some section and part of the wall slid aside. They moved on deeper into the maze. Twice more walls slid open for them, shut almost soundlessly behind them. Finally they came into a place which widened out into a huge low-roofed area. To Jonton it looked as if it could have once been a shopping mall of the olden days.

The boy bearing the light moved forward, Jonton following obediently. Now he could see that there were a number of children waiting. All had the same lean predator look and the off-world man thought he'd rarely seen a more dangerous-looking group even in the cheap low Port bars.

He was thrust towards a far wall where a girl of about fifteen sat enthroned on a pilot's seat. The two children with guns moved up to flank her. Jonton looked as well as he could at her without seeming to stare. She was fine-boned, wearing a one-piece black jumpsuit, a knife rode in a belt-loop and she had the look of one who knew her own value and abilities. If he'd ever seen a child of the upper classes before, then this was one. She addressed the smallest girl.

"Tell it."

"I was begging down bar-street. He was with a coupla others. Rebels they was. That Candara an' Gerand. Talking 'bout how they was gonna git down here. I followed an' when I knew his way I went back an' got Beck. We opened a wall an' hit him when we hadda chance. First I thought he was one 'a them stinking Empire viera. He ain't. Not all cozy with Candara an' them."

A boy stirred. "We don't have to wonder. If he won't tell us easy, I can ask the questions."

Jonton hid a shiver. There was a chill certainty in the childish voice that spoke of practice. The enthroned girl turned to look.

"You hear Sharrio. Who are you? Where do you come from? Why are you down here?" She sat back to wait as he thought swiftly. No

Empire-lovers here. The truth could serve him best. They would already guess part of it from what the child said.

"My name is Jonton. I lead a mercenary group from the Federation. Your rebels called me in to help in a rebellion. I don't mind doing the Empire a bad turn so I came." He saw the disbelief. "I got paid up front for the trip and my people get exclusive trade rights if the Empire's people are run off-world and stay off. If we just free the city I get first pick of all but food and arms."

The girl eyed him. "Sounds true. But what have you got in mind? The outers won't fight. They've been so beaten down that God himself couldn't put fire back into their spirits."

Jonton gave her a considering stare. "Just how many of you live down here in the—ah—dens. How many of your people have good weapons and would fight?"

Jarra glanced at a smaller girl. "Linni, you're armory, tell him true."

"'S just over a hundred of us. We all got weapons. Only nineteen guns in shape to use. Rest are for parts. Everyone got good knives though and we got a case of mixed grenades."

Jonton blinked. He wondered just how these kids had come by grenades.

Jarra took up the talk. "And we'll fight. We're dens. Where do you think we got the Empire clothing, Empire guns and gear? Sometimes we hunt Empire to get money to buy medicine and food."

Linni giggled suddenly. "Sometimes in the bad months they *are* food."

Jarra glared. "Only when we have no choice. Only twice two winters ago when we'd have starved." She turned to Jonton. "What's your idea, Federation man?"

"I want you to talk to the rebels. I think we could use you, particularly if you have a way up into Cer Mora's complex. You'd get a fair share of the loot if you did that. I'm sure Candara would give hostages if you want that while you're outside talking to them." There was a mutter of disapproval but Jarra slashed a hand for silence.

"All you'd lose is me and we'd have a hostage like he says. Could be a way out for all of us if the Empire goes. We could have a different life, you want to be den rats forever?" She shifted back to stare at Jonton. "Keep talking, let's see how you think."

He kept his plans brief, adding a few suggestions, listening in turn to what the girl said and even more, evaluating her command over the others and her determination. After a couple of hours she signaled to the boy.

"Blindfold him, Sharrio. Lead him out by the same entrance." Her eyes met Jonton's before the blindfold dropped. "You get someone down here to talk to us, or give a hostage and I'll come back with you and talk to the rebels."

Jonton arrived at the rebel meeting place several hours after he found himself back above ground. Candara was already there waiting with Gerand. They listened until they understood Jonton planned to attack the Governor's complex from below—with a gang of children. Then Candara's description of the mercenary became fluent enough to melt control panels. He stared her out, his eyes hard and empty.

"You haven't got one person in your so-called rebels with half the guts or ability of this kid. I've met her. Those brats would follow her into hell and hold the gates if she gave the word. You wanted a way to get in to Mora's complex. You wanted fighters you could rely on. I'm giving you both. Now you want to back out because they're kids and could get hurt. So they're kids. Who says they aren't as ready to die as that pack of cautious cowards Gerand leads? Those kids aren't living down there in the tunnels for fun. They have some guns and they know how to use them. Give them enough other weapons and they'll fight. If we don't do this then I'm out and my group with me."

Candara looked at him warily. "You sure they'll fight?"

"Jarra says they will and she'd know. Now, you come down and talk, or she wants a hostage from you if she comes out. What'll it be?"

"I'll come down with you."

They slipped unobtrusively into the ancient sewer entrance, branched off into the underground ways and halted. A wall shifted in the torchlight and Linni appeared.

"This way."

They followed, into a bewildering maze of tunnels and paths that wound through moldering piles of rubbish and rubble. At a large open area Jarra was there to meet them.

"Sit. May I offer food or drink?"

Candara was staring at the rows of waiting children. "Jarra, this is wrong. I want you to know I don't agree with Jonton or what he plans. You and these children are too young, they can't truly understand they could die. And there's no way they could fight trained Empire troops and win against them."

Jarra moved up to stare into her face. Candara shivered, as something deadly seemed to move behind the girl's eyes. "We've fought and killed Empire troops for years. The dens have taken more troopers' lives than your rebels ever dreamed of. And we've paid the price, or did you think none of us have ever died before? They don't hand over what we want for the asking, we take it. The rats will fight; they'll accept death if they have to so long as the odds are good. It's my decision and I lead."

Her two seconds moved up to back her as together three pairs of feral eyes stared Mirri Candara down.

Jonton cleared his throat and Jarra's gaze shifted back to him. "I'll be with you." He turned back to Candara. "Our Tac-Officer put it on the computer. Odds are two-point-nine-eight to one that we succeed if we arm the kids properly. Jarra knows an old path into the heart of Cer Mora's communications center up there. If we hit at the right time we can hold long enough to get everyone in. Jarra's never tried because they don't have enough guns. But note well, Candara. If they'd had the arms, they'd have tried. What have your bunch ever done to equal that?"

Her head lifted angrily. "Nothing, I guess. I'll tell them though. I'll shame them that children fight the Empire while they hide. I'll drive them into Cer Mora's Palace with my own guns if I must. We'll back you when the time comes. Jarra, if I get all of your people good Empire-issue weapons, can you use them?"

"We train everyone as they come to us. That way if they manage to steal one they don't blow their heads off trying to use it. I want double the number of weapons for us too, that way we can have spares available."

"Done. When can the dens be ready to fight?"

"A good meal, a good sleep, a light meal and time for me to go over all this with them. Twelve hours, ten if we have to."

Candara nodded. "I'll bring the guns down in a couple of hours. Jarra, the children really do know they could die in this attack?"

"They know death. One thing. When the fighting stops, if we've won, we get Cer Mora. There's rats who'd like to meet him. There's no give on that either. We get your promise or we don't fight."

"If you have a use for him, he's yours," Jonton said, smiling slightly.

She looked up. For a fraction of a second hell glowed in her eyes. "Then we fight."

Ten hours later Jonton was sharing out the contents of cases dragged laboriously through the underground pathways. Good Empire guns for every child here and almost sufficient spares for a second for each child, ammunition for an extended firefight. Even a couple of dozen flameproof shirts. Jarra was smiling as she doled the items out.

"I've talked this over with everyone. Cer Mora clinched it. We'll break through an old door. It's under so many layers of junk now in a back room they don't use; that they've never known it's there. We lock the door to the corridor, clear the junk back into a side tunnel and cram about thirty of us into the room before we have to move on. After that the others will be right behind us as soon as there's room to follow."

Jonton checked his timer. "We'll move out in two hours. Candara's people will be in position outside by then. It'll be early dawn, not many people about. The guards are more likely to be bored and sleepy. Go and eat now while there's time."

The rats formed up silently when the hour came. They padded through familiar tunnels to arrive at a blank wall. Jarra's fingers flickered over the wall and Jonton suddenly wondered how she knew there was a door here. He asked the question softly.

Her smile was dangerous. "I grew up in Cer Mora's complex, mercenary. My parents were House Marrigan; they served Cer Mora until he had one of his paranoid fits. They had just enough warning to hide me before the guards came. I had to watch everything until they left with the bodies. Then I got out into the tunnels through that door. I had an older friend in here already. His parents were murdered by Mora two years earlier and I'd been smuggling him food. When I arrived he took care of me until I learned den ways. Mora's troops killed him a while back." She broke off to peer into a tiny spy-eye in the wall. "The room's empty. Let's move."

They slid through the hidden entrance, locked the storeroom's door and moved the room's junk to allow a clear passage. Once that was done Jonton opened the door. Beside it was an alarm panel, not connected to this door but to beams across the corridor. It would sound an alarm if any passed who were not cleared. He grinned. Old equipment. His fingers moved with quick sureness as he bridged it. There'd be no alarm now. He nodded to the waiting girl.

She straightened, her voice low but razor-edged with command. "Rats! No mercy but take Mora alive if possible. Move out."

The door swung open as a wave of lean savage-faced children poured through. Like armed ants boiling up from a nest, more and more joined the out-rush. Jonton nodded to himself, there were more than the hundred Jarra had claimed. No doubt she'd lied, a wise fighter always kept a few secrets and reserves to herself.

An Empire Officer rounding the bend died gape-mouthed before he could sound an alarm. Jarra's picked team raced ahead with Jonton, heading for the communications center. Troops finding themselves faced with children, some barely nine or ten, often hesitated before firing— and died for it. Jonton flung himself at the control panels as they reached communications. With a sweep of his hand he barred all personal doors. Many troops would be trapped in their rooms to be removed at leisure.

Another movement and passage doors were locked open, the main front door gaping in invitation to those who waited there. Jarra leapt for the center door calling her rats. Guns steadied in small hands as they began to sweep the building level by level killing as they went. Leaderless troops tried to rally, there was confusion, children died, but still more fought. Viciously willing to die if only they could take some of the hated enemy with them. Jonton could only hope Candara would get her rebels in before too many rats died. Jarra was back just as he saw another small figure fall. Then he heard the call.

"Cer Mora! We've found Cer Mora!"

There was a terrible chilling triumph in the childish voice. Jarra jumped for the door. "Bring him here. He's ours."

Jonton looked at her face, then away. "If the kids can hold another few minutes, Candara's people should be here."

Her smile twisted into a snarl. She reached for the communications com and snapped words in a street-dialect he couldn't understand. In the distance he could hear cries of acknowledgment from all down the passages.

"What was that about?"

"Said we'd got Mora. Said we could keep him if we held a while longer. They said they'd hold 'til death or World's End."

Jonton nodded, his head lifting abruptly as he heard the noise. In the corridors guns blazed as more Empire troops died. Mirri Candara flamed into the center with Gerand and his rebels a pace behind. The mopping up was bloody but swift. After that word spread. Empire minions and hated collaborators died everywhere, first on the island continent, then all over earth.

Two days later Linni reported to Jarra and others. "We lost fifty-seven out of one hundred and seventy-eight who fought. Most 'a the rest who's hurt are gonna be okay. We got a real stack 'a weapons an' canned food down in the tunnels now. That rebel who used to be a teacher 's joining us. She says she can have us all reading an' writing in a few months. Those of us that can't. Of course," she added proudly, "I already can."

Jonton sighed. "So we get trade rights but damn all loot."

"It wasn't our fault there wasn't much there," Gerand snapped.

Jarra stepped forward, holding out her hand. Linni placed a small box on the out-stretched palm. "These are from the dens to you. They'll provide some repayment."

Fighting back surprise Jonton opened the box. Probably a few old coins. Pickings the kids had collected. It was kind of them, but what would they know about the expenses of running a mercenary group? He looked down and forgot to control his emotions.

"Great Burning Fires of Hades! Where did you find this lot?"

The box was compartmented. One side dripped the purple fires of Zanri gems from Inshi. A necklace, bracelets, ear and nose-studs, rings and a pendant. There must be a ruler's ransom. The smaller, shallower compartment held a credit chip. He touched the read-out patch and studied the total. It left him completely speechless.

Jarra grinned. A wide happy evil smile. "Mora. He offered them if I'd let him go unhurt. I swore on the name of my House that I would if he cleared the chip's access. So he handed everything over."

"You lied?"

The girl shook her head. "I gave my House word. He went free."

Something in the way she spoke alerted him. "Just how free?"

"Have you see vieras? They brought them to Milbin a generation ago to clean out the rats. The rats won but there's still vieras about. They're down in the tunnels. They don't give us any trouble so long as we aren't helpless or anything."

Jonton remembered. He'd heard about the nasty little scavengers once. Sometimes they ran in packs of twenty or so. On their original planet of Trelane they'd been used in a couple of the more vicious rulerships as a punishment. Unfortunate prisoners had died, literally eaten alive. Vieras didn't breed well on any world but their own so they eventually died out anywhere but Trelane.

"Cer Mora?" he reminded her.

"I gave my word. We took him down to the deepest tunnels where the viera hide. Shallio had a med-laser. We cut his wrist and ankle tendons painlessly. Then we left him there. Viera are fast and with the blood scent they go crazy. We backed up the tunnels a while and waited. I gave my House word. He wasn't hurt and he went free. People who take House word should be sure what it was given on. He died loud and not too fast. The dens feel it was fair."

Candara who'd been listening looked sick. "How could you do

that?"

"Easily. All we had to do was remember families and friends he'd tortured and murdered. Did you know that if he caught us from the dens we were sold to kid-brothels—or given to his pals with the same tastes? If some of the rats had their way he'd have died a lot harder. Now it's over. We can be other things if we want to be."

Candara eyed her. "What about you?"

"I have plans. I'm leaving with Jonton's group."

"What?" Candara was stunned. "Where? How about your friends?"

"Linni and Shallio are taking over the dens. I'm going to school out on the rim. I'll live with my kin at House Marrigan. Jonton sent word to them and they say I'm welcome. After that we'll forge records and slip me into the Empire Space Officer school on Lythere."

"But—but—why?"

"I've been a rat in Milbin walls for almost seven years. I'd like to see in how many other places rats can bring down the Empire."

She turned on her heel heading for Jonton's shuttle, fingering the credit chips in her pocket as she went. Clever Mora. So many secret funds stashed away, but he'd talked. One chip for Jonton, two for her rats, and two more for her and her House. Jonton paused to look at Mirri before following Jarra towards the ship.

"Happy revolution, Mirri Candara. Look out for Jarra. In another ten years she could be running the Federation—or the Empire."

He walked briskly in the girl's wake. Candara and Gerand found they were grinning. They were still smiling when thunder raised the ship. Terran skies faded into black star-glittering space around the ship, as a rat left her world.

And in the great cities of the Empire on a thousand terrorized subject worlds, the rats moved in their tunnels and walls. Hating, watching, and waiting—always waiting.

Printed in the United States
98531LV00003B/153/A

9 780978 514853